To Paul with my best
wishes.

Nasir Khansab

01-12-2014

SILENT TREES

SILENT TREES

A NOVEL
OF AFGHANISTAN

Nasir Shansab

Bartleby Press
Washington • Baltimore

Published and distributed by:

Bartleby Press

8600 Foundry Street
Mill Box 2043
Savage, Maryland 20763
800-953-9929
www.BartlebythePublisher.com

Library of Congress Cataloging-in-Publication Data

Shansab, Nasir.
  Silent trees : a novel of Afghanistan / Nasir Shansab.
     pages cm
  ISBN 978-0-910155-93-9
  1. Afghanistan--Politics and government--Fiction. I. Title.
  PS3619.H3557S55 2012
  813'.6--dc23
                              2011050809

To Aaron and Kate

Prologue

2001

Maggie Reed awoke at once. She could clearly hear a tapping noise. Was it in her head, the remnant of a dream? No, she was sure it was coming from outside her bedroom door. She listened carefully. Someone was walking along the corridor. A notion dashed through her head, the prospect of it jolted her like a strong electric current coursing through her body. Habib Dhil, she thought. It's Habib Dhil?

The steps came closer and stopped right before her bedroom.

She raised her head from the pillow and stared at the door, straining her eyes to penetrate the darkness. Her heart raced. She felt hot. Beads of sweat formed on her forehead.

She trembled at the thought that Habib could enter her bedroom any moment. Without thinking, she put a hand up to her breast, feeling her nipple erect against her fingers.

This wasn't a dream. She was wide awake and this was

1

reality. She filled with joy as she anticipated Habib's return into her arms after such a long absence.

Seconds crept by. Nothing moved on the other side of the door. The house was cloaked in perfect silence. Only the sound of her own breathing disturbed the windless summer night.

Maggie dropped her head back onto the pillow. Never had she felt Habib's presence so strongly.

Her hand trembled as she reached out for the bedside lamp and found herself surrounded by nothing but familiar objects. She slipped out from beneath the covers and rose from her bed. Gasping for air and barely able to keep from collapsing, she dragged herself to the kitchen and fetched a bottle of water from the refrigerator. She walked out onto the porch and sat down on one of the white lawn chairs.

Immersed in the stillness of the night, she leaned back and turned her head upwards. An impenetrable darkness hid the sky. Trying to regain her sanity, she closed her eyes, raised the plastic bottle to her lips and let the cool water pool into her mouth.

She sighed. Perhaps it was a dream after all. Or maybe a spirit—Habib's ghost, coming to inform her that he had already left this world, the world of the living, and that she should end her search for him.

Too much television, she told herself, halting the anxiety taking further hold of her.

She closed her eyes and Habib Dhil appeared before her. They were together at the old fort outside Baghlan in the north of Afghanistan. Before long, however, her picture turned painful.

Habib Dhil was suffering; sweat and dirt covered his face. Blood dripped through his fingers onto the thirsting earth as he pressed his hand against his stomach. The same fingers, she thought, that had slid over her skin and caressed her ever so gently.

She took another sip of water from the bottle. She had to face the facts. It wasn't going to be too long before she would be considered an old woman. And what then? Her years would be spent working in her garden and volunteering at the Women's Club.

Yes, she decided. She would make the trip to Pakistan one more time, probably for the last time. She would again search the refugee camps in Peshawar, hoping to find a trace of him.

But first she would visit the central immigration office in Arlington, Virginia and go through the files once more. Habib might have applied for asylum since she had last checked the records.

She looked at the back of her hand. In the soft light streaming out through the sliding door, she saw tiny dark spots on her skin.

So much time had passed. The collapse of Communism and the disintegration of the Soviet empire had turned the world upside down. Yet, she had been unable to find Habib Dhil, not even a trace of him. Could he have died, murdered by someone who was jealous of his wealth? Given the everlasting turmoil in Afghanistan, that was a distinct possibility.

Strange, she thought. Until a few minutes earlier, she had not, even for an instant, thought of him being gone. Whenever she tried to imagine where he could be and what he might be doing, he always appeared on the move, as if he could not find a place to settle and had to travel continually.

Now the tragedy of September 11th had forced America's hand and another war seemed poised to descend upon the destitute Afghan people. She became determined to visit the refugee camps again, making one final attempt to find him—or at least discover a trace of him, a sign, any sign that helped her find peace of mind.

Chapter One

1978

It was July 14th. Bastille Day. Habib Dhil walked along a pebble-covered walkway through the French embassy's festively decorated courtyard. Despite Kabul's warm, dry summer, the grass looked fresh and the lush foliage of the majestic chestnut trees radiated vigor and health.

The sun had already turned downward and the leaves rustled softly as a fresh breeze drifted by. Lamps, covered in colored paper and fixed on top of tall steel poles, lit the spacious yard.

Dhil looked around. The other guests, glasses in hand, stood in clusters or strolled about, evidently enjoying the pleasant evening.

Powerful spotlights were turned on, flooding the elevated concrete platform in front of the embassy's main building with shirll illumination. Handlers put up a microphone stand in the middle of the elevated area.

Moments later, Jack du Borque, the French ambassador, came out from the building in the background, stepped onto the lit platform and walked over to the microphone stand. Dressed in coattails, the front part of his coat heavily embroidered with silver threads, he looked as if he had come from a different time, a time long passed and forgotten. Photographers rushed to where the ambassador stood and focused their cameras on him.

Signaling with a nod to one of his attendants, Ambassador du Borque positioned himself before the microphone. An assistant pulled open a tall glass door and Abul Jabar, the Afghan Minister of the Interior, walked through it. His shoulders too narrow for his big head, his thin brown hair combed sideways to cover the top of his balding skull—he peered through oversized glasses and walked toward the ambassador.

After the two men shook hands, the minister took his place beside the ambassador and faced the audience. When the ambassador began speaking, the minister, displaying a dour expression, stiffly turned sideways to observe him.

Dhil's school-taught French was inadequate to really follow what the ambassador was saying, but toward the end of the speech, Dhil figured out enough to realize that the French government had bestowed the Legion of Honor upon the Afghan minister.

Disappointed that France would so formally pay tribute to a senior member of such a corrupt and deadly regime, Dhil turned his head in disgust and saw a woman standing a few feet away from him. She was watching him and her gaze remained steady as their eyes met.

He had no idea who she was, but her features seemed familiar and a delightful sensation of warmth gushed over him, and he felt as if he already knew her well. His attention converging on that woman's strikingly beautiful face, he momentarily forgot his incredulity over the French ambassador's absurd act of venerating a man whose hands practically dripped with blood.

Dhil smiled. The woman's face, framed by shining blond hair, was unusually attractive. Even if she couldn't match Miriam Khan's extraordinary beauty, her blue eyes seized him and kept him tightly in her grip. Dhil was convinced she was sending him a message. The bright glitter in her eyes seemed to transmit that she, too, had been taken by him.

Dhil wasn't sure how long they had been staring at each other. Seconds? Minutes? His paralysis was only broken when a tall man appeared at her side. Wrapping his arm around the woman's delicate shoulders and whispering something to her, he pulled her away.

Without resisting the man's embrace, she let herself be led away but not without turning her head to look at Dhil one more time. He thought he saw her smile faintly as she disappeared into the crowd. A sense of panic seized him as he considered the alarming possibility of never seeing her again.

Chapter Two

Dhil had accepted an invitation to the home of his friend Salman Rashid. He looked forward to the invigorating conversation Rashid always offered.

Rashid's servant met him at the door and let him into the house. As soon as Rashid saw him, he took several large steps toward him, stretched out his hand and said, "Salam, my friend." Taking his arm, Rashid pushed him toward the small cluster of people standing in the center of the large, high-ceilinged living room. Dhil recognized among them the woman he had seen at the French embassy a few days before.

There she is, he thought. He struggled to stay composed.

To Dhil's relief, Maggie took the initiative, "My name is Maggie," she said. "Maggie Reed. I saw you at the French embassy."

"Yes, you did. I'm Habib Dhil."

She smiled. "This is Charles, my husband."

Charles shook Dhil's hand. Dhil took notice of his firm grip.

Maggie grabbed on to her husband's arm. "I was just re-marking to Charles and Salman how handsome I think Afghan men are."

Dhil could feel himself beginning to blush. He smiled shyly.

Before he could say anything, Charles spoke up. "My wife is always trying to get a rise out of me—ah, getting me to become excited."

"It works," Maggie said.

"Of course, dear," Charles said, putting his arm around her waist.

Noticing how happy they seemed, Dhil sensed his attraction to Maggie lessen, but only slightly.

"Habib," Charles said, "Salman tells me you are a person one must know here in Kabul. There's nobody more connected." He winked. "Outside of the regime, of course."

Dhil nodded at his friend. "I am sure Salman is exaggerating my importance. In truth, I am just benefitting from what my grandfather built."

"In any case," Charles said, "I hope we can all get to know each other well."

Charles and Maggie Reed came from Buffalo, New York. High school sweethearts, they had gone to college together and gotten married after Charles entered the Foreign Service. Afghanistan was their first overseas assignment, where Charles was the second-in-command of the economic section at the American embassy.

Although far from home, they were pleased with their post-ing. They liked the dry weather and admired the majesty of the snow-capped Hindu Kush range. But they also missed the lushness of upstate New York.

"Kabul's arid landscape is too austere," Maggie said. "It of-fers the eye no respite at all," she added, her blond hair falling straight on her small shoulders and the vibrant energy in her large blue eyes reflecting the fervor of her curious mind.

It was toward the end of summer, a period when the season's heat began receding while the cutting cold of northern Afghanistan's remorseless winters remained far off. The Reeds were visiting Dhil's farm in Baghlan—a small town perched on a hill in a fertile, rolling region of the country's northern plains, built around and thriving from Dhil's family-owned mill.

They first stopped at Dhil's company guest quarters to unload their luggage and rest for a while. Then, after Maggie pressed to see where Dhil had spent his childhood, he reluctantly drove them over to the farmhouse. Majid, one of the caretakers, let them in, and Dhil gave Maggie and Charles a quick tour of the house.

Since Dhil stayed at the company's visitor compound whenever he came to Baghlan, the farmhouse had not been lived in for quite some time. The air inside was a little stale, but the polished stone floors were spotless. Dustsheets covered the furniture, and the rugs had been rolled up and stacked along a wall in the living room.

"This is a lovely house," Maggie said, as they walked down the gravel walkway through the large garden back to the car. "Why don't you stay here when you come up?"

"The guesthouse is more convenient," Dhil replied. "The cleaning staff is there. And a cook is always on duty."

But that wasn't really the truth. Six years ago, driving back to Kabul after his grandfather's burial, he'd made a decision: On his overnight stopovers in Baghlan, he would stay away from the farmhouse—his grandfather's house. He didn't really have a specific reason to stay away from the house, just a general sense of the need to keep his past separated from the present. Despite periods of ambivalence and even pain, his childhood in Baghlan seemed a time of some decency and security. Perhaps, he didn't want to contaminate his memory of it with his present feeling of eroding dignity and the presentiment of escalating turbulence.

Should he share this sentiment with Maggie? No, he thought. Anyway, he wasn't at all sure his unease made any sense, even to himself. How could he explain it to Maggie in a comprehensible manner?

The next day, Dhil kept his guests busy. Getting up early, they went horseback riding. During lunch, Dhil suggested they visit the *Ziarat*, an old fort where, according to legend, a *Shahid* by the name of Mansur Darwishi was buried.

"What is a Shahid?" Maggie asked.

"The Shahid was some sort of a saint who could heal the sick and perform other miracles," Dhil explained. Looking at Maggie through the rearview mirror, he smiled and added, "I don't take it seriously. But many people do."

It was early in the afternoon and the sun shone brightly when they left to see the remains of the ancient fortress. They drove for several miles on a worn-out gravel road that caused Dhil's Land Rover to shake and rattle, leap high and fall back hard on the road's rutty surface. Finally, they crossed the old bridge over Baghlan River. Hitting the paved highway, they turned right and headed toward Mazar-e-Sharif, Afghanistan's northern-most city.

"There isn't much left of the fort," Dhil said, pressing the accelerator, letting the Rover rapidly gain speed.

"Why are we going there if there isn't anything to be seen?" Charles said, his athletic body filling the front passenger seat.

"It's not so much what you see that gives the site its significance," Dhil said, his eyes focused on the road. "It's what you hear and perceive in your imagination that has made this place famous." He paused, a little unsure about whether to continue. "Rumors have it that with concentration and some luck, the old

Shahid may reveal himself to you. Some pilgrims, who come to pray for sick family members, claim to have seen him."

Maggie leaned over the front seat. "Have you seen him yourself?"

"I haven't," Dhil said, his gaze wandering to the rearview mirror, watching Maggie's long hair mussed by the wind rushing through the open window. His heart jolted when her large blue eyes met his.

He turned his attention back to the road. "It's commonly held that the Shahid appears to those who are close to Allah. To those who do God's work." As he left the freeway and turned onto a dirt road, he cranked up his window to stop the soaring dust from penetrating the car's interior. Smiling impishly, he added, "I'm not sure I possess those qualifications."

"Habib means it's nonsense," Charles said, his perpetually tan face exuding confidence and contentment. "It's just a fantasy. Nobody in his right mind would believe such a story."

Maggie was not satisfied. "But there must be many who do," she said. "Otherwise, the myth wouldn't have lasted." She leaned back into her seat as if she needed to reflect on her comment.

They drove for a while along the dirt road that followed a straight line through the dry flat desert. At last, Dhil stopped the car in the shadow of a beech tree beside the collapsed outer wall of a long-vanished structure. The ruins stood amidst a flatland that continuously stretched in all directions.

While the two men went on an inspection tour of the remnants of the aged building, Maggie, mesmerized by the idea that the saint could reveal himself to her, climbed to the top of the slight elevation, where the long-gone structure once stood. Surrounded by crumbling walls, aged weeping willows, and the nothingness of the endless steppe, she stood still, closed her eyes, and focused her thoughts.

A cool breeze blew over her face, stirring her hair. The wind carried barely audible whispers, which seemed to come from the far edges of the horizon. The soft current gained force, evolving into a shrieking gale. It hit her so hard that she thought it would knock her over. Growing into an uproar, the mayhem came closer and filled the air. Screams of men and the thunder of hooves swept over the plain.

Maggie wasn't sure how much time had passed when a roaring current lifted her, removing her outside the present, taking her into a different time—an age of swords, shields, steel-meshed harnesses, and man-to-man fights. She found herself in front of a massive fortress in the center of a large garden. The moon stood high, glistening cold and sullen in the black sky, blanketing the countryside with a mantle of silver. Uncounted bodies covered the ground. The wounded lay bleeding in the dust, their moans growing weaker with each passing minute.

A fierce pain ran through her heart when she saw Dhil among them, fallen on the dusty ground, pressing his hand against his stomach, blood trickling through his fingers. It took her a few moments to grasp the horrifying meaning of what she saw. Death had fixed its hideous eyes on Dhil. A vicious torment befell her, virtually sapping life out of her.

Dhil watched her intently, seemingly wanting to tell her something. When he stretched out his blood-smeared hand toward her, she extended her own and rushed forward to grab his. But as much as she labored to reach him, she could move only slowly ahead. And before she could get to him, a horseman—his powerful shoulders drooped, his head bent, his long hair covering his face, his armor reflecting the moonlight—rode by, blocking her way, forcing her to halt her agonizingly slow steps altogether.

The horseman's reins hung loosely around his horse's neck. His bloodstained sword dangled from his right hand, swinging gently with the movements of the horse's sluggish trot.

When he raised his head, two ebony eyes gaped at her, his gaze searing all the way to the core of her being. Like a tornado, a strong force swirled around her. It enclosed her, absorbed her, and shook her savagely. An enormous thrust tossed her upward. She rose endlessly as if soaring from the dark depth of the sea toward the intensifying rays of daylight.

Panic-stricken, she opened her eyes, barely keeping herself from collapsing to the ground. All her strength had been sucked from her body.

In the distance, she saw Charles and Dhil still wandering about the ruins. She wanted to walk towards them but couldn't move.

"What's the matter, Maggie?" she heard Charles say, as he drew closer to her. He studied her face. "Are you all right? Your eyes are all red."

"I'm fine," she said, bending her head, looking at the ground, walking away from her husband.

"Perhaps she's tired," she heard her husband say, as she drifted away from the two men.

"Maybe we should go back," Dhil suggested. "Let us get some rest before dinner."

Maggie walked down the knoll toward Dhil's car. She needed to sit down and recover her strength. When she heard the men's steps approaching, she shut her eyes and pretended to sleep. She didn't want to look at Dhil. She wasn't sure she could see his face without sensing that unbearable pain she had felt as she found him, slouching on the windswept ground, his blood draining onto the arid soil, the powdery dust swallowing his life.

Chapter Three

Showered and changed, Dhil sat outside in the garden, waiting for his guests to come down and join him for dinner.

Maggie had combed her hair back into a ponytail. She did that sometimes after they had gone to bed and she took a quick shower before leaving his house.

She looked young, even younger than Miriam. Dhil, amazed at her easy transformation, couldn't take his eyes off of her.

Dhil motioned for his friends to sit and Maggie answered with a smile that filled him with vitality and happiness.

At first she avoided his gaze, averting her eyes, staring at the tabletop as if her thoughts had gone to some long-past event in a faraway place. She looked small and lost, and Dhil wondered if she was ill. It would explain her earlier behavior.

At last she turned to him. No trace of her exhausted

expression remained. Instead her face radiated a delicate tenderness he had not seen in her features before.

The sun dipped behind the hills. The air cooled down rapidly as the night's black canopy spread over the hushed valley. On the other side of the river, more and more lights came on in the company houses. Dhil imagined the occupants moving inside the small, detached, stucco dwellings, doing their ordinary chores, walking from room to room.

The muted roar of the distant rush of water flowing through the turbines of the hydroelectric power plant and bursting out on the other side of the dam was the only sound during the calm early evening.

"It's so peaceful," Maggie said, speaking softly, forcing Dhil to lean forward to catch her words. "I could imagine living here and being perfectly happy."

"I'm pleased you like it here," Dhil said, instantly worried that he sounded too formal. His attraction to Maggie made him insecure. He always felt uncomfortable when the three of them came together. He liked Charles and a sense of betrayal seized him in his presence.

"Have you ever thought about leaving Kabul and moving up here?" Maggie asked, leaning back in her chair, the strength of her voice restored.

"It wouldn't work," Dhil said. "In this country, you can't do anything without government permission. I need to be close to the authorities to run my business."

"You own the property," Maggie said. "You know you could relocate whenever you wanted. At least, you have that security."

"I wish I were that certain of it, Maggie," Dhil said, wanting to change the subject.

"Why would you say that?" Maggie asked, her eyes wide with surprise.

"I wish I knew." Dhil said, knowing it wasn't much of an

answer. He found it hard to explain his feelings without risking overdramatizing the situation. Trying to give his voice a lighter tone, he went on, "It's my gloomy mentality. I've never been confident about the future." He shook his head. "Although in Afghanistan, there's never much to be confident about. Chaos and even bloodshed are never that far away."

"Long-term," Charles said, "I would agree with you. That's if you Afghans don't change your ways. But nothing will happen in the foreseeable future."

"The future?" Dhil said. "I see only calamity ahead."

"Come now," Charles said, leaning back on his chair, taking a sip from his drink. "The only thing you have to worry about is political instability. There's nothing on the horizon to suggest that."

Dhil didn't respond. He stared at his drink, letting the ice cubes clink inside his glass. Then he spoke up. "For one thing, we're less than a hundred miles away from the Soviet border. With Carter in the White House, Brezhnev seems to be getting away with everything he does. Or at least that's what most of the rest of the world believes."

Dhil took a deep breath as if he needed to gather his strength. "But as bad as that sounds," he then said, "it isn't my immediate concern. The real problem is with my own government. The brutality and corruption they inflict on our people will eventually tear the country apart."

"I don't know what you base your assessment on," Charles said, frowning. "We at the embassy consider this a stable country. The King is liked and Khan's regime is safe. And don't underestimate President Carter. He's a kind man and may take long to decide, but he also has a will of steel."

"Don't ask me why," Dhil said, "but I see it differently. I can't give you a single concrete reason. It's just a hunch."

The steady roar of water permeated the mild, late-summer

air. The sun had disappeared. Darkness gradually overwhelmed the day's dying luminescence. The shrieking voices of playing children reached them from the company houses across the river.

"Habib," Maggie said, "why don't you leave if you're so sure that you have no future here?"

"He can't just pack up and go," Charles said, sitting up, grabbing his glass and taking a large gulp. "His money is tied up in plants, equipment and real estate."

"I think," Magie said, "he should leave if he is that unhappy."

"Maggie," Charles said, "don't upset the good man. Nothing's happened." He took another swallow from his scotch and said, "Habib, I really think there's nothing to be worried about. The Communists and fundamentalists exist on the fringes and there is no other opposition worth mentioning." He leaned toward Dhil. "We do know what's going on in this country."

"The opposition?" Dhil said. "No, I worry about a general breakdown. I think the country will disintegrate into chaos. Everything here depends on a few people. Remove one of them and the whole edifice comes crashing down."

Charles smiled. "You really are a gloomy character. Nothing will happen." His face turned serious. "If one of your leaders were eliminated, another leader would take over. Probably one of your generals, they're not a bad bunch."

"I'm convinced the people will rise up one day," Dhil insisted, feeling immediately foolish at his outburst of idealism. "Frankly," he added, without really wanting to say it, "I would be disappointed if they didn't."

Charles got up, went over to the trolley with the drinks, and poured himself another scotch. He stared into the distance for a moment. "I don't know exactly how much our various intelligence agencies spend on studying other countries. I know it's a shit-load of money. The State Department alone spends a few billion dollars every year on collecting information. We often have more insight into what's happening in other countries than their own leaders."

"A typical American response," Dhil said, laughing. "You throw money at problems and think that will take care of them."

"Habib's right," Maggie said. "How often have we messed things up in foreign affairs? Especially in this part of the world."

An itchy silence came down upon them. Dhil hoped he had not stirred up a hornet's nest.

"In any event," Maggie said, gazing at Dhil. "Should you ever want to leave your country, come to the States. Americans understand the plight of those who lose their country."

After dinner, when Maggie and Charles had retired to their room, Dhil tried to reconstruct the discussion they'd had earlier in the evening. An affectionate sensation seeped through him when he thought about how Maggie had not argued with him when he expressed his concern for the future. She had nodded in agreement when he had spoken of his uncertainties. She obviously trusted his judgment without hesitation and even worried about him. It always pleased him to see her accept his way of thinking; it intensified his fascination with her.

Later in bed, as he drifted between consciousness and sleep, he sensed her in his room. Lifting one corner of the cover, she slipped into his bed. When he began caressing her body, she held his hand. The silky skin of her other hand stroked his chest, and her moist lips touched his mouth. Like a velvety blanket, her body's warmth enclosed him and they made love. At the point of her climax, her delicate body shivered and writhed as if pained by an agonizing joy.

He wasn't sure how long they had been lying together, breathing rapidly, their sweaty bodies pressed closely to each other. He had fallen asleep, when a movement awakened him, and he heard the muffled clink of his bedroom door gently closing.

Chapter Four

Miriam Khan sat on the edge of her bed. Looking out the window, she watched how the heat of the midday sun gradually broke up the thick cloud cover. Rays of vivid light pierced the scattering scraps of vapor, allowing blue patches to appear in the sky.

Zarina, Miriam's personal servant, opened the door. Putting her head through the crack, she said, "Lunch is served." Her usual black chador covered her graying hair.

Miriam didn't move. She expected Habib Dhil's call at any minute. She worried she could miss it if she left.

"Bibi's waiting," Zarina said. She did not like it when things didn't run smoothly. Her voice took on an irritated tenor. "She's already at the table," she insisted.

Reluctantly, Miriam rose. Walking along the corridor to the other end of the sprawling mansion, she agonized that she

might not reach Dhil in time to tell him to meet her in Paghman tomorrow.

"I wouldn't go to Paghman," Miriam's mother said when she
realized what her daughter intended to do the next day. "The car
could get stuck in the snow." She put a little rice on her plate,
pouring a spoonful of meat sauce over it. "Why don't you drive to
Jelalabad instead? The warm weather there would cheer you up."

Driving to Jelalabad was out of the question. It was the last
place Miriam could expect to find privacy. Lured by the area's
mild climate, many of her relatives spent the winter in Jelalabad,
a small town without any cultural or recreational facilities, a place
that offered little for visitors to fill their time. Bored to death, the
younger people had nothing better to do than to walk the bazaars
along the main road and to haggle with the vendors over the
prices of their wares. It was a virtual certainty that somebody
would notice her presence as soon as her car entered the town.

She had no choice but to go to Paghman, the summer retreat,
some ten miles west of Kabul. Deserted for its unforgiving cold
in winter, Paghman would keep prying eyes away. There she
always felt freer than anywhere else, a little less restricted by the
impediments instilled in her since childhood. Hard as she tried,
she could not always prevent those inhibitions from lingering
in the corners of her mind. To her surprise and anguish, she
sometimes had the thought that sleeping with Habib Dhil was
a filthy vice, an unforgivable sin in God's eyes.

In those moments, she felt trapped in a world that had stolen
her soul, forcing her to commit acts of immorality. The struggle
to overcome these feelings of failing and shame exhausted her.
The desertion of Paghman in winter, the utter silence of the
snow-covered landscape, and the purity of the nippy mountain
air helped her forget the questions of sin and damnation. There,
she could relax, even if only for a short while.

Poor Mother, she thought, watching the dry skin of her mother's hand as she dug her fork into the brown rice on her plate. More than half of the rice fell off the fork before it reached her mouth. Sitting at the head of the long dining table, she appeared lonely and isolated. Would she suffer a heart attack if she knew her daughter went to Paghman to sleep with a man? Perhaps not. Maybe she, too, had had an affair when she was young and her skin fresh and her body desirable. Yes, Miriam decided, it couldn't be beyond the realm of possibilities. Perhaps she should share her secret with her mother. She might understand.

As Miriam observed her mother, she realized how much her mother had shrunk lately. Her oversized eyeglasses made her look owlish, adding to the rapid aging of her countenance. Was she dying, Miriam wondered, or was it her own dejected mood that made her see everything in a dismal light?

"What's the matter, dear?" her mother asked, as if sensing that something bothered her.

For a split second, she was tempted to tell her mother about her affair with Dhil. But the desire to open up toward her mother dissipated. "There's nothing you can do for me, Mother," she said, unable to hide her exasperation.

"What do you mean?"

"Why does father insist on it?"

"You mean your engagement?"

"What else is there?"

"You know how men are," her mother said, placing her fork carefully on her plate. "They do what they believe is right."

"Not when it concerns me."

"Obeying your father is not just a custom. It's Allah's will that we do as the men in our lives tell us." Miriam's mother stretched out her hand, placing it on her daughter's forearm. "When I was given to your father, I wasn't asked. And I was terribly worried about who this man, with whom I would spend the rest of my life, would be."

Miriam looked at her mother. She wanted to believe her, trust her. For a moment, her mother's face more resembled the once beautiful woman she had been.

Bibi slowly nodded her head. "In the end, it all worked out. You'll see. Before you know it, you'll get used to him. And when the children arrive, they will bring you joy. They'll make up for your suffering."

"You can't justify something simply because it has been done in the past," Miriam said, brusquely moving her arm away from under her mother's hand. "I simply don't accept that God doesn't want us to have our own minds. Besides, things change, Mother."

"But, my dearest, nothing has changed here."

"I have. And I'd sooner die than marry Reza Bahaadur."

"Your father wants to strengthen the bond between the king and himself." She took her napkin and dabbed her thin lips with it. "He's doing it for you. He wants you to be safe when we are gone."

"My father has done enough for me. I can take care of myself."

"Your refusal will complicate our relations with the King and his family. The religious leaders would be concerned if your father gave in to your demands. And tribal chiefs would exploit a rift, confounding your father's work. It's so much more important than you realize, my child."

"Father should know that I won't get married to please the mullahs or anyone else. And nothing will happen between the King and my father. They depend on each other. They can't afford a squabble."

"We still have to follow Allah's commands," Miriam's mother said. "That will never change."

"Why did you send me to school abroad if you intended to treat me the same way your parents treated you?"

"I had nothing to do with your going to school abroad," Miriam's mother said, picking up grains of rice from the table, putting them on a small saucer. "I was afraid you would change and refuse to accept our ways. I mentioned it to your father. But he was adamant. He wanted to make a modern woman of you."

"Then, why doesn't he treat me like one?"

Bibi's eyes grew moist. Her hands began to shake. "Men do what they want," she said, her voice breaking. "You better accept it before you ruin your life."

"I'm not going to. This is my life. I won't let anyone destroy it."

"You can't deny your father his wish. He won't let that happen."

"He must," Miriam said, taking her napkin from her lap, twisting it, and putting it back on her lap. "Remember, Mother. It's me, his daughter."

"If you deny your father his wish," Miriam's mother said, avoiding Miriam's eyes, looking down at her plate as if she were speaking to herself, "it will end badly. I know him. He's going to get very angry."

After a moment of silence, Miriam tossed her napkin on the table and left, slamming the door shut.

Back in her room, she threw herself on her bed and picked up from her night table *The Arab World Today*, the book she had been reading. She tried to read but feeling painfully on edge; she couldn't concentrate. The conversation with her mother had left her aggravated. How could she expect her to deny her own self for the sake of her father's wishes—for the sake of political expediency? Despite her mother's advice and the potential consequences for the two families if she refused to marry Amir Bahaadur Shah's son, she resolved not to let herself be treated as a prized possession, one that the owner could sell off whenever an advantageous opportunity presented itself.

She knew she had to make a stand. Feeling very determined, she climbed from the bed and lifted the phone.

Chapter Five

Pushing aside the thick stack of correspondence, Habib Dhil rose from behind his desk and strode to the window, watching Kabul's dreary jumble of decrepit houses, crowded streets, and shimmering mountains. Snow covering the street down below had turned black from the exhaust of passing cars and trucks. Massive crowds, mostly wearing heavily worn overcoats bought from the old-cloth bazaar, populated the sidewalks.

Dhil always wondered how such teeming masses appeared in such a sparsely populated country. Just where did they come from? But the scruffy throng couldn't retain his attention for long. His thoughts returned to that sun-drenched afternoon in Paghman three weeks before. He found it impossible to take his mind off Miriam's relaxed, sweaty face as she lay beside him in her bedroom where Paghman's brilliant daylight, muted by the drawn curtains, faintly lit the room.

He didn't know how long he had been standing before the window when he heard a knock. It was Hadi Omar, his newest assistant. He looked something like a stick figure a child might draw. His expression was pained.

"Excuse me, Sa'heb," Omar said. "Someone just called. He said the director of the Central Depot has locked up Zeb."

"Locked up Zeb? What for?"

"Apparently, he had a confrontation with the director," Omar said.

"Who did you say called?" Dhil asked, still not sure he understood what Omar was saying.

"I don't know who it was, Sa'heb. He didn't introduce himself."

It had been almost two years since Dhil had been purchasing staples—sugar, cooking oil, tea, powdered milk, and the like—that could only be acquired from the *Enesarat-e-Dowlati* for resale to his employees. In that way, he had hoped, everybody would be a little better off. His decision, he thought, had been a success. His employees were happy not having to endure the time-consuming and often humiliating chore of buying those products themselves. Company operations had improved as absenteeism had declined noticeably.

The scheme had worked so well that Dhil had expanded the service, even maintaining a limited supply of merchandise for emergencies. Of course, winter was the time for the greatest demand. As soon as the first snow fell, he instructed his procurement department to replenish the company stocks.

Agha Zeb, Dhil's procurement manager, had been at it for weeks, securing permits from the *Enesarat-e-Dowlati*, making the required payments to the *Enesarat-e-Dowlati's* account at the Central Bank, submitting the Central Bank's receipts to the relative department of the *Enesarat-e-Dowlati*, obtaining the necessary release vouchers authorizing the *Enesarat-e-Dowlati*'s Central Depot to release the goods.

Zeb would have mentioned an impasse with any of those offices, no matter how insignificant, Dhil thought. He wasn't sure what to make of the ominous news.

"Is this serious or is someone playing a game with us?" he said, unable to imagine Zeb starting a fight. Experienced and clearheaded, he would be the last person to provoke a confrontation.

"The caller sounded sincere," Omar said. "He warned that the director would file charges if something wasn't done immediately. He urged you to come personally."

Dhil would have preferred to have one of his employees handle the task of negotiating Zeb's release. This was quite unusual.

"Of course," he said calmly, not wanting to betray the undefined sense of alarm he was feeling. He loathed the thought of having to go to the Central Depot and a sudden fatigue came over him. The flow of melting snow down the waterspouts had quickened. In the quiet of the early afternoon, the rush of water sounded like a creek running through a narrow gorge in a serene spot out in the countryside. For a moment, a wonderful whirl filled his head, and he wholly forgot Zeb and the Central Depot. His mind emptied itself from the disconcerting prospect of having to confront the Depot's director, and he found himself behind the wheel of his Land Rover as it eased through the narrow lane and came to a stop at the black-painted, wrought-iron gate.

He remembered how his conscience had jolted. He wasn't sure whether it weighed on him for being disloyal to Maggie. Maybe he just felt guilty for having left his work so early in the afternoon to meet clandestinely with Miriam while the rest of the world wrestled with the tedious business of survival.

On that uncharacteristically mild day in an otherwise harsh winter, the snow-covered countryside had sparkled as the sun's rays blazed fiercely down from a dazzling sky.

Miriam stood on the other side of the entrance, inside the compound of her family's summer house that sat on a sloping ground against the massive silhouette of mountains perched above the small hamlet of Paghman.

The guard opened the gate just wide enough for Dhil to walk through. Miriam—her black overcoat hugging her slim figure, her shoulder-length, chestnut-brown hair framing her pale face—smiled when he stood before her. She grabbed his hand, and they rushed up the hill toward the house. They couldn't afford to waste a single minute. The next day, Miriam would accompany her mother to London for her yearly medical checkup, and she had to dash back home for the farewell party her father had planned for them later that evening.

Omar cleared his throat. The sound of it jolted Dhil back to the present. He found Omar scowling as he waited for instructions.

"I'll go myself," Dhil said. "But stay by the phone. I want to be sure that I can reach the office immediately." Walking along the hallway toward the exit door, he heard the phone for his direct line ring. He slowed down, deliberating whether he should go back and answer it. It couldn't be Maggie. She rarely called. He normally had to take the initiative. That was the deal they had worked out. It made it easier for her, she had once said.

Suddenly, he stopped. It could be Miriam. He rushed back. But when he picked up the receiver, the caller had hung up.

For the last several months, Dhil had noticed a gradual deterioration of his company's relations with government authorities.

Processing simple applications had been getting costlier and more time-consuming. Increasingly, he had to take matters into his own hands and go all the way to government ministers to get simple jobs done. The cost of obtaining services had become astronomical. Besides, his debt didn't stop at that. Inevitably, officials returned for additional personal favors.

He had never gotten completely used to shelling out money for perfectly normal and legal transactions. It greatly disturbed him, even though his grandfather taught him that paying kick-backs was an important part of dealing with the government bureaucracy. His grandfather was right. Over time he had grown used to it, resigning himself to the fact that he could neither ignore nor change such an entrenched habit and had to live with it. When he could avoid participating directly in those deal-ings, the transactions remained impersonal, even anonymous, and barely stuck in his mind. But, when forced to personally involve himself, their nagging, corrosive memory caused him anguish. The debauchery signaled to him the degeneration of his own life. He had a sense of being injured, mangled by wounds that never healed.

He didn't know the reason for the growing impasse in his dealings with the bureaucracy. Inevitably, he wondered whether his relationship with Miriam had something to do with it. But he always rejected the thought. They had been too careful for anyone to find out. Maybe it was the time he spent with the two Americans. But nobody should care about his relationship with the Reeds. After all, the Americans supported the govern-ment with subsidies and technical assistance. Perhaps he should search for the reason within the government itself. He often felt that anyone living in Afghanistan knew instinctively that it could, and probably would, all end, suddenly.

A gathering crisis within the government would explain the extra harassment. Once bureaucrats sniffed a potential catastrophe coming, they grew scared and became greedier, wanting more money—fast money before upheaval swept over their lives. Still, Dhil had to admit that he would have heard if trouble was stirring.

A shiver went through Dhil's body. Turning the heat all the way up, he drove across town to get to the Central Depot, which was located in the industrial sector on Kabul's eastern outskirts, just before a shantytown began its untidy spread all the way to the foothills of the mountains that soared dark and steep into the sky. Low clouds gathered. Snow began to fall, the flakes gliding down soundlessly, muffling the dissonance of the street noises.

Cars, trucks, horse-drawn *gadis*, and bicycles—innumerable bicycles—crammed the street. The black limousine of a high government official and an olive-green Russian Volga of the Ministry of Defense cut off other motorists, zigzagging wildly through the thick traffic. Military trucks loaded with ragged army recruits on their way to work on some government construction projects steered ahead regardless of what moved in front of them. The noisy engines of their battered Moskovitchs and Volgas puffing out inordinate amounts of fume, the taxi drivers relentlessly pushed forward, adding to the jumble and hazard in the street. Buses, overflowing with people, some barely hanging on to a door handle, sported bright paintings of large rivers flowing through fertile valleys, lush-green jungles disgorging herds of wild animals, among them lions and tigers, their jaws wide open, their eyes full of fury.

Smiling at this extravagant display of fancy, Dhil carefully steered his car through the confusion, barely avoiding a bicyclist who was remarkably oblivious to the deadly dangers around him as he employed daredevil maneuvers in a rush to get ahead.

Dhil drove along Central Avenue through the crowded downtown commercial district, the chief location for the karakul pelt traders, dried fruit sellers, tea merchants, and rug exporters. Then he passed the palace, its high encircling walls hiding the acclaimed Delkusha Gardens. Would Miriam spend her life there, as Bahaadur Shah's daughter-in-law?

Dhil's muscles stiffened, and he smashed his fist against the steering wheel. How could he allow such a thought to enter his mind? That would never happen. He had not given up on her. He would never give up on her.

When the press had announced Miriam's engagement to Reza Bahaadur last fall, Dhil was shocked and grievously wounded and had pressed Miriam to see him immediately. Although he knew that it would take her some time to find an excuse and make the necessary arrangements, he would not relent. It took a day before she could prepare the ground to get away and, as had been their habit, they met in Paghman.

As soon as the house door had shut behind him, Dhil had shouted at her, "How can you marry him?"

"I had nothing to do with it," she screamed back. "I can't stand Reza Bahaadur. I'd sooner die than be his wife."

Her words deflated the explosive pressure that had been building in him. He took her in his arms and stroked her hair. "Will you be able to withstand your father's power?" he asked, knowing that she, in many ways, was quite traditional and inclined to submit to her father's will. "Your father would be concerned about what the religious leaders and tribal maliks would think if you broke the engagement."

"My father knows me well enough to realize that I won't get married just to please them."

"What about the politics behind your engagement? There will be repercussions if you refuse."

"Nothing will happen," she said. "My father and the King

can't afford a squabble. They depend on each other. Nothing will happen regardless of what I do."

It wasn't difficult for Dhil to concur with her assessment. After all, a breakup of the two leaders' political affiliation could lead to a fierce struggle for power among them and their supporters. The quarrel could be messy, ending in bloodshed—including their own. Wouldn't they want to avoid that at all cost?

But as much as this conclusion seemed to reflect reality, Dhil was not placated. Aside from the potential political implications, the families' honor was on the line. Miriam's renunciation of the marriage would be an intolerable insult to both the King and his son. And Prime Minister Khan's acquiescence to his daughter's rejection of the marriage to Governor Bahaadur would humiliate the whole Bahaadur clan. The consequences of the resulting hostility would most likely cost Khan his job and could, and probably would, spawn a blood feud that would continue for half a century or longer. It would be foolish to believe that Miriam could get away with it.

In any event, Prime Minister Khan would never give up his high office. Holding on to power and protecting his position would always be his first priority, a precedent he would place even above his daughter. As long as he believed that marrying off his daughter to Amir Bahaadur Shah's son would forever cement his political future, he would never agree to dissolve that union.

Dhil had no illusions. If he tried to disrupt Miriam's marriage to Reza Bahaadur, her father would destroy him. A shadowy tribunal would charge him with treason, and he would be taken straight to some isolated spot and shot dead.

He pressed the accelerator. As the Land Rover lunged forward, he almost ran over a pedestrian crossing the road. A little further down, along Helmand Street stood the great Eid

Mosque. A veil of white blurred the outline of its tall, slender minaret, and its snow-mantled blue dome loomed large over the structure. At the end of Helmand, he turned left onto the wide Dar-ul-Alam Boulevard, which led to the city limits and connected with the East-West Highway.

As he headed out of the noisy central part of the city, traffic thinned out and the town's boisterous confusion gave way to sleepy streets and shabby dwellings. A few pedestrians hurried to their destinations, bent by the biting cold and wearing long chapans, the scarves of their turbans wrapped tightly around their throats. Half-starved stray dogs roamed about, sniffing at bones, eggshells, pieces of hard, moldering bread, anything that promised to be edible. Two boys—despite their tattered sweaters, their thin cotton garments, their bare feet inside ripped shoes— rolled iron hoops and romped together in youthful indifference.

Chapter Six

Colonel Alam Gol returned from his lunch break. He had gone to the small kebab place two blocks from his office and eaten too much. He felt bloated and craved for hot green tea. He settled in behind his desk and rang for the office sergeant to get the tea. After a minute or two, he buzzed for the sergeant again.

Where was the damn sergeant? The aide was not to leave his station without authorization. But Gol refused to be angry. He was not about to let some petty infraction spoil his pleasure about his good fortune. He opened his desk drawer, fingering the envelope with fifty thousand afghanis. It was the first time in six months since his promotion that he had been able to take private advantage of his office.

The sergeant had just brought his tea when Secret Police

Chief Nabi Dost came into Gol's office. As he rose to greet Dost, his mind searched feverishly for a reasonable explanation for Dost's unexpected visit. Gol's hasty review of his actions over the past several days failed to dig up a potentially objectionable deed, one that could have prompted the secret police to investigate him.

The only thing that could have come to Dost's attention would be the fifty thousand he had collected from Akbar Nouri whom he had helped obtain government approval for the purchase of a parcel of publicly owned land that lay adjacent to his property. But that should not have triggered an investigation. Before agreeing to help Nouri, Gol had carefully researched whether some important person had shown interest in that particular acreage. Only after he had been convinced that no higher-up wanted it had he expedited the procedure.

Still troubled that the Secret Police Chief's visit might be in conjunction with an investigation of him, Gol directed his visitor to the small conference table by the window. He pulled up a chair and invited Dost to sit down.

The secret police chief's plump body bulged out from both sides of the chair, his short legs barely touching the floor, his smooth cheeks shimmering a healthy pink. His eyes were remarkably alert, beaming an extraordinary amount of energy from behind thick, rimless glasses. Gol couldn't help but notice that the Secret Police Chief, despite his obesity and diminutive build, had a dominating presence.

"May I offer you some tea, sir?" Dhil asked.

"Yes, please." Secret Police Chief Dost turned to the file he had been holding in his hands, flipping playfully its pages. He looked up briefly when Gol put the cup in front of him.

"Thank you, Colonel Gol," he said, turning back to the page that seemed to have caught his attention. His eyes remained fixed on it for what seemed to Gol several terribly long minutes.

The only sound was Dost's rhythmic breathing. Gol felt hot, wondering whether those neatly typed pages contained damaging information about him. Who might have fabricated it?

"Colonel," the Secret Police Chief finally said. He turned his puffed-up face toward Gol, watching him intensely. "Arranging the sale of state-owned land isn't a part of your job, is it?"

A strain of chill dashed across Gol's head. Dumbfounded, he remained still for a time and struggled to steady himself. When he spoke his voice trembled. "May I explain, sir?"

"Don't," Dost cut him off. Raising his hand in which he held the file. "Everything I need to know is here." He put the file on the table.

"We all need money; I understand that. But you don't do it on your own. You must come to me first. Then you will get what you want."

"I am sorry, sir," Gol said, his uniform clinging uncomfortably to his perspiring skin. "It won't happen again. I promise, sir."

"Well then," Dost said, taking a sip from the tea cup. "The Prime Minister thinks highly of your late father. He was a patriot and a friend to all of us in the government." He looked down at his fleshy hands resting on the table. "It's time that you show the same loyalty to the regime."

Gol began to sense an opening, a chance to alter his predicament. "Sir," he said, "I have always served the government. I am ready to do anything that is demanded of me. I assure you of my fullest cooperation."

"Well, then," Dost repeated. His tone was conciliatory. "Let's forget the land deal and the money. You've been paid for it. What was it, fifty thousand afghanis?"

The stress that had been accumulating within Gol evaporated like air escaping a punctured balloon. His stiff muscles relaxed.

He shifted in his chair, finding a more comfortable position. "Thank you, sir," he said, softly.

"We've got a nasty problem to deal with in Kunduz," Dost said, growing serious again. "Last night, Governor Bahaadur tried to have sex with a conscript."

Gol watched Dost carefully. Neither the tone of his business-like voice nor his features revealed what he personally thought of the Governor's behavior.

The chief took another small sip of tea, "The soldier freed himself from the Governor's grip and attacked Bahaadur's body-guard, snatching away the guard's pistol. He then attempted to shoot the Governor."

Dost paused again. Gol couldn't help himself becoming impatient. But Dost was not going to be rushed. He finally continued, "Governor Bahaadur pulled his own weapon and shot back. In the melee, the bodyguard was killed and a bullet pierced the Governor's left hand. The recruit, who is from the Kunduz area, was able to flee.

"According to my agent in Kunduz, the renegade soldier has gone to his village and is hiding in his parents' house. When the local police tried to detain him this morning, the villagers surrounded the hut and prevented the police from entering." He raised his voice and leaned forward. "This is unacceptable. We can never permit people to defy our authority. Especially in this case. The Governor isn't just anybody. We're dealing here with the King's son."

Gol agreed that it was a serious matter. He waited for the rest he knew was coming.

"Here is the strange part of the story," Dost continued. "When the Prime Minister suggested dispatching troops to arrest the conscript, the Governor declined. He insisted he could solve the problem himself but refused to elaborate how he planned to go about it.

"The Prime Minster has ordered me to handle the matter, and I have decided to entrust you with the task. This is your opportunity to prove your loyalty to the Prime Minister."

Gol felt paralyzed. There had to be unforeseen consequences for interfering in something the Governor had chosen to deal with himself. Maybe he had his father's support. Gol decided to be cautious.

"This is a very important assignment, sir" he said. "I'm not sure I can handle it."

Redirecting his attention to the file, Dost turned its pages again, taking his time glancing through them, gliding slowly his stubby index finger over the type-written lines. He put the dossier back on the table and raised his head. His eyes looked cold. "You're an ambitious man, Colonel. If you want to get ahead, you must accept risks. Above all, you must prove your loyalty." He fell silent. "Show your mettle," he said very softly. "And you will be rewarded beyond your imagination."

Dost looked at his watch and, as if having misplaced something, looked around. He suddenly rose from his chair. "I've got to rush," he said. "In a few minutes, I've to see the Minister of the Interior. Meet me in an hour in the hall before the Prime Minister's office. He wants to give you your orders personally."

Gol was not even given a choice. He quickly resigned himself to that fact. Now, without any details, Gol began to imagine all sort of scenarios. He wondered whether Khan wanted the Governor dead but dismissed the idea. Even with Khan's propensity for violence in dispensing of problems, the thought of him orchestrating the Governor's assassination appeared highly far-fetched. It seemed implausible that Khan would accept the political risk that was involved in murdering the King's son. The fallout could be a furious clash between them and their followers.

He returned to his desk. No, he thought. It was more likely

that Khan would order him to detain the renegade soldier and arrange for his public execution in Kunduz City. The only danger that remained was the possibility that the Governor would make it difficult for him to carry out his orders, leading to a confrontation the outcome of which he simply could not fathom.

Balancing the negative against the positive, Gol began to consider the more encouraging possibilities. If discharged successfully, he thought, the special assignment could lead to rapid promotions. He could almost see himself replacing the colonel's crossed sabers on his shoulder pads with a general's stars.

Still, he could not prevent himself from worrying. Prime Minister Khan was a dangerous man. If Gol failed him or crossed him, even inadvertently, Gol's career or even his life could be at risk.

Gol returned to his paperwork to keep his mind off the impending meeting with the Prime Minister. But a fluke thought brought back the scene of his first encounter with Khan. An eternity stood between now and then. Having successfully put the occasion away for a long time, he loathed its re-emergence before his mind's eye.

Chapter Seven

Gol had recently graduated from the National Military Academy, when Prime Minister Khan, on an official visit to the Northern Provinces, stopped at their family farm in Baghlan. Gol had never seen Khan close up. Standing beside his father's imposing physique, Khan didn't look like an omnipotent ruler. In his tight, English riding breeches and shining black boots, he rather appeared somewhat like a clown.

Gol couldn't understand why people feared this squat, pompous man. And fear him they did. When his father's friends gathered in their house for an evening of card games and, usually during dinner, discussed politics and complained about the brutality of Khan's government, Gol often noticed how they lowered their voices, even looked around, seemingly making sure nobody else was listening.

The extensive preparations preceding Khan's visit disrupted

Gol's normal routine. One day prior to the Prime Minister's arrival, his father told him neither to visit nor to ride out with Habib Dhil, his childhood friend from the neighboring farm, who had come up from Kabul to visit his grandfather. He should be available, Gol's father had said to Gol, in the event that he would be needed for one thing or another.

Not knowing what to do with himself, Gol had lingered about in the stables. He was chatting with the groom who was sprucing up the horses and polishing the saddles, when his father sent for him.

The cook Dhil's grandfather had sent over to oversee the culinary arrangements had decided that the meat of the two sheep would not suffice and a third one had to be slaughtered. He also wanted one more sack of rice and another barrel of cooking oil. And the butler Dhil's grandfather had also loaned out to help with setting the buffet table and serving the guests, had disapproved of their utensils and wanted to return to Dhil's farm to get napkins, tablecloths, silverware, and dishes.

Gol's father instructed Gol to ride the *gadi*, make the purchases in the bazaar, and then accompany the butler to Dhil's farm, helping him carry the items that he wanted to pick up there.

All of that had annoyed Gol greatly. But what had him feel ashamed and angry was his father's submissive manner in Khan's presence. And then there was the moment when the Prime Minister shot a bluebird.

His father directed Gol to show the Prime Minister the new rifle his father had bought him as a graduation gift.

"It's an excellent piece," Khan said after examining the gun. Khan put a single round in the chamber and aimed at the lush foliage of the nearest tree. The rifle's sharp report shattered the tranquility of the summer afternoon. Frightened birds rose from the treetops, soaring high above them, forming dark, reeling clouds in the sky, filling the air with the nervous flapping of their wings.

One bluebird plunged to the ground and Gol's father rushed to where it had fallen, the loose end of his turban fluttering in the air. He picked up the dead bird, holding it from its wing tip, its head hanging loosely, its reddish-brown breast torn apart by the bullet. "What an extraordinary shot, Your Excellency," he called out, raising the dead bird high above his head. "Truly, a formidable shot."

Despite his tough, weathered face, his long, gray beard, and huge build, his father looked ludicrous. The respected master of so many tenant farmers had been no more than a silly creature, laughable, insignificant. And all that had happened while Dhil and his grandfather witnessed the shameful scene.

Chapter Eight

Chief Dost was waiting for Gol outside the Prime Minister's office. He looked at his watch as Gol approached.

"Good," he said. "Well, Colonel, have you prepared yourself?"

Gol was not completely sure what he meant, but assumed he was being asked if he was committed. It didn't matter. There could only be one answer. "Yes, sir. I am ready."

Dost grabbed Gol gently by the arm. "Let's go to his office then."

Prime Minister Wali Khan sat behind his writing desk, his face turned downward, the index finger of his right hand tapping the desktop. The sun, flooding through the large windows and transparent curtains, bathed the room in a soft pastel. Apart from the nervous thumping of Khan's manicured fingernail hitting the clear top of the desk, quiet reigned in the office.

Only an expensive-looking penholder and a dagger with a deep-red ruby attached to its hilt were on Khan's desk, and the meticulously polished desktop reflected the muted rays of light.

How could any ordinary man fail to be intimidated, Gol thought. However, inside this office, Gol could also feel himself drawn to the power on display so close to him. He could already visualize being a part of this powerful man's inner circle. Would his father be disgusted or proud of him?

He clenched one hand tightly in the other, forcing himself to focus. All other thoughts were silly and irrelevant.

"Sir, Colonel Gol has arrived," Dost said.

Khan looked up and nodded. Gol was surprised to see that, except for flabbier cheeks and slightly duller eyes, the Prime Minister hadn't changed much since he had visited their farm in Baghlan so many years back.

"The Governor of Kunduz has betrayed our trust," Khan said. "We must remove him to protect the nation."

Gol found his voice's grave ring sounded precisely like one of his television speeches.

"We must also make sure that the peace in the country is not disturbed," Khan said. "Traitors always use moments of tragedy and uncertainty to provoke instability."

Gol noticed that Khan used words similar to those he employed in public declarations when he justified the elimination of opponents. Invoking peace and stability surely meant to rationalize yet another execution.

"I entrust this historic task to you, Colonel."

Khan's words reached Gol in a strange way as though coming from a far distance but hitting him with the full force of their import. He shuddered. Not only had he to bring the fugitive soldier in for punishment, the job required him to kill the Governor, too.

"I know of your family's commitment to our nation and its

leaders," Khan said. "I am convinced you will prove worthy of my trust."

Khan stared at Gol without adding anything to what he already had said. Gol felt like Khan's eyes were trying to bore inside his mind.

Finally, Khan spoke again. "I have no personal vendetta against the Governor, or the King." His voice was now utterly devoid of emotions. "The decision to liquidate the Governor has been painful to me. My close family ties and long-standing friendship with His Majesty are well known."

Gol wondered why Khan felt the need to explain himself.

"I realize this is an act against my own friend and family." Khan banged the desk. "But, as Prime Minister, I must uphold the interests of our nation. Regardless of the cost to myself, I am compelled to eliminate any and all sources of betrayal and to protect the good of our country."

Son of a bitch, Gol thought. He felt his revulsion for Khan resurface and, at the same time, was fascinated by his unyielding use of complete control. He instinctively turned to Secret Police Chief Dost, watching him for any reaction but found his features frozen, his sweaty face empty of any sentiments. Standing stiff, his large belly protruding from under his uniform jacket, Dost's unmoving eyes were fixed on Khan.

Prime Minister Khan said nothing else and looked away. Wordlessly, Dost signaled Gol to leave.

Gol and Dost drove back to the Chief's office at the Ministry of the Interior. Dost remained silent the entire trip which only magnified Gol's anxiety.

At last they reached Dost's small office. "Sit down, Colonel," he said curtly. And barely had they settled in, when a captain entered, handing Dost two sealed envelopes.

"Here are the documents you must take with you," Dost

said, passing the letters on to Gol. "One is the Defense Minister's order to the Commandant of the Kunduz Mechanized Division. The other is from the Minister of the Interior to the Kunduz Chief of Police. Both are instructed to put their resources at your disposal. You can deploy their men and equipment as you see fit."

Dost's attention turned to the many folders cluttering his desk, and he began organizing them, piling them up and sorting them out. After a while, he looked up. "Oh yes," he said. His face had an expression as if he had only now remembered the reason for Gol's presence in his office. "Later today, an Air Force plane will fly some equipment to Kunduz. I've arranged for you to travel along. One of my drivers will pick you up at six and drive you to Amir Bahaadur Shah Military Airfield. As soon as you're on your way, I'll instruct my representative in Kunduz to notify the local Army Commander and Police Chief of your arrival."

Dost didn't wait for Gol to leave. His attention immediately returned to the files on his desk. He grabbed one, opened it, and began to read.

Chapter Nine

It was still early in the afternoon when Gol headed home. He would put on a new shirt, he decided, and polish his shoes, clean his pistol and ask his sister, Nadia, to iron his uniform. She would probably want to know the cause for his sudden departure. He would speak of an emergency, but only in general terms. And not to cause her anguish, he would add that it wasn't anything important. Nothing to worry about, he would insist.

In any case, she wasn't aware of much that was going on in the outside world. She sat in the house, waiting for someone to come and take her away. She had taken too much after their father. What had looked merely imposing in the old man made her appear frighteningly unpalatable. How would a man feel holding her large hands, Gol wondered. He couldn't imagine a suitor wanting to spend a lifetime fucking a woman of her size.

Gol shook his head and remembered his mother, who, in a moment of anguish and disappointment, had looked to the heavens and cried out, "Oh, All Mighty! Thanks for what you gave my husband and for what you denied my child."

And there was nothing Gol could do about it. Lacking the right name or the money for some unfortunate soul to be enticed into asking for her hand, Gol realized he had to accept that she would always be there when he returned from work, looking expectantly, hopefully, yet resignedly at a lot not of her choosing.

Driving through the quiet streets, he realized his mission could directly affect Habib Dhil. Initially, it had all been mere rumors that he fucked the Prime Minister's daughter. Then, about a month ago, Gol found out that the talk about Dhil's affair with Miriam Khan wasn't just gossip but fact, and the information came directly from Chief Dost.

They were at a funeral for Ahmad Welayati, the old air-force General and had by chance been standing next to each other. The mullah—a slight man, a loosely-cut black gown hanging over his shoulders—placed himself at the head of the open grave and began his sermon, evoking Allah's wrath and admonishing the assembled mourners to repent.

Dost, a bored expression on his face, looked up at Gol. "You know Habib Dhil, the cloth manufacturer, don't you?" he whispered. "Isn't he from your province?"

"We are neighbors in Baghlan," Gol said, looking down at Dost's red, fleshy face. He warily added, "I knew him when we were boys, haven't seen him for quite a while."

"The man's playing with fire," Dost said sharply. "He sleeps with the Prime Minister's daughter."

Gol's first thought was one of admiration for his old friend. After all, Miriam Khan's beauty was legendary throughout the country. But he knew this was nothing to joke about.

Dost used his hand to shield his eyes from the sun's blazing light. His tone softer, he said, "He's from a good family. He shouldn't risk his safety for the daughter of a leading personality. For that matter, he shouldn't jeopardize his security for any woman."

Dost pulled a white handkerchief from his pants' pocket and wiped the sweat from his face. "Tell him, we know he maintains a shady association with a man from the American embassy. The man's wife visits Dhil in his house. I'm willing to look the other way in regards to what he does with the American woman. But he must end his affair with Miriam Khan at once. We observe every move he makes. Tell him that. Tell him, he can't hide from us."

Gol nodded, acknowledging that he understood.

While Gol had occasionally met Dhil at parties and other social events of various kinds, he could not remember the last time he had seen him privately. On the way home from the funeral, he decided to visit Dhil right away. Dhil's place of work would be a better, more impersonal place. Gol would just say he was in that part of Kabul and taking advantage to visit his old friend. He was sure Dhil would be pleased to see him.

Dhil's office was located in a three-story, recently constructed building. While the building's architecture appeared quite non-descript, its façade gave a solid impression.

Behind the tall entrance door was a well-lit reception area. Light-gray marble covered the floor and, toward the back of the large space, a young Hazara man sat behind a desk. Except for a black telephone, the desk was clear.

Gol approached the young man who rose to greet him.

"I'm Colonel Gol," he said. "I would like to see Mr. Dhil."

"Do you have an appointment, sir?" the receptionist asked.

"No, I don't. I'm an old friend. Tell him I was passing by and decided to see him."

The receptionist picked up the receiver and dialed a number. Turning his back toward Gol, he whispered into the phone, making it impossible for Gol to hear what he said. When he turned back toward Gol, he replaced the receiver and, smiling shyly, said Mr. Dhil's secretary was on her way down.

The secretary, a middle-aged woman, came down the red-carpeted stairs. Looking up at Gol, she stretched out her hand. "I am Khadija Ghorban, the president's secretary."

Gol noticed her Hazara accent. He grabbed her hand, which felt tiny in his big palm. "Salam," he said. "I hope I am not disturbing him in his work."

"Not at all, sir. The president's delighted that you've come."

They climbed to the second floor. Crossing the hall, Gol noticed the large Persian rug that covered almost the entire floor.

The secretary knocked at one of the three doors on this floor and opened it. Gol had barely entered the room, when Dhil rushed to him, embracing him warmly, kissing him on both cheeks. "My friend, it is so good to see you."

He motioned for Gol to sit and rolled down the sleeves of his plain white shirt. Gol couldn't help but notice its perfect fit. Probably English or French, he thought.

Having made himself comfortable on the couch, Gol slid his hand over the soft cushion's expensive-looking satin cover. His eyes moved quickly around the room, taking in the oil paintings on the walls and the elegant wood paneling behind Dhil's desk. Dhil must be busy, Gol thought. Many files were stacked one upon the other on Dhil's desk.

Although Dhil always surrounded himself with expensive things, the opulent appointments in his office surprised Gol. As they talked for a while and exchanged past memories, Gol noticed a nervousness in Dhil's movements. But when Gol asked him whether he had a relationship with a girl, Gol clearly noticed Dhil's embarrassment. And he lied outright, denying that he was involved with anyone.

Dhil's butler served tea and biscuits. Moving noiselessly, he had not even once looked at Gol. Better dressed than many mid-level government officials, the discreet servant reminded him of the differences between their two households when they had still lived in Baghlan. In Dhil's house, a reserved silence prevailed, interrupted only for the most necessary communication. And the servants never joined their masters in the living quarters.

In Gol's own home, servants and a multitude of farm-hands entered the house at all times for a host of different reasons. Even the women who came to assist his mother with the laundry and the occasional housecleaning, didn't carry themselves like servants. They worked hard but also lingered about, sitting and talking, without the slightest deference for the mistress of the house. Unlike Dhil's mother, who had an unapproachable air, Gol's mother had felt a sense of sister-hood with the maids.

But those differences had not mattered to either of them. Their friendship had its own ground rules. Despite all the activity on their farms, they considered farm life dull. What fascinated them was the wide countryside, where the wind whispered baffling tales. They wanted to explore the scents and vaguely discernible sounds of the distant mountains, dry ravines, verdant hills, and the expansive stretches of wheat and barley fields. Without company, the serenity of Baghlan seemed dead and the mysterious lisping of the wind terrifying. The adventure had to be sought out with somebody who felt the same longings. Together, roaming about the rolling countryside was a joyous occupation.

As the butler refilled his cup, Gol tried to summon up the feelings he'd once had for Dhil. But hardly anything stirred within him. The intimacy that in years past had existed between them had faded.

Baffled, even hurt, Gol gave up trying to bring up the real purpose for his visit and decided not to transmit Dost's message to Dhil. He realized the danger to Dhil if he didn't warn him and acknowledged the cruelty of his omission. But, all of a sudden, he wasn't really concerned and decided not to be involved.

Pushing the rights and wrongs of his decision out of his mind, he concluded that Dhil's affair with Khan's daughter was his own business; a personal act that, should it have any consequences, would entirely be his own responsibility.

Changing the subject, Gol said, "I sometimes wonder what would have happened if we had never left Baghlan."

"We would probably be the happiest landlords in all of Baghlan Province," Dhil said. "We'd spend time with our horses and punish our children, whenever they abused them." He remained quiet for a moment, then asked, "Do you remember the day your father got mad because we had worked the horses too hard?"

"How could I forget?" Gol said, aware that he had carried the memory of that day with himself for far too long.

Dhil and he had gone horseback riding. Spring had arrived early that year. A warm sun shone from a cloudless sky and a cool breeze stroked their faces. Their horses were in a nervous, challenging manner. Enticed by the liberating freshness of the air and tempted by the charged vitality of the animals, they had, contrary to Gol's father's instructions, stayed out too long.

The sun had just disappeared over the horizon when they returned. Soaked in sweat and foam dripping from their mouths, their overworked horses breathed precipitately.

From afar, Gol saw his father pacing impatiently in front of the house. As soon as they reached the large, freshly painted green stable door, Gol's father came over to him. Grabbing the reins of his horse with one hand, he pulled him down with the other. When he dropped to the ground, his father took a whip and began beating him.

Gol cringed whenever he recalled how the whip's hard leather cut into his flesh. But what hurt him even more was what happened next. Letting go of him, his father turned toward Dhil who stood terrified, anticipating his own share of the whip. But Gol's father—his anger seemingly dissipated, his voice laden with concern—asked Dhil, "Are you all right?" Without waiting for an answer, he added, "Run along now. Your grandfather is worried about you."

Gol had been angry with his father for singling him out for punishment. He also scorned Dhil for having avoided retribution. But years later, he had realized that Dhil had nothing to do with the way his father had behaved.

Time to end his visit, Gol thought and got up.

"Let me show you my latest acquisition," Dhil said, grabbing Gol's arm and leading him to another room.

A well-polished dining table, surrounded by eight chairs upholstered with dark green velvet, dominated the adjoining chamber. Ample light flooded in through two large windows.

Dhil stopped in front of an oil painting of a woman against a murky red background. She had waist-long black hair, large eyes, a shapely figure clad in a long flowing dress. She walked barefoot and turned her head, looking back as if she feared being followed. Her tiny image against the vast background of the turbulently shaded red canvas amplified her solitude.

"Isn't she beautiful?" Dhil asked. His smile made him look years younger.

"It's a stunning piece," Gol agreed.

"Look at her eyes." Dhil walked a step closer to the painting. "Watch how she looks back. She's afraid of being pursued."
Dhil seemed lost in the canvas. "What appeals to me most is
the grace of her movements," he said.

"Is it from a local artist?" Gol asked.

"No, I bought it in Delhi. It's the work of a little-known
painter from India. Our artists don't paint women. And they
wouldn't dare venture in areas of forbidden love. You know
Islamic restrictions wouldn't allow that."

Thinking about how friendships change over time, Gol left
the main road and turned into the quiet street where his house
was situated. Dhil had seemed like his own self only during
the few minutes when he had shown him the painting in the
room adjacent to his office. And, at that moment, Gol had once
again sensed the depth of their friendship.

He wondered whether he had been right not to warn Dhil
that the secret police knew about his affair with Miriam Khan.
But he dismissed his apprehension. Whether he had said anything to Dhil or not would, in the end, not have made much
of a difference. Whenever Khan decided to let Dhil's head roll,
he would do so without heeding anyone or anything.

Chapter Ten

A noisy collection of men crowded the Central Depot's snow-covered courtyard where speculators offered their valid purchase vouchers for sale at inflated prices and buyers—no longer able to bear their children's hungry stares and to look into their wives' silent eyes—counted their last afghanis to check whether they could afford those exorbitant rates.

Hunger must force them, Dhil thought, imagining them saying to themselves, 'There still remains a few days till the rent comes due. By then, God will show a way out. Allah knows the answer to everything.'

Despite the outwardly tumultuous scene, Dhil noticed a conspicuous order dominated the actions of the throng. As soon as a sale had been completed, the speculators handed their vouchers to waiting government officials. In turn, the *mamours* crossed out the owners' names on the vouchers and replaced them with those of the buyers, validating the changes by placing their signatures at the bottom of the documents. Then, cash changed hands, slipping swiftly into pockets.

Dhil worked his way through the multitude and passed by the dozens of soldiers who, in their tattered uniforms and dull faces, lingered about, apparently dazed by the bustle in the courtyard. The atmosphere of gloom that hung around them gave the impression that the Central Depot was an asylum where insanity had taken possession of both the guards and the guarded.

"Excuse me," he said to the soldier standing closest to the door. I need to find the director's office."

"I can take you there myself," the man replied. "Help me out with fifty afghanis. I haven't had a meal today."

"Here's ten," Dhil said. "Just tell me where it is. Quickly!" The soldier grumbled something inaudible. He grabbed the bill, stuffed it in his coat pocket. "It's at the end of the hallway. You can't miss it."

Grime covered the cement floor of the Central Depot's administrative building. The white of the walls had turned gray. Cold air blew through broken windowpanes.

When the broad, tall door that led to the director's office closed behind Dhil, he felt trapped in a wall of bodies. Forty men or so packed the room. Overheated by a large, coal-fired oven, the place stank from the strong smell of sweat.

Nobody spoke. No one moved. All eyes were glued on the director. A seemingly debilitating silence had settled over the crowd. The director—a military officer, a big man with a thick mustache—sat behind a cluttered oversized desk. The scratching of his stylish fountain pen was the only sound audible as he scribbled his instructions on an application.

Standing at the director's right, a civilian, apparently the director's assistant, constantly scanned the supplicants. As soon as the director had written his instructions on an application and signed it, the assistant signaled another person among the crowd, motioning him to step forward and hand over his petition. He read the document, then, speaking in a muffled voice, explained its contents to the director. The director, his broad-shouldered torso inclined forward, listened carefully and, without reading the application himself, wrote his directive beneath the applicants writing and signed it.

Immediately after getting back their applications for some rice or sugar or cooking oil, the petitioners rushed out as it worried that the director might change his mind and yet deny them the delivery of the little food he had just approved.

Dhil did not understand by which method the director's assistant chose the applicants whose petitions he processed. But he concluded that the civilian held his superior's confidence and seemed to be in complete command of who got selected. Attempting to attract the director's attention would be futile, he thought, and decided to try his luck with the assistant.

Gently but firmly, Dhil pushed aside the other petitioners, ignoring their grumbling as he passed through them. After a few minutes, he had made his way to the middle of the room. He stood opposite the director's assistant and their eyes met. Before Dhil could say a word, the assistant motioned him to wait outside. Dhil didn't know what was going on. Did the assistant know him? He had little choice but to follow the man's instruction. He retracted his steps, making his way through the throng back to the door and out of the overheated room. Outside, he took several deep breaths to cleanse his lungs from the foul air he had been breezing inside the director's office.

The chill in the freezing corridor had just begun to numb the skin of his face when the director's assistant appeared.

The customary long-drawn greeting and empty exchanges

of mutual respect prevented Dhil from coming straight to the point. At last, when he addressed the reason for his visit, he couldn't control a measure of gruffness in his voice. "Is it true that your director has locked up my manager?"

"Your employee started an argument with my superior," said the director's aide.

"Is that reason enough to lock him up?"

"I'm afraid it's a little more serious than that," the assistant said, speaking slowly, emphasizing every word. "Your employee is accused of threatening a military officer and slandering government leaders."

"That's preposterous. Zeb would never start a fight."

"What has happened is unfortunate," the assistant said. "The matter is between my director and your employee. I've nothing to do with it. But I'd be available to mediate in this unfortunate situation."

"What's there to mediate?" Dhil said, sharply. "Before I can discuss this further, I want my manager to be released."

The assistant cocked his head. His eyes hardened as he locked them on Dhil. "It would be better to settle the matter before an official report is filed."

Noticing the change in the assistant's posture, Dhil realized the assistant would not be too easily intimidated. He looked him over carefully. With his smooth haircut, spotless white shirt, and cheap, but well-tailored brown suit, he stood out incongruously amid the squalor of the Central Depot. He couldn't afford western-style attire with the salary of a low-level government official. Dhil concluded that this official could be bought without too much difficulty.

Dhil was confident. The Central Depot of the *Enesarat-e-Dowlati* handled an enormous volume of goods. The assistant must have paid a small fortune to secure his position. Naturally, he needed to create enough revenue to recover his investment and make a decent profit himself. The director had to get his share and only God knew who else had to be paid off.

Money would solve the problem, he reassured himself. He would reduce Zeb's detention to a simple business proposition and the director's assistant would agree to the deal.

"Mr. Deputy Director," he said, "I'm not interested in a confrontation. I hope we can solve this matter among ourselves."

"I agree," the assistant said. "But my director's very upset." He got close to Dhil. Taking on a conspiratorial air, he said, "We have to find a good way to satisfy him. I'm afraid it will take some doing."

Dhil smelled the man's cheap cologne. It reminded him of a whore at the whorehouse on Jade Maiwand. He moved back a step. "What do you want me to do?" he asked. "Should I talk to him?"

"I don't think that would be a good idea. Somebody he knows, somebody he trusts, should do the negotiating."

"Could you do that?"

"As I said, I'm available to assist but can't guarantee anything at all."

"I'll reward your effort handsomely, Mr. Deputy Director. All I want to know is what would persuade your superior to release my manager."

"I'll talk to him. But you have got to be patient and let me handle the matter."

"Where's Zeb being kept? Can I see him?"

"My director has given orders not to let anybody speak with him."

"I want to assure him that we are working toward his release."

The assistant deliberated. "You're a special case," he said. "I'll make an exception. My director will understand."

He instructed one of the two soldiers, who guarded the entrance to the director's office, to let Dhil speak with his procurement manager. The conscript, his shoulders hunched in the freezing cold, led Dhil to a door at the end of the hallway. He pulled a single key out of his pocket and, hardly able to move his numb fingers, unlocked the door with great difficulty. At last, the door swung open, and Dhil went inside. Evidently used to store coal for the Central Depot's heating, the small room was dark and damp. Zeb cowered near a heap of coal, his slight frame shaking, soot covering his hands and clothing, the palm of his right hand bleeding.

"What's all this about?" Dhil asked, forcing a smile, so as not to appear too gloomy.

"I could kill the motherfucker with my bare hands," Zeb shouted.

Dhil took out a handkerchief and cleaned Zeb's scraped hand. His manager explained what had happened: For the past two days, he had produced his release voucher at the Central Depot's storage hangar. Although he had paid the customary baksheesh to all of the officials, each time the supervisor at the distribution hangar had told him to come back the following day. "This is the third day I've come to pick up my consignment," Zeb said. "All the departments have approved it. It is fully paid for. I gave the bank receipt to the official in charge. He issued the release vouchers." Zeb's voice quaked as he went on, "Today, when they refused delivery again, I decided to complain to the director himself. But the director refused to listen and had me locked up."

"The director's assistant claims you used strong language. He says you threatened the director."

"I did nothing of the sort. I only pushed a guard aside when he tried to stop me from going up to the director's desk. That's all I did."

"It's not important what they say. We will pay them off and get out of here."

Zeb's face tightened. "I wish you would complain to the Minister. They had no reason to give me the run around."

Dhil knew he couldn't do anything to restore Zeb's wounded pride. The damage had already been done and could not be undone. Besides, he didn't know the Minister of *Enesarat-e-Dowlati* well enough to approach him directly. Appealing to him via mutual acquaintances would take time, time Dhil didn't have. He had to act quickly if he wanted to prevent the director from filing a formal complaint. Being charged with having ridiculed the country's political leaders was as bad as it could get. The Ministry of Justice prosecuted harshly any impertinence toward the government. Under no circumstance would the authorities show leniency in such cases, insisting on the accused receiving a stiff sentence. Making concessions in such cases, they always argued, could be construed as weakness.

"It would take too long to bring it to the Minister's attention," Dhil said. "We don't have that much time. The director could file charges any moment. Once the complaint is put on paper, it'll take forever to clear you from the accusation."

"The motherfucker shouldn't get away with it," Zeb said, his face growing even paler. Wringing his hands, he continued, "The son of a bitch humiliated me in front of all those people. He shouldn't be rewarded for it. He should have to pay for it."

"We can't change the system," Dhil pleaded, determined not to let Zeb's pride get in the way of making a deal with the director. "He's in uniform and this goddamned place is his little kingdom. The best we can do is to make sure we get the hell out of here without the asshole filing charges against you."

"You've the power to put that piece of shit in his place," Zeb said. "But that would cost too much effort, wouldn't it?"

Zeb's abrupt change of demeanor took Dhil aback. He felt the urge to match Zeb's angry outburst. A quick survey of the surroundings made him realize that Zeb must be close to hysteria. Dhil forced himself to keep his calm.

"I'm doing what I can. Don't expect me to turn out a damn miracle."

"I didn't mean to hurt you," Zeb said, letting his head hang and starring at the ground for a moment. He raised his head and said, "Whatever you decide is fine."

Dhil stood quietly, not sure what more he could say. He noticed a large rat in the corner.

Finally, Zeb broke the silence. "It's dirty in here," he said. "You better wait outside."

Dhil left the dark storage room. Zeb was right, he thought. It was wrong to reward the director. He sighed. There was nothing more he could say to Zeb that would make him feel better.

When Dhil stepped back into the drafty hallway, the squalor around him and the bleak expression on the soldiers' faces reinforced his desolation. The bitter cold, pouring in through the jagged windowpanes, chilled him. He desperately wanted to leave this place and, despite his sympathy for Zeb, decided not to let his procurement manager make matters even more difficult by starting another fit.

He thought of Maggie, a good way—the best way he knew of—to direct his mind away from the desolation of the situation. When they lay in bed and pressed their bodies tightly to each other, her natural sense of security, her strength and independence seeped out through her soft skin, streaming through his pores inside him, making him forget the precariousness of life and the arbitrariness of survival in this barren, frosty world where a giant fisted hand, heaved high above, was ready to strike mortally anyone at any time.

He understood that Maggie would not break up her marriage, and he couldn't expect to have a permanent place at her side. Yet at moments of despair and hopelessness, his thoughts, instead of wandering to Miriam, invariably brought Maggie before his eyes. He couldn't comprehend why his mind functioned the way it did. Perhaps it had something to do with Miriam's close link to the country's political leadership and her complete denial of government cruelty. But with her father being the prime minister, repudiating the true nature of the administration seemed the only way she could accept her situation and enjoy the privileges bestowed upon her.

Chapter Eleven

The director's aide came out of his boss's office wearing a big smile. The director wanted fifteen thousand afghanis. Dhil hadn't expected to have to pay so much.

"Fifteen thousand?" he said, raising his eyebrows. "Does an office clerk's minor transgression now command such an exorbitant price?"

"It was a serious offense," the aide said. "It's just and fair compensation."

Dhil ignored the absurdity of the comment. His main task now would be to make the transaction go smoothly. "Very well, I will meet your request. I will deliver the money shortly. You will have to release my man immediately."

"Well, of course." The man looked to the ground. But, first..."

"Yes?"

"My director also demands that your employee apologize to him."

"Mr. Assistant Director," Dhil said, his face beginning to feel warm. "Humiliating Zeb beyond what he has already endured is not right. I'm willing to pay what you demand, but don't insist on an apology. Zeb has done nothing wrong. I can't ask him to apologize."

The assistant shook his head. "My director's set on it."

"Tell your superior I'm willing to pay more. Let's say twenty-five thousand afghanis. He shouldn't persist in an apology."

At the mention of the higher amount, the assistant looked hesitant but again shook his head.

"Don't refuse my offer. It's a good chunk of money. And God Almighty will reward you for your help."

"I would like nothing more than take your money and let your employee go. But I can't persuade my director. Your man has brought this on himself."

"I'll apologize on my employee's behalf," Dhil said, making one more attempt at bringing the matter to a conclusion. "Isn't that more useful?"

The aide shook his head.

"Please, let him be. He has suffered enough."

"What do you know about suffering?" the assistant said, his face flush, his gaze hostile. "You have no idea what real suffering is."

Dhil sensed his anger boiling and painfully churning his guts. Was he now to be insulted by this low-level government worker and pay for the privilege? Struggling to remain calm, he closed his hands into fists inside his overcoat pockets and pressed as hard as he could. The most important thing to do was keeping Zeb safe, he said to himself.

He took a deep breath. "Mamour Sa'heb," he said, taking

care to keep his voice steady. "I'm not at issue here. Let's focus on how we can resolve the problem at hand."

"If you want to take your employee with you today, you'd better persuade him to apologize. I know my superior. There is nothing I can do."

Dhil felt beaten. "Very well, show me to a phone so that I can make arrangements for the money to be brought over. And then bring me back to Zeb. I'll have to prepare him."

The assistant grinned and, with a wave of his hand down the hall, said, "Sa'heb, this way to place your call."

The same soldier who had opened the door to the storage room before walked sluggishly toward the chamber, again unlocking the door with excruciating slowness.

Zeb hunched in a corner of the dark cell. When he saw Dhil, he jumped up, rushing to meet him.

Dhil sensed Zeb's growing anticipation while he searched for the best way to explain the director's ultimatum. Seconds seemed to stretch into minutes—or was it hours? Still Zeb waited silently.

Finally, Dhil decided being direct would be the most palatable. "In order for the director to release you, he insists on you apologizing to him."

"He doesn't want my apology." Zeb's eyes filled with tears. "He wants money."

Dhil smiled, then shook his head. "I'm giving him all the money he wants. He wants you to apologize on top of that."

"I haven't done anything wrong. What do I have to apologize for?"

Dhil had no answer. The cold, the grimy piles of coal around them, the hurt in Zeb's face, and his own sense of humiliation made him feel sick. He understood Zeb's predicament, yet this man should recognize that Dhil was doing everything he could to help him. "I know it doesn't make any sense. But I don't see a way out of this. I did the best I could."

"I understand," Zeb said.

"We haven't the time to negotiate a better deal," Dhil said in a calm voice, hoping his composure would flow to Zeb and help pacify him. "I think we should do whatever it takes to get out of here. I've already called the office to send the money. Let's go to this director and get it over with." He clutched Zeb's shoulder and spoke in a tone as light as he could muster. "Later, once this is over and done with, we will laugh about it."

Zeb nodded. Dhil wasn't really sure that Zeb was convinced.

"Look at this son of a bitch," the director yelled as soon as they entered his office. Gesturing toward Zeb, he went on, "He thinks he can push around an officer in uniform and get away with it because his boss can help him buy his way out."

Dhil realized at once his miscalculation. The director intended to humiliate Dhil himself. To what end, he wasn't sure, but knew the director wouldn't dare attack him directly.

Dhil grasped Zeb's arm and could feel Zeb's muscles contracting. He tightened his grip, hoping to convey a message of calmness to Zeb and silently implored him to hold back, just for a few more minutes.

When Zeb turned toward him, Dhil could see in his eyes that it was too late. Zeb's patience had reached its limit.

Pulling his arm free, Zeb pushed the crowd aside, leaving Dhil behind, bolting forward, hurling himself at the director. With one hand, he grabbed the director's throat. Using his other hand, he began furiously beating the official.

The director was a large man but, startled by Zeb's abrupt ferocity, was unable to fight back. Trying to protect himself, he crumpled his massive body together, held his arms over his head, and exposed his back to absorb Zeb's blows.

"Guards!" he screamed. "Guards! Get this motherfucker off of me."

The assistant jumped up and down like an overexcited child, shouting. Three soldiers rushed in, pulling Zeb away from the director, holding him firmly in their grip. Back on his feet, the director struck Zeb across the face, knocking him to the ground and began kicking him. Zeb groaned.

Even from the back of the crowd, Dhil could see blood gushing from Zeb's nose and welts appearing on his face.

"It's enough." An elderly man, one of the supplicants, had stepped forward. He positioned himself between Zeb and the director. "Let him go." His voice was neither pleading nor demanding but firm. It had an immediate effect.

The director stopped beating Zeb and regained his bearing. Straightening his uniform, he observed the supplicant. "Step back," he ordered, but with little force. The man obeyed and disappeared back into the crowd. "Take this criminal out. I'll show him a lesson he won't forget," he shouted. "I'll personally deliver him to the Ministry of the Interior." He gesticulated to the crowd in his office. "Out," he yelled. "Get out. All of you."

Dhil stood motionless for a few moments then worked his way out with the bewildered petitioners. There, in the hallway, he saw Omar who had arrived with the money in a small canvas bag.

He was about to explain to Omar what had happened when the director's assistant appeared.

He was willing to ignore the episode, the aide made clear. He eyed the bag that Omar carried. But the director would not budge. He had to save face, the assistant explained. Zeb would be sent to the Ministry of the Interior and handed over to the political unit of the ministry's special police.

"I told him it was too late to file charges," the assistant said. "My director agreed to delay that until tomorrow."

Dhil took this as a hint. The delay might make the official malleable. It might take more money but by tomorrow the director might have sufficiently calmed down to give him another opening at freeing Zeb.

Dhil requested that he be allowed to drive Zeb to the Ministry of the Interior rather than sending him there under police escort. He emphasized that he would be "most grateful" for this simple favor.

After a few minutes, the aide returned. The director had agreed under the condition that his assistant accompany them, apparently to make sure Zeb would indeed be delivered to the Ministry.

Dhil again felt hopeful. With this sign of the director's willingness to compromise, the chances to come to an understanding with the director the next day seemed to have improved measurably.

The guard opened the door to the same dark chamber. This time, Zeb staggered out, barely able to stand. Dhil grabbed hold of him. The assistant also stepped forward to help.

"It's all right," Dhil said, waving him away with his left hand.

He moved toward the exit, heaving Zeb and pulling him along. The assistant followed. When they left the crumbling building, a gust of cold air swept over Dhil, burning the skin of his face. Zeb leaned heavily on him as he struggled to cross the courtyard.

A few soldiers roamed about in their shabby uniforms. Otherwise, the enclosure was empty. The speculators, the mamours, and the destitute buyers had called it a day.

The aide motioned for a soldier to come forward, whispering in his ear. The soldier followed.

It had stopped snowing. The temperature had fallen. The

hardened snow crunched beneath Dhil's shoes. Breathing heavily under Zeb's weight, he opened the car's right front door and asked the assistant to hold it. He helped Zeb inside and opened the rear door for the assistant. The soldier unexpectedly climbed in the other side. Dhil didn't care.

No one spoke. Dhil could see through the rear-view mirror the eyes of the aide dancing about the Rover with obvious admiration. The soldier seemed afraid to even move.

Zeb clasped the sun visor and squeezed it. Dhil imagined the pain and anger that must be burning inside Zeb.

"I realize how bad the situation looks to you," Dhil said, quietly. "I'll do all I can to get you out. By noon tomorrow, you'll be back in the office."

"Who knows what might happen between now and tomorrow?" Zeb said, letting go of the sun visor, its beige cover smudged with soot and blood. "I'll be locked up in a cell. I'll be defenseless there."

Dhil didn't know what to say. After all, he wasn't going to spend the night in jail. For the first time since he had seen the shivering Zeb inside the storage room, he understood that no matter how deeply he considered himself involved in Zeb's trouble, he would, in the end, be no more than a spectator.

The sudden awareness of this absolute separation from Zeb brought him a surprising touch of relief but also engendered within him a sense of shame, as if he were now implicated in what had happened to Zeb. Tomorrow, he said to himself, he would get him out of there. Tomorrow, he repeated to himself, as if needing to reinforce his determination to not let anything else come in between.

High clouds covered the last rays of sunlight. Night settled rapidly over the city. Lamps in front of roadside shops provided passersby with a little illumination. Dhil put on the headlights and concentrated on the evening traffic.

Chapter Twelve

When he was a cadet at the state military academy in Kabul, Colonel Alam Gol had often flown to Kunduz to visit his family in nearby Baghlan. He knew well that rough weather governed the sky over the desolate peaks of the Hindu Kush. Savage gales perpetually blasted across the vast empty terrain of naked stone.

A bumpy flight over the mountain range was to be expected. But this time, the storm was unlike anything he had ever experienced. The raging winds threw about the Russian-built An-12 CUB like a toy, causing the huge military transport to sway and rattle ominously.

For a time, Gol wondered whether he would ever make it to Kunduz. The idea of ending up spread out on top of one of the brooding peaks or lying in the dark of a bottomless ravine contributed to the unsettled feeling in his stomach.

The plane continued its arduous upward flight and the shaking gradually came to an end. Reaching its cruising altitude, the aircraft leveled off and headed straight north.

The reassuring buzz of the plane's engines and the growing steadiness of the ride soothed Gol's frayed nerves. He loosened his grip on the metal bars along the sides of the narrow seat in which he had squeezed his body. Shifting, he threw his weight to the left to release the pressure from his right side that had grown numb. He looked out of the small window beside him but couldn't see the bleak, barren wasteland below. Shrouded in darkness, the snow-clogged passes, the narrow gorges, and the endless succession of jagged peaks remained invisible.

He was badly in need of some rest but found it difficult to fall asleep. Governor Bahaadur was not far from his mind.

Gol had never been in battle, never experienced the sensation of killing someone, personally one-on-one. But he had witnessed many executions and even commanded a few firing squads. Then, each step had been rehearsed; the final operation seemed almost mechanical, machine-like.

The condemned never got to see their end, never fought back, and, in general, died swiftly and quietly. Would the Governor be so compliant?

He was sure the hardest thing would be to look the Governor in the eye. Face to face, would he betray his intention? Trying to suppress such thoughts, he resolved not to agitate his mind. Those were things he could neither foresee nor control.

He wished he knew who had selected him for this critical task. Dost had suggested, it had been his decision alone. But was he telling the complete truth? As much as he coveted a rise into the echelons of the government, he dreaded even more the danger of being associated too intimately with Chief Dost. Should the Secret Police Chief ever fall from favor, he could go down with him.

Gol smiled to himself. A foolish thought. Every schoolboy knew that Dost had been with Prime Minister Khan and Bahaadur Shah since they had, as they claimed, saved the nation when King Rahmatullah had been assassinated. Dost's loyalty to the two leaders was legendary. Two leaders? The two so-called pillars of the Afghan nation. In an instant, Gol realized the full implication of his task. He had taken sides.

Where Khan ran the nation by fear, Bahaadur Shah had the power of his title, of the people's acceptance of his right to power.

Yes, he did work for Prime Minister Khan, but so did thousands of others. Now, on this day, it had changed. He had been given an important, secret task. And at the very least, Khan had given his approval.

He put aside his misgiving, concentrating on the trust that had been placed in him. He had no doubt that Prime Minister Khan had now taken him into the innermost circle of his government.

And what of the King? Prime Minister Khan surely had a plan to bring everyone together as one people with a common purpose.

At long last, his many years of service would pay off. If successful, he would not have to fear the security forces ever again. Instead of keeping tabs on his movements, their watchful eyes would look out for him and protect him from his enemies.

His confidence leaping, he closed his eyes and leaned back in his seat. He no longer noticed the hard squeeze of the steel frame against his body. Soon, the humming drone of the aircraft's engines coaxed him to doze off. His mind surged out into the silent darkness and empty enormity of space. Feelings of immense ecstasy and contentment filled his heart. Virtually freed from earth's gravity, he floated in the electrifying state of weightlessness.

Roaring at full throttle, the aircraft engines' loud whir woke Gol. The droning clamor of the turboprop motors and the reverberation of the fuselage caused him an excruciating headache. He felt as if a thousand needles penetrated his skull.

Flying low in preparation for landing, the plane circled over Kunduz City. Apart from the flimsy city lights, it was ink black outside.

Whenever he flew over the wide, parched land of Kunduz Province, he counted himself fortunate to be from Baghlan. Although less than a hundred miles away, his family's farm lay in a rolling countryside where the soft soil always yielded a bountiful harvest. In Baghlan, the cows' colossal udders burst with milk; large flocks of sheep dotted the gentle slopes of green hills; horses, working their hefty muscles, dashed boisterously along their fenced grazing grounds.

Condemned to work a hard, dry land, the peasants in Kunduz were too poor to own horses. Their sparse grazing grounds could barely feed their emaciated cows and tiny flocks of sheep and goats.

As a youngster, he'd always had an immense sense of pleasure when he approached his horse in the semi-dark stable and slipped the bridle over its head, watching the horse's mischievous shaking of its head and listening to its gentle whinnying. Whenever he would think about the boys in Kunduz, he would pity them for not being able to afford their own horses.

But Kunduz was not entirely without its own beauty. Stretching endlessly in all directions, the region's vastness possessed its own peculiar magnificence. If nature had robbed the earth in Kunduz of water and if the sun incinerated its meager vegetation, the panoramic sweep of the province's wind-swept landscape could take one's breath away.

Suddenly, the aircraft dropped for several seconds, jolting Gol out of his reverie. The cavernous fuselage shook as if it were about to break into several pieces. Every one of his muscles rattled along with the aircraft's vibration.

He took a deep breath and sat upright in his narrow seat inside the vast, empty belly of the military transport. Through the partially open cockpit door, he could see its lit interior. The captain laughed and said something to the co-pilot.

The pilot's relaxed demeanor convinced Gol that no life-threatening danger had come over them. His strained muscles relaxed and his thoughts returned to the tranquility of Baghlan and the certitude he had felt there. Far removed from Kabul's intrigues and intricate living, life's simplicity on the farm had been refreshing.

Again, he could not keep his thoughts from his mission. He realized that he was sweating so profusely that he wondered whether the temperature inside the plane had caused his body heat to rise. But his sense of reality made him realize that it was his own fear of the unknown that made him perspire.

Flying low over the airport, the plane made its final approach. A flood of lights from strong overhead lamps illuminated the terminal building. A large number of people, predominantly military officers, stood on the tarmac. The polished brass stars on their shoulder pads and the brass buttons on their uniform jackets reflected the brilliant glitter of the lights.

The airplane's tires screeched for only a moment as they touched the ground. The plane, jerking and rattling at the impact, rolled for a short distance before coming to a stop. Descending the steps, Gol recognized the two top uniformed officials of Kunduz waiting for him: General Saeed Asil, Commander of the Kunduz Mechanized Division, and General Hamid Nawaz, Chief of the Provincial Police.

They shook hands. Gol sensed resentment in their blank-eyed faces and stiff smiles. He understood. They had been ordered to receive a lower-grade officer without even being informed of the exact nature of the Colonel's urgent visit.

He had come to arrest the conscript, they must have concluded. Naturally, they were offended that the government had dispatched a junior officer to resolve a local problem they could have easily handled themselves.

Gol overlooked their resentment. The only important thing was to concentrate on the assignment. He must act decisively and let nothing distract him from completing his job flawlessly.

He couldn't resist a moment of pleasure seeing the two officials' envy. With it, they acknowledged his preeminence. From now on, he would encounter jealousy more often. He would have to get used to it and accept it as a part of being among the chosen few.

After arriving at the division house, Gol retired to his room to wash up. He decided to shave and pulled out his kit, when he heard a knock. Opening the door, he found Chief Dost's local representative before him. Although the agent looked younger than he had visualized him, Dost's description was quite accurate. His medium height, slender build, and young face gave the appearance of child-like innocence, which struck Gol as odd considering the work he did. He seemed overly polite speaking each word as if it had been practiced, each movement planned in advance.

"I know it's late and you must be tired," the agent said. "But I have orders from the Chief that I must share with you before you join the others for dinner."

"I could do without dinner tonight," Gol said. "I'm not particularly hungry and don't really feel like eating."

"That would not be wise," the agent said. "You would offend General Asil. He has made elaborate preparations for you."

Gol disliked this man telling him what to do. But he made sure not to sound irritated. "What are my new orders?"

The secret police agent moved closer to Gol, stretching to bring his face as near as possible to Gol's. His breath smelled of garlic. "You're ordered to liquidate the Governor tonight," he whispered. "The General and the Police Chief are not to be involved in the Governor's termination."

"Shit," Gol said. "I was hoping to consult with General Asil and Police Chief Nawaz. This doesn't give me any time for preparations. Chief Dost had assured me that the details would be left to me."

"It's not the first time the Chief has changed course at the last moment."

"How much do General Asil and Police Chief Nawaz know about the assignment?"

"They've been told you were dispatched to oversee the execution of the renegade soldier and any mutinous villagers. They also believe you will try to persuade the Governor to travel to Kabul for medical treatment." He smiled shyly. "Considering the Governor's temper and his distaste for the Prime Minister, nobody envies you."

"What about the soldier?"

"You must lead the assault on the village first thing in the morning. The Chief wants everything to be done by noon tomorrow, in time for the 1 PM TV newscast. The aim is to wrap up everything in one single broadcast. When the Governor's death is disclosed as an act of treason, the execution of the assassin and the other ringleaders must be announced simultaneously. We can't leave any unanswered questions hanging over the country."

Gol looked at his watch. Time was running out. Yet, he still had no idea what to do, where to begin. "You know the area better than I," he said. "How do I approach the Governor?"

"After dinner," the agent explained. "Take General Asil's car and drive to the Governor's mansion. Don't let the General's chauffeur take you. Tell the General that you plan to drive yourself."

"What about the guards at the Governor's residence?" Gol played the scenario inside his mind.

"The Governor's guards will not stop you," the agent emphasized. "They know the General's staff car. And they have been informed that the Governor will have a visitor. The Governor also knows you will be calling on him tonight to deliver a message from Prime Minister Khan."

The agent paused, dropping his head and gazing at the carpet. "The job must be finished before you leave the Governor's mansion. After you've left, I'll take care of the rest. You must return straight to the guesthouse and inform General Asil that the Governor had committed suicide. Don't forget to tell the General that you will leave on your mission to arrest the deserter early in the morning. But don't go into any details. He has already been informed of how many men and what type of equipment you will need."

The agent started to head for the door, then turned around. "One more thing. You should know that I'm known here as Fahd," he said. "Officially, I'm the director of finance for the Kunduz Provincial Government."

Chapter Thirteen

A pleasantly warm gust of air drifted over Habib Dhil as he entered the lofty entrance of the three-story building housing his office. The pale-gray marble floor was impeccably clean. The light of the two ceiling lamps bathed the walls' off-white color in a soft shine. Returning from the dilapidated condition of the Central Depot, Dhil found the sight unreal.

Omar jumped up as Dhil entered the hall and followed him into his office. Omar's presence disturbed Dhil who wanted to be alone to go over the events while they were still fresh.

He wished Omar would leave. They couldn't do anything until tomorrow. Besides, the night got rapidly chillier, and the danger of exposure to Omar's emaciated body during the ride home in an unheated city bus increased with every passing minute.

Two months earlier, Saland Ghausy, deputy minister in the

Ministry of Finance, had introduced Dr. Zia to Dhil, explaining that Dr. Zia had run out of space in his practice and needed a larger suite to accommodate his increasing number of patients. Ghausy asked whether Dhil could assist the doctor, adding that Zia extended free treatment to needy patients and should be given a generous break in the amount of the lease.

Dhil couldn't deny Ghausy, an influential official, what amounted to a personal request. He let Dr. Zia move into one of his commercial buildings and, as his contribution to the physician's charitable work, agreed to let the doctor occupy the space for free.

He had hoped that that would be the end of it and that, having done his part to satisfy both Deputy Minister Ghausy and the doctor, they would leave him alone. But within days, Dr. Zia began asking him to pay for some of the medications he dispensed free of charge to needy patients. Among them was Hadi Omar, a recently released political prisoner. He had a form of hepatitis, Dr. Zia explained, and needed to be treated with something called gamma globulin. The drug was not available locally. Dhil made contact with Richard Dean, his American business agent, in New York and made arrangements to supply the medicine.

Later Dr. Zia had asked Dhil to consider hiring Omar. "There's no use treating him and dispensing expensive drugs to him when he can't afford to feed himself," he pleaded.

Dhil had been very reluctant. "You know there's a ban on his employment," he made clear. "If I hire him, the authorities will make my life even more difficult than it already is."

"They aren't that efficient," Dr. Zia insisted, obviously intent on not giving up easily. "It'll take some time before they'll notice. Make it a temporary assignment. Meanwhile, I'll try to find something else for him."

Unconvinced and against his own judgment, Dhil yielded. His grandfather would have not approved, he thought.

Now Hadi Omar, the object of that decision, leaned against the wall as if he lacked the strength to support his own weight.

A satchel in his hand, he looked haggard and frail, the skin of his face yellowish. He must have realized that Dhil was observing him. He straightened and smiled. As his crusted lips parted, they exposed his teeth and Dhil, for the first time, became aware of their abnormal length. They hung loosely from his receding gums and seemed about to fall out of his mouth any moment. But Omar's eyes frightened Dhil the most. Lusterless, they resembled two extinguished candles with two burnt-out wicks in the center. The combination with the rest of his appearance made it appear as though death were already at work within him.

"Are you the only one in the building?" Dhil asked.

"Except for the security men," Omar said, "everyone else has left."

"There's no reason for you to stay on, Omar. We can't do anything till tomorrow."

Omar nodded. "Good night, Sa'heb."

In the silence, Dhil returned to the incident at the Central Depot, doubting his own actions. Would the director have been more conciliatory had he offered him substantially more money? On the other hand, he had perhaps been too readily inclined to give in to the director's demands.

Perhaps there were other complications he didn't understand. Had he possibly had a previous encounter with someone in the director's family. Why had the director agreed to negotiate when he was unwilling to settle the dispute? There was the possibility that the director's assistant, wanting to keep a large share of the money to himself, misrepresented to his superior the actual amount Dhil had agreed to pay?

Failing to find a satisfactory answer to what he could have

done to obtain Zeb's release, he finally gave up looking for one. He couldn't undo what had happened. He had failed and that was that.

Acknowledging his own responsibility strengthened his resolve to let nothing prevent him from securing Zeb's release. Tomorrow, first thing in the morning, he would go to the Ministry of the Interior and leave no stone unturned until Zeb was safe.

It also occurred to him that now that the Ministry of the Interior was involved, he had to approach the matter differently. He needed to enlist the support of someone with sufficient clout to persuade the director to withdraw his complaint and, if necessary, to be willing to force the director's hand.

He thought about a suitable person for the job. The answer came to him immediately: Alam Gol. Although they had drifted apart as childhood friends often do, Dhil felt there still was a strong connection. And, as one of Prime Minister Khan's military adjutants, Gol could be in a position to make the director of the Central Depot listen to reason.

Would Gol help? Would he demand a payment, like any other government official? Or help in return for some future favor? Dhil would refuse him nothing. Still, Dhil hated the idea that this would come between them. It would alter their relationship forever.

He sat for many minutes at his desk unable to move. Was there another way? He knew he needed to act but was frozen. Suddenly, Zeb's tormented face appeared before him. Inhaling deeply, he grabbed his personal phonebook and looked for Gol's home number.

Chapter Fourteen

There were times when Dhil thought Alam Gol was his only friend. Even when they didn't see or even spoke with each other, he always pictured Gol as his protector, his confidant.

Dhil had been the youngest in the class and Gol, the big boy from the neighboring farm, had protected him, fighting off bullies and making it clear to everyone else that he was not to be messed with.

Dhil followed Gol's rise through the ranks of the military and wished he could see him more often.

So it was a real pleasure, although a great surprise, when Gol, wearing a dress uniform, had showed up at his office on that hot June day.

Dhil rushed to great him. They embraced. "Alam Jaan. This is such a pleasure. What brings you here?"

"What an office," Gol said, slowly gliding his gaze over

the paintings on the walls and the deep red Bukhara rug covering the gray marble floor. "It looks like a picture cut from a magazine."

"You haven't been here before, have you?" Gol looked heavier but, as usual, confident. "You should come more often."

"That's true," Gol said, continuing to scan the office. "We're all too busy and have lost sight of what's really important in our lives. We should see more of each other." Gol stared at Dhil softly but intently. "You know, I always think about our time in Baghlan. That was a happy period. Nothing compares with it."

"Just my thoughts," Dhil said. "I also miss those years." He patted Gol's massive shoulder, leading him to the couch. "How does it feel working for the Prime Minister? Being so close to the center of power?"

Gol laughed. "More like the edge of power, my friend." He spread out over the couch. "I really work with General Momand. I've never been called in into the Prime Minister's office."

Dhil considered this. "I am sure this will change. It's only been what – seven or eight months?"

"Only six months," Gol replied. "But it's already routine. A job like any other."

"Only six months?" Dhil said, sitting down on the armchair closest to Gol.

"What is happening in your busy life," Gol said. "I know you work hard. But tell me about your private life. When will you take a wife?"

"Work is all there is in my life," Dhil said, feeling slightly uncomfortable. He went to his desk and buzzed the butler to bring tea and biscuits.

He returned to his armchair. "I spend most of my time bickering with your civilian colleagues about all sorts of authorizations. Export licenses. Import permits. And other boring stuff. The government has its hands in everything."

"What do you expect?" Gol said, smiling broadly. "We've responsibilities. We've rules to uphold."

"Too many rules stifle initiative."

"That's what businessmen think. Civil servants see it differently."

"I don't expect them to be sympathetic to our plight." Dhil couldn't completely suppress a measure of scorn he felt.

"Of course," Gol said with a faint smile, "the armed forces are impartial. We have no opinion one way or another. But civil servants are sick of barely scraping by, while the business community eats the cream."

"Have you ever added to their salaries the baksheesh they collect?" Dhil said, his face heating up. "They've no reason to complain." An awkward silence followed and Dhil regretted his harsh remarks. "Everything considered," he finally said, "it isn't easy to do business here."

"Come on, my friend," Gol said, without showing the slightest reaction. "Don't tell me life is difficult for you. You're wealthy enough to make your own rules."

"Is that what you think?" Dhil said. "I never thought I had any power at all."

"Oh, well—" Gol stopped in mid sentence, his hand sliding over the blue satin cover of the couch he sat on. Smiling, he tapped Dhil's knee. "Be grateful to God Almighty. You aren't starving."

They'd drifted into a touchy area, Dhil thought. Even as boys, they'd been divided on certain issues. True to his family's conservative tradition, Gol had been a staunch supporter of the political leadership.

Dhil decided to drop the subject. "I couldn't agree more. I make good money. That's what counts in business."

They shared a laugh. Dhil noticed a broad smile in Gol's face and took it as a welcome sign that their brief disagreement was over.

"I hear you're seen all over Kabul," Gol said. "And always with the prettiest girls."

Dhil laughed nervously. "Where in God's name did you hear that?" he asked.

"You know. People talk."

"Actually, I don't go out much."

"That's not what I hear."

"I wonder why anyone should show any interest in me," Dhil said, uncomfortable at the idea of having to discuss the details of his own existence.

"I suppose you can't stop people from talking, can you?"

Leaning back, Dhil folded his arms over his chest. Trying to appear indifferent, he said, "Tell me what they say."

"They say you spend enormous sums of money on the women you go out with."

"Typical," Dhil said. He shrugged, trying to dismiss such talk. "Spreading around nonsense is what people like. My life's boring. There really isn't much to tell. Let's talk about you. What have you been doing with yourself?"

"What can I do on an Army officer's salary?" Gol said. "I just survive." He paused. Then, his face grew pensive. "Finding a woman is my problem. This is no place for single men."

"What about marriage?" Dhil said, relieved that the focus of their conversation had shifted away from him. "There are many beautiful girls in town."

"They're not for me."

"Why not?"

"Their families would never accept me. I'm just a peasant boy from the provinces. And, by now, I'm too spoiled to want to live with a girl from my village."

"We're both from the country," Dhil said. "Remember, I was born on a farm, too."

"Your folks are city people who own land in the country-side," Gol said. "I'm the real country boy."

"Well, there are other, temporary possibilities. Have you heard of Farida's establishment? Maybe you should give it a try."

"You mean the one on Maiwand Street?" Gol asked.

"That's the one."

"That's the most expensive whorehouse in town," Gol said, sighing. "I was there once. It cost me a month's salary. "That's more a place for you. I bet you're one of their regulars."

"I haven't been there in a long time."

"I see," Gol said, smiling oddly. "You're involved then. Which family is she from?"

"No, no." Dhil laughed to hide his sense of alarm and worried that the unnatural ring of his laughter would expose his anguish. "I'm not involved."

"Come on," Gol said. "Don't hide her from me, my friend. Who is she?"

"Really, there is no one."

Gol bent over the coffee table and brought his face close to Dhil's. "No one at all?"

Did Gol know about Miriam? No, it was impossible. Dhil struggled to appear relaxed. Maybe he could just tell him right now. Alam would understand. He did not want to hide the truth from his friend. But his relationship with Miriam was too sensitive. "Honestly, there's no one."

"Well," Gol said, taking a sip from his tea and settling comfortably on the couch. "My sister, Nadia is living with me right now. We would be honored to have you in our family. "

"Thank you, my dear friend. But you are a horrible matchmaker."

They laughed easily.

"Who knows," Gol said. "Perhaps we both will find some-one one of these days. After all, some of our friends have two wives and we have none."

Suddenly, Gol chuckled. Crinkles appeared on his broad face.

"What is it?" Dhil asked.

"I just remembered your maid. The Uzbek girl from the refugee community."

"You mean Roshana," Dhil said.

"What happened to her?" Gol asked.

"She married a young worker from the factory."

"I always suspected that you fucked her. She blushed when-ever she saw you."

"That was a long time ago," Dhil said.

"Well? Was I right?"

"Actually, she fucked me," Dhil said. "At least the first time she did."

"How did it happen?"

"One day," Dhil said, "she asked me to help her lift a mat-tress to its place in the linen storage room."

"I remember that narrow, windowless chamber in the rear corner of your house," Gol said. "A red rug covered the ce-ment floor."

"We did it on that very rug."

"Did you do it on the day you helped her with the mattress?"

"That day she only pressed herself against me as I lifted the mattress to put it on top of the pile of the other mattresses. When I turned she rushed out of the room. Only after several tense and hurried encounters of touching and kissing, did she let me. And I was so nervous. I didn't feel anything at all."

"Did the relationship last?"

"The final three years of high school. She was my winter-vacation gift from heaven."

"You lucky devil," Gol said, laughing.

Even today, Dhil didn't know why Gol had suddenly appeared unannounced on that hot summer day. Perhaps he had passed by Dhil's office and, on the spur of the moment, decided to pay him a visit.

Remembering their youth and the sense of companionship that had given them the courage to embark on discovering the origins of the howling winds that blew across the wide fields and over the green hills of Baghlan, Dhil rediscovered his friendship for Gol and felt close to him.

He picked up the receiver and dialed Gol's home number.

"The Colonel left for Kunduz a short while ago," said a woman.

Dhil recognized the voice of Gol's sister, Nadia. She had never married. Maybe nobody wanted her because of her massive size. When her mother died, she came to Kabul and moved in with Gol.

Dhil refrained from introducing himself. He hadn't seen her for quite a while and didn't have the patience to engage in a lengthy reminiscence about their childhood. "Do you know when he will be back?"

Nadia didn't answer.

"Hello, are you there?" Dhil said.

"There's some type of an emergency in Kunduz." Nadia spoke slowly as if she were reluctant to pass on the information. "He wasn't sure when he would return."

Replacing the receiver, Dhil reproached himself for not making better use of his connections. He could make things so much easier for himself and his company if he better nurtured his contacts with government officials. That was the way things worked. His grandfather always taught him. You helped them; they helped you. As the saying went, one hand washed the other.

To safeguard their assets, his grandfather had worked closely with the government. He repeatedly counseled him to preserve their family's close bonds with the political leadership and cautioned that only in that way he could maintain their holdings.

But when he took over the family business, he had resisted, thinking he should do things his own way. Reviewing the endless chain of troubles that seemed to plague him, he now wondered whether he had made the right choice by not strictly following his grandfather's advice?

As for Zeb's problem, he had no way out. He had to tackle it on his own.

Getting up to leave for home, he realized that night had descended. Outside the range of the yellow light of the lamp on his desk, darkness had spread about in the rest of his office and over the city outside the windows and above the mountains beyond.

The temperature had plummeted. Water from the melting snow had stopped flowing down the waterspouts.

Perfect quiet reigned in the room.

Chapter Fifteen

Habib Dhil climbed down the steps and walked across the snow-covered front yard. His Rover was by the entrance where Ghani, the driver, had parked it. The night watchman came out of his cabin, offering the keys.

Dhil paused. "I'll walk," he said, hoping the hike would restore his spirits and help him overcome his anxiety. "Give them to Ghani when he comes in the morning. And tell him to pick me up."

"I would take the car, Dhil-sibe," the watchman said. "It's too cold to walk."

"I'll be alright," Dhil said. Pulling up the collar of his overcoat and sticking his hands in his pockets, he set out plowing through the biting winter chill. The ordeal at the Central Depot persisted in his mind, nagging at him. It distressed him that he had nobody to back him up tomorrow. He felt thoroughly inadequate for having blinked once again at the first sign of trouble and found satisfaction from the anonymity of the night. Darkness gave him the security of not being recognized as the fraud he thought he had turned out to be.

The image of Zeb locked up in that cold storeroom made his own degradation brutally plain. The arbitrariness of Zeb's detention reinforced his own fear of a world where he felt exposed to countless dangers while the randomness of luck seemed to be the only guard he could count on.

His growing alarm of life's unpredictability made him often wake with dread in the morning and left him with a feeling of queasiness at the end of the day. In the face of that intense sense of uncertainty, he had begun pondering the possibility of leaving, emigrating to some other country, far from this oppressive place.

Each time it crossed his mind to abandon the country, he tried to visualize the prospects of such a drastic move. Would he be alone or would Miriam consider joining him? He thought for a moment about Miriam leaving her family behind, residing in a foreign country, surrounded by people she didn't know and with whom she had no common background. He wondered whether she would ever accept that.

Money also played a major role in those broodings. He knew by Afghan standards he was a very wealthy man. But even if he could convert a large chunk of his assets, he would have to do with less and questioned if he could manage with dramatically reduced financial resources. Would it be enough to go to some other place and buy himself another life?

And where would he go? Or, rather, where could he go? Italy had once come to his mind. As a teenager, he had gone skiing there and had fond memories of it. He remembered the beauty of the Italian countryside, the warmth of the people, and their elegance and carefree ways. But then, after thinking about it in some depth, he understood that visiting a country was entirely different from living in it. Not knowing the language, he would forever be handicapped and could never claim equality among Italians, a people that would feel superior to him, a society that would allow him to settle only at its edges, safely removed from it.

Perhaps he could settle in Britain. The anonymous life of a faceless, solitary immigrant in the midst of the bustling millions of Londoners wasn't wholly abhorrent. But it wasn't altogether appealing either. Americans often claimed they were a nation of immigrants. Perhaps they meant it. If true, that would give him and them a common ground, a kinship that could make life endurable, possibly even enjoyable.

It wouldn't hurt making some inquiries about the different ways of immigrating to America. He had thought about speaking with Maggie and Charles but decided against it. Maybe it was best not to get them involved. After all, they counted on good relations throughout Afghan society. Dhil might upset that. Finally he resolved to discuss it with an immigration attorney during his next trip to New York.

He came by a fruit and vegetable shop. The shopkeeper—covered with a heavy, cotton-filled blanket—sat cross-legged, heating up an oval-shaped flat bread on the fire that burned in a small round oven before him. The smell of bread pulled Dhil over to the shop, and he asked the shopkeeper whether he could buy it.

"It's my dinner," the shopkeeper said but, without hesitation, tore off a large piece of the warm bread, offering it to Dhil. When he refused to get paid, Dhil separated a small portion from the chunk the shopkeeper had offered him and returned the rest. He resumed his hike, eating the bread and thinking about life in far-off places.

Coming from the opposite direction, a pedestrian brushed Dhil's shoulder, causing him to emerge from a delirious-like mental condition. Lost in thought, he had unwittingly changed course, walking away from the paved streets and open spaces of his own district and entering a maze of dark, narrow alleys in a ramshackle settlement. The moon and the stars hardly broke through the hazy sky. The snow on the ground gleamed dimly.

People scurried about noiselessly, cowering in the cold, carrying oil lamps whose trembling lights distorted their features to gruesome grimaces.

Dhil turned and hurried back toward his own quarter. The streets had emptied. The buildings along the roads loomed dark and ghastly. No light or noise seeped through the tightly closed shutters. Only the frozen snow crunched under his steps.

As he strode through the hushed neighborhood, he had a strong sensation that he was being observed. Although he could not see a single soul anywhere, he heard shrill laughter—not a joyous laughter, but a taunting, belittling one. Yet nothing moved and all doors remained closed. Not a single window had been opened and the somber house fronts continued to loom shadowy and impenetrable. He could neither see the human face behind that diabolical laughter nor locate the place it came from. Magnified a thousand times by the stillness of the night, the gruesome noise mocked him and he accelerated his pace.

The black sky hung low and seemed about to crush him. Despite the freezing cold, he sweated profusely and choked as if invisible hands squeezed his throat. He strained to walk even faster.

At last he returned to the lighted streets and familiar homes of his own precinct. He took a deep breath and slowed down his stride.

It was fear, he thought. Plain, simple fear. He had neither been observed nor had there been any laughter. Fear had prompted it all. And fear had been responsible for the humiliating fiasco at the central depot. Since Zeb had done nothing wrong, he should have taken his side and remained resolute in dealing with the officials. Instead, he had capitulated, submitting Zeb and himself to the whims of the depot's director.

He wished Anwar Haq were here. He had made it so easy when Dhil needed help with one government department or another. Whenever he went over to his office, Haq would invariably make him sit down, instruct his office boy to serve tea, and relate funny stories. He wouldn't do anything until Dhil relaxed and enjoyed his jokes. Only then would he pick up the phone and begin working on the problem. And without fail, he would find a friend, a relative, or an old colleague who would be glad to help out.

Dhil tried to imagine what Haq was doing at that very moment. It was early in the morning on the American east coast. Haq had probably completed his nightshift at the hotel in Arlington, Virginia and gone to bed in that smelly room of his at the end of the dark, narrow corridor, in that squalid little building in a rundown neighborhood.

When Dhil had visited him at his place, he had admired him for his determination but had not fully agreed with him about the imminence of civil war in their country. But now Dhil's own sense of a looming danger had intensified and the external pressures had begun to terrorize him. Fear had become his constant companion.

Fear had also shaped his affair with Miriam. He knew he needed to come to some conclusion about her. But he was afraid to confront the complications if he did take action.

Images of Miriam—her face, her sensual lips, and her slender body— drifted before him. He missed her. He missed the feel of her warm, slim hands and the soft touch of her pale skin.

His failure to free Zeb and the nightmare of tomorrow's

struggle to get him released began fading away and the heaviness in his chest subsided.

When he opened the door to his house, he heard Zaman, his servant, come out of the servant's quarters, entering the house through the back entrance and switching on the lights.

The telephone rang.

"I'll be in Paghman tomorrow," Miriam said quickly. "I'm planning to spend the whole day there. Will you come?"

Remembering his promise to Zeb, Dhil hesitated.

"Did you hear me?" Miriam asked.

"I'll be there," Dhil said.

"I must go now. I'll see you tomorrow."

Life stirred in his body again. The weight that had been pushing him down finally evaporated. He didn't feel lonely anymore. He was alive.

Chapter Sixteen

The expensive furniture in the reception room of the division guest house confirmed to Gol that in the provinces, too, the military enjoyed the government's favor. In the dining room, a huge red Bokhara rug stretched out under the dining table and the fine silverware glistened under the light of a low-hanging chandelier.

A tempting aroma filled the air when recruits carried in three large maroon platters heaped with mounds of steamed rice, chicken, and mutton. But Gol, unable to take his mind off the task before him, didn't feel like eating and put just a little of each dish on his plate. While forcing the food down, he looked around.

General Asil and Police Chief Nawaz had remained quiet. Gol took their silence as a signal of their aversion for him.

The charged tranquility made him feel awkward. The glaring

lights inside the dining room hurt his eyes, forcing him to deliberate what the pitch dark outside the house was holding for him. The uncertainty of what stood before him reinforced his feeling of edginess.

Observing General Asil and Police Chief Nawaz, he concluded that Asil was less troubled by his presence than Police Chief Nawaz. Gol liked General Asil's sincere face. Dressed in a well-fitting uniform, his graying hair carefully groomed, the General possessed a pleasantly dignified appearance. By contrast, Police Chief Nawaz's strained countenance exposed his resentment. Stuffing large portions of mutton and rice into his mouth, he nervously scrutinized Gol.

Gol realized he hadn't made even a perfunctory attempt at conversation. "Sorry for having disturbed your evening," Gol said, shattering the overbearing silence. "I wish I could have started off tomorrow morning and arrived at a more convenient time. But the urgency of the situation made delaying my trip impossible."

"Fuck the late hour, Colonel," Police Chief Nawaz said. "Tell us what really brings you here. I don't see any emergency. We could have easily handled the incident ourselves."

"I bear a personal message for the Governor," Gol said, pleasantly surprised at the ease with which the words came out of his mouth. He had not been told how to respond to such aggressive questioning. Nor had he prepared himself for it. Yet he spoke with authority. "The message is from his family."

"Don't try that collegial shit on me, Colonel," Police Chief Nawaz said, his stocky face twisting with animosity. "You're here to lead the assault on the rebellious village. That's your main objective, isn't it? You're here because the government doesn't trust us."

"It's not a matter of trust," Gol said. Nawaz's outburst did not anger him. He remained calm, actually enjoying the opportunity to test his own mettle and size up the two officials.

"My main concern is to persuade the Governor to fly to Kabul for medical treatment. His family is worried about his health."

"There isn't the slightest danger to the Governor's life," Nawaz said, his angry face pushed forward, his hands pressed into fists. "The man's pretending. His wound's superficial."

"Stop it." General Asil said sharply. "You are out of line, Chief Nawaz. The Colonel is doing his job. It's not for us to question the leadership's decisions."

He smiled at Gol. "Don't mind Chief Nawaz, Colonel. It's been a long day, and we're all a little tired."

"I understand," Gol said, eager to dismiss the matter. "It's getting late, and I need to head to the Governor's mansion."

"My driver will take you there," General Asil said.

"I would like to drive myself, General. But I would appreciate the use of one of your staff cars."

Driving through the outskirts of Kunduz, Gol observed the bright beams of the car's headlights flash over dilapidated house fronts and perfectly deserted streets. The mud of the flat-roofed, one-story buildings, the dusty alleys, and the surrounding desert were indistinguishable from each other. The eerily vacant roads and the lack of color invoked a sense of desolation. It seemed as if a calamity had swept over the town, extinguishing all life.

Speeding through the ghostlike streets, Gol reviewed his mission. Since he had been given this assignment, he had allowed himself no time to map out his moves and decide how to approach the task. Now that he tried to visualize the scene and plan his actions, he couldn't imagine how he would go about it and what he would do once he stood face-to-face with the Governor.

He loosened his tie and opened the top button of his shirt. At that moment of confusion and anguish, he remembered his mother telling him stories when he was a boy. Transfixed, he had listened to her melodic voice recounting episodes of that medieval knight, Rostum, of his mythical deeds, his valor and invincibility.

Once, on the northern bank of the Amu River—he remembered his mother's hypnotic tone and her storytelling word for word—Rostum's troops faced a horde of warriors from Uzbekistan. The dispute was over land. As a relentless sun shone over the parched dunes, the two armies stood in formation, ready to charge into battle. Rostum, tired of all the bloodshed he had seen over the years, called over to Morad, his adversary, challenging him to settle their dispute in a duel to the death instead of letting their legions fight it out in a long, messy contest. The Uzbek leader, renowned for his mastery of the sword, took up Rostum's challenge.

Gol tried to picture the two armies. He could see the soldiers, silently observing their leaders' mortal contest, the scorching sunlight reflecting brightly from their shields and breastplates.

In his usually offensive fighting style, the powerfully built Rostum charged forward but, during the very first moments of their skirmish, recognized Morad's swiftness and virtuosity with the saber. Abandoning his aggressive fighting routine, Rostum settled for a cautious, defensive bout. He had to wear down his opponent, Gol's mother had explained. He had to counter the Uzbek's technical superiority with tenacity and endurance.

The two men fought all day long. The sun had plunged into the crimson horizon and darkness was about to enclose the two combatants when, all of a sudden, Morad's knees gave way under the heavy weight of his armor. For a fleeting moment, he tottered. Rostum observed how Morad's weary eyes drifted to his silently waiting legion, searching, questioning. Could he be panicking?

The seasoned Rostum recognized his moment of opportunity. Raising his sword high up, he lunged forward and hurled down his heavy weapon, hitting the Uzbek's neck. The razor-sharp blade cut effortlessly through flesh and bone, severing

Morad's head from his body. The decapitated warrior collapsed. His heart continued to pump for several more seconds, forcing blood to gush out from his neck, soaking into the hot sand. Morad's head rolled several feet over the baked earth before it came to rest, his eyes strangely alive, his mouth wide open as if he begged for a drink of water.

A feeling of destiny arose in Gol's breast, and he lost his sense of foreboding. He recognized a clear parallel between his assignment and Rostum's fabled deed. With his victory along the leisurely flowing waters of the Amu River, Rostum had saved countless lives and changed the tide of history. Gol, too, had embarked on a historical course. His action would cleanse the government from the poison of the Governor's depraved conduct. Involuntarily, he pressed the accelerator as though time moved too quickly and could run out on him.

The sentry outside the Governor's residence peered through the small window of the guardhouse. Recognizing General Asil's staff car, he rushed outside and, Kalashnikov slung across his shoulder, lifted the black-and-white striped bar.

Gol entered the walled compound and drove slowly through the large garden. When the narrow gravel path made a sharp turn and he saw the contours of a house behind the trees, he stopped the car. The vehicle's engine running, its headlights cutting a blazing trail through the trees, he took his pistol out of its leather case and examined it carefully. Assuring himself that it was loaded and ready, he replaced it in its holster. He fastened his collar button and tightened his tie before resuming his ride. Driving slowly through the heavily wooded yard, he speculated about what the Governor might be doing at that instant. According to Chief Dost, the Governor should have had his dinner and, as was his habit, settled in his living room, giving himself over to drink. Gol was confident that he would find exactly that.

He parked the car at the main entrance of the sullen structure. He had studied the layout of the sprawling mansion from the plan Dost had shown him. Entering the house, he recognized the door that led to the living room and strode towards it. As he crossed the hall, he forced himself to walk with a firm step.

The door was slightly ajar, letting a slim shaft of soft light escape into the foyer. When he pushed it open, he saw the Governor sitting in an armchair and looking toward the entrance as if he expected Gol to turn up at that very moment.

"Come in, Officer," the Governor called out, raising his hand, motioning Gol to enter.

Fahd had stressed the importance of getting it over with quickly. "Do it fast," he had told Gol. "Concentrate on the task and let nothing else enter your mind."

Slowly moving his hand toward his pistol, he stepped into the room. But as he drew closer and saw Governor Bahaadur's ashen, frail features, something, a feeling he couldn't specify, came over him, and he hesitated.

The Governor's large, agitated eyes bored into Gol with such intensity that he shuddered and a feeling of frailty gripped his mind. Suppressing his sense of ambiguity, he fixed his mind on the Governor whose pallid skin looked as though he never went out in the sun and whose strong neck over his narrow, drooping shoulders appeared like a bad patchwork of an incompetent craftsman.

Without getting up, the Governor extended his hand. When Gol grabbed it, its moist and deathly-cold feel caused a tremor that he sensed in the core of his being. And his heartbeat accelerated, pounding evermore wildly. Worried that his heart's loud throbbing could arouse the Governor's suspicion, Gol hastily said, "I'm Colonel Gol, Your Highness. His Excellency the Prime Minister has sent me to—"

"I know why you're here." Governor Bahaadur cut him

short, motioning him to sit down. "You've come to catch the runaway conscript."

Two gray rugs with dark blue flower patterns covered the floor. Heavy chairs lined the walls and a beige couch set was arranged around a rectangular mahogany table. Drawings of horses and two large landscape paintings covered the walls.

The intimate surroundings made Gol feel inadequate and finding himself so close to Bahaadur bewildered him. The rulers of the nation were to be admired, never known. He remembered how his father talked about them, recounting stories of their refined pastimes, intrigues and harsh rule, their vengefulness and their benevolence only towards those loyal to them. Visibly mesmerized by their seemingly invincible powers, his father had put his large, heavy hand on Gol's shoulder and said, "Remember, my son. They're a breed unto themselves. Never confront them. You will do well to be on their side. Work with them, and you will succeed."

Sitting together with a member of the ruling family in the same room replaced his initial feeling of inferiority with one of importance. This new sensation pleased him and he now wished to prolong it.

"Your Highness," he said. "The Prime Minister is concerned about your health."

"Fuck the Prime Minister's wife," Governor Bahaadur said. He grabbed the tall, crystal glass that stood on a small table in front of him and took a large gulp from it. He set the glass down, running his finger along its rim. For a moment, he seemed withdrawn, his eyes focused on the rug's flower patterns. He raised his head, his features taut. "Prime Minister Khan doesn't care about anybody. The only thing he cares about is his own power."

Gol remained still.

"What do you think, when you look at me?" the Governor asked, slurring slightly.

"I don't understand what you mean, sir."

"I know what you think. You think I'm drunk." The Governor took another swallow from his drink and put the glass back on the table. He wagged his index finger. "You're right. I am drunk. But even in this condition, I can read your mind, Colonel." He lifted his glass and, in a sudden, nervous move, knocked back its contents. He took the bottle that he had put beside his seat and refilled the glass. After taking several rapid sips from his drink, he remained quiet.

Now, Gol told himself. Get it over with. His face heated up. Gradually, he slid his hand toward his pistol but, at that very moment, the Governor aimed his gaze back at him.

Raising his left arm, the Governor displayed his bandaged hand. "You look at my superficial wound and ask what the fuss is about? You're right again. I'm not seriously injured. I'm alive and well." Closing his eyes, he again fell silent. As he hung his head forward, his thinning brown hair revealed a reddish scalp. Then he lifted his head and opened his eyes anew, taking another swallow from his drink. He stared at Gol intensely. "I'll tell you why you have come," he went on. "His goddamn Excellency the Prime Minister is infuriated. He's not angry over my wanting to fuck the conscript. He's enraged because I have broken a holy edict. By not killing the soldier, I have cast doubt on our strength. And he has sent you to catch the soldier and hang him from the nearest tree."

It reassured Gol that the Governor felt completely safe. A little delay might be to his advantage. Let the Governor have a few more shots of his liquor, he told himself. The more alcohol the Governor poured into himself the better.

"He must punish the conscript," the Governor rambled on. "The Prime Minister wants people to believe we are sacred. Like the mighty Hindu Kush, we're elevated above the rest and cannot be challenged. That, to the Prime Minister, is the secret of our survival. He has worked diligently to cultivate this view and will stop at nothing to safeguard it."

One part of Gol wanted to put an end to the life of this self-indulgent pig, yet another part was craving to hear more, to let the Governor reveal more of himself. Gol was sure he would never have another opportunity like this.

"You're puzzled that I'm telling you all this, aren't you?" the Governor said, as if reading Gol's mind. For a moment, his eyes appeared clear and vigil. And then, they seemed unfocused and drowsy again. "I don't have to worry about you," he continued. "I can see you are an ambitious man. You want to move ahead. You know you have to do it with us. Everything revolves around us. Without us, you're a nobody. That's why I can tell you what I want. You know better than to reveal what you hear in this room. Let me disclose a—"

Suddenly, Gol felt an intolerable revulsion for the Governor. Ceasing to listen, he refocused his thoughts on the reason for his visit. He refused to be humiliated any further. He leaped to his feet, pushing back the heavy armchair with such a force that it tumbled backward.

Bewildered, the Governor stared at him.

Gol grabbed his gun, the Governor's eyes following the movement of his hand. Despite his apparent drunkenness, the Governor's eyes looked sharp and penetrating, his face revealing a dogged determination.

In those critical seconds, Gol heard his father's insistent warning, "Work with them," he said. "Never oppose them. They are invincible." But he also saw his father run like a fool to pick up the bluebird that Khan had shot dead.

He pulled his pistol out of its holster. The Governor hurled his glass at him. It missed but the whiskey splashed Gol's face.

The Governor jumped out of his armchair. Gol was surprised, he, too, held a weapon, a revolver, in his hand.

Without any more hesitation, Gol fired his pistol once, then again.

Breathing heavily, the Governor remained on his feet. The air made a ghastly sound as he sucked it in. His wildly protruding eyes resembled those of a hunted animal in the jaws of its predator, halfway between life and death, still alive, still holding a glow.

Gol thought to fire yet again, but at last, Bahaadur collapsed, falling heavily on the small table before him. Its legs shattering under the impact, the table crashed to the ground.

Bahaadur's body writhed momentarily. Then complete stillness settled over the house. There was no sound, no hurrying foot-steps, no anxious voices alarmed by the loud crackle of gunfire.

The Governor's open, lifeless eyes stared toward the ceiling. Blood from his chest seeped through his clothes.

Gol heard a click and turned. It was Fahd. He motioned Gol to remain silent as he bent over the Governor, carefully examining the body.

"It's best that you drive back to the division guesthouse," Fahd said, standing, turning away from the Governor's remains. "Don't forget to report the Governor's suicide to the general and the police chief."

Gol was uncertain. Clearly, anyone observing the body would know he had not killed himself. He stared down at the Governor.

Fahd must have realized Gol's concern. "Don't worry," he said, "I'll take care of him." He smiled. "This took you a while. I was beginning to wonder what you were up to. But you did well. Everything's fine."

Gol crossed the hallway and left the house. Walking down the slate-stone steps to the staff car, he noticed the stillness in the garden and the complete silence of the trees in the perfectly windless night.

Chapter Seventeen

The sting of guilt for reneging on his pledge to Zeb and the thrill of seeing Miriam had combined to keep Dhil awake for a good part of the night. At long last, a muted gray began seeping into his bedroom and the muffled commotion of the awakening city trickled in through the shut windows.

A long time ago, his grandfather had told him that this neighborhood once had consisted exclusively of private houses and been considered far out of town. But over time, as the city's perimeters had slowly and inexorably expanded, businesses had settled here, including Dhil's own office which was located at Ariana Square in a three-story building he had built only two mile or so down the road.

Recently two nightclubs and a trendy Thai restaurant had opened nearby. But it was the elegant women's clothing store, housed in a freestanding building that had become the talk of the neighborhood. Its expensive apparel reportedly came straight from the best boutiques in Paris.

All that activity, while energizing the area, had detracted from its original appeal as a quiet residential district. Dhil had seen many of the original inhabitants sell their properties and move to other, newly developed, suburbs. Although he had been ambivalent about relocating, he hadn't been able to resist the popular current and had completed the building of a new house in Kabul's new Wazir Akbar district.

As his moving time grew nearer, he, to his surprise, found it difficult to think of leaving the old house. It was the first time he realized how attached he was to it. He also preferred the old home's proximity to his office over the new house's exclusive locality. In the end, he decided to stay where he had spent most of his life.

But he hadn't regretted his investment. On the contrary, it gave him a sense of satisfaction, even accomplishment, to know that his mother, who preferred an active social life, would live in the new house and enjoy its abundant space and modern facilities.

Worn out by the lack of sleep, Dhil staggered over to the window and pulled the curtains. Fresh snow covered the yard. Only the maple and mulberry trees, the flakes wafting off their bare skeletons, had remained unwrapped. The evergreen, the one breathing vegetation in the center of the garden, had to endure the full weight of the snow; its vibrant, elegantly curved branches pressed downward in a silent bow to the snow's fleeting prowess.

Dhil liked snow. When winter came, and the annual snowfalls failed to make their timely appearance, he felt anxious and even a little guilty that he enjoyed nature's winter fury. He particularly appreciated snow for its cleansing effect. In

Kabul's lengthy summer, when the Kabul Darya dried up and the riverbed turned into the hot season's public toilet, the reek in the city's business district became unbearable. But when winter arrived and snow covered the riverbed and all the other open sewers in Kabul's old town, the infested earth seemed to heal again. The foul odor of dried excrement vanished from the atmosphere, and breathing became easier.

Opening the window he took a deep breath. Cold, pure air filled his lungs. It was a joy to inhale fresh, uncontaminated air. He wished he could keep it inside himself forever, never having to breathe the city's fetid air again. He smiled at the impossibility of the idea. As soon as spring arrived and the warming sun heated up the ground, the stench would invariably rise up again and, like a curse from the depth of hell, encase most of the city. You couldn't escape it no matter where you lived. Contrary to everything else in this afflicted country, foul air enjoyed unencumbered freedom of movement, and there was no force to keep it bottled up.

He finished shaving and moved his head closer to the mirror. There was no ignoring a growing number of white strands among his full black hair. He had detected the first few gray hairs when he was sixteen, and his grandfather had told him before he turned forty his hair would be completely gray. "My hair went gray when I was in my late-thirties," he had said. "Your father's, too. It's in the family."

But that was not the only thing Dhil had inherited from them. Along with endowing him with their genetic makeup, they had bequeathed him this house, the mill here outside Kabul, and the older mill and the farm up north in Baghlan. But in one thing he definitely differed from his elders. While he saw everything slipping away from him, they'd had the strength to prevail and prosper. Especially, his grandfather with his indomitable spirit had worked hard and left behind substantial wealth. Yet, within

Dhil, his predecessors' drive and determination had mutated into a sullen, almost fearful, languor, making him feel painfully insufficient. He doubted he would ever match, let alone surpass, his forerunners' dexterity.

Trying to rationalize his pungent sense of insufficiency, he argued that these were different times and circumstances stacked against him. But then, doubt sneaked back into his mind and obliged him to inquire whether there existed other reasons for his ineptitude. Whenever those troubling thoughts mocked him, he wondered whether something had gone awry with himself and his own lack of qualification caused his drift. Or was it simply his spirit of negation that made him drift to a lonely corner of his society?

He shook his head as if wanting to rid himself from those disturbing contemplations and refocused on his image in the mirror. Taking another look at the growing numbers of gray hair on his head, he realized they didn't upset him. Perhaps it was a sign of a new maturity. Besides, Miriam seemed to like it.

One more piece of business and then he would drive straight to Paghman to see Miriam. First, he had to convert the dollars he had received for his last shipment to New York. Local sales having been unusually slow lately, he needed all the cash he could put his hands on to beef up his reserves to carry his company through what looked like rough times ahead.

Chapter Eighteen

Gol sat silently next to General Asil in the back of the Russian-built Volga. Police Chief Nawaz occupied the front seat next to the driver.

They stopped.

"This is the deserter's home," Asil said, looking straight ahead. "You're in command, Colonel."

Gol nodded. He waited for the driver to open the door, then stepped into a hazy, bitter-cold dawn. The inhabitants of the neighboring huts had come out, grasping their children by the hand, watching the convoy of five armored troop carriers with blank stares.

He realized that General Asil and Police Chief Nawaz made no move to leave the car. Gol didn't care and confidently walked toward the conscript's house and ordered an officer to knock at the door.

The woman who answered was middle-aged. She wore a

long red dress that hung loosely over her black, baggy pants. A white chador covered her hair. Accompanied by a teenage girl and a boy—no older than twelve, holding a slingshot in his hand—the woman's sharp green eyes took in the swarm of officers, soldiers, and military vehicles. She turned her weather-beaten face toward Gol. "What do you want?"

Gol had expected at least some respect for his authority. The simple question seemed defiant and caught Gol unprepared.

He hesitated. After all, he didn't want to provoke a messy confrontation. He knew these rural folks and how they cherished their privacy. The right course was to avoid the impression that he intended to pry into the family's private matters. Otherwise, he would offend the sensitivities of the villagers.

Without taking his eyes off the woman, Gol motioned for the soldiers to step back. "Mahder," he said, "we have come to take your son to Kunduz." He made sure to speak simply and calmly. "We need to question him in a police matter."

"He can't go with you," she said, her voice firm, her attitude bold.

Gol smiled. The woman was not even going to bother to lie and say her son was not at home. "It's not up to him to make that decision. He must come with us."

"I know what you will do with my son." The woman raised her chin defiantly. "I won't let you take him."

"We have to question him about an incident two nights ago," Gol said. He was already losing his patience but strained to sound reasonable. "Your son has acted illegally. He must stand trial for what he has done."

"He did no such thing. He was defending his life. Nobody can object to that."

"He shot the Governor. The Governor's seriously wounded."

"The Governor's a wicked man. My son had no choice."

"Nonsense," Gol said firmly. He was pleased with the authority in his voice. "Your son was never in danger. He has lied to justify his criminal deed. He must come with us. Otherwise, we'll use force to take him."

There was a little pleading in the woman's voice. "The Governor's evil. He forced my son to undress. He listened to his heart and told him he wanted to tear it out of his chest."

"Stop it!" Police Chief Nawaz quickly approached from behind. "Stop it," he repeated. He stood next to Gol. "We have no time for such talk. Either your son comes out now or we will send in the soldiers and drag him out."

A foolish woman, Gol thought. She thinks she can face down the military the same way yesterday the villagers had forced the police to retreat. But he still believed he could defuse the situation. "Let's give her one more chance," he said to Nawaz in a low voice.

Nawaz looked surprised. "I'm telling you," he whispered, "if we don't wrap this up right now, we'll have a riot on our hands."

Gol turned around. The male villagers had come closer and gathered around the military men. Some had their old Enfield rifles slung across their backs. Others carried homemade, silver-plated guns. The boys held their hand-carved slingshots as if ready to pelt the soldiers.

"I understand, Chief, but let's see whether we can resolve this peacefully."

Nawaz shook his head, barely controlling his rage. "Colonel, I've been in this type of situation before. We must get the soldier out now if we want to avoid a clash. There is no middle ground in these matters."

Disregarding the Police Chief's warning, Gol addressed the woman, "I wish to speak with your husband."

"My husband's ill. He has been having a high fever for weeks. He's too weak to move."

"We can't wait any longer," yelled Police Chief Nawaz. He

took several steps toward the woman. "We must take your son to Kunduz now. We will put him in chains if he resists."

The young boy freed himself from his mother's hold, picked up a stone, put it in his slingshot and shot, hitting Nawaz squarely on the forehead. Doubling over, Nawaz covered his forehead with his hand. One of the officers jumped forward, grabbed the boy and began beating him.

The boy's mother scuffled with the officer, shrieking, scratching, trying frantically to free her son from his grasp. Another soldier stepped forward and with a forceful blow tossed her to the ground. Her chador slipped off her head, revealing two long, thick plaits of black hair.

The conscript appeared at the door. Rushing past Gol, he hurled himself at the officer who held his younger brother. Under the impact, the officer fell to the ground, pulling the child down with him.

Police Chief Nawaz pulled out his pistol and aimed at the boy. Probably realizing that he could not fire without also endangering the officer, Nawaz turned to the older brother whose back was now turned toward him and pulled the trigger. Stunned, the conscript spun around. Nawaz fired twice more. The wounded man staggered then fell heavily to the ground.

His mother screamed and flung her arms at Nawaz, her high-pitched wail shattering the strange quiet that had descended on the scene. Someone began shouting at the troops. Brandishing their weapons, the villagers closed in on the group of soldiers and officers in front of the house.

Before Gol could figure out what to do next, somebody grabbed him by the arm and pulled him away. Turning, he saw General Asil. As they rushed towards the nearest armored personnel carrier, several shots rang out. The general bellowed to his men, instructing them to withdraw immediately.

Chapter Nineteen

It was a little after seven when Dhil left the house to walk to the office and take his car. Normally, Ghani picked him up at 8:30. Today that would be too late. Before driving to Paghman to see Miriam, he had planned a visit with Ishaq Suleiman, the currency dealer. Suleiman had agreed to meet him at an earlier hour than was customary.

Dhil had known Suleiman since his teenage years. The old man had been taking care of the family's foreign currency dealings for many years. On a number of occasions, his grandfather had brought him along when he met with the currency dealer. Once, Dhil had asked why he didn't sell his foreign money to the bank.

"Banks pay less than independent money exchangers," his grandfather had said as they walked up the stairs to Suleiman's second floor office. "I don't like working with our banks. They're inefficient. It takes them ages to complete a transaction."

Nothing had changed since. In a place where trust and efficiency were rare commodities, Suleiman was a reassuring exception.

Dhil felt a prickling sensation as the chill morning air enfolded him. Thick clouds covered the sky but didn't seem too threatening.

The night watchman lay on the couch in the guardhouse. When Dhil knocked at the windowpane, the dozing guard opened his bloodshot eyes. Seeing Dhil, he jumped up and opened the door.

"I'm sorry I woke you," Dhil said.

Obviously startled at seeing Dhil so early, the guard—his hair messy, his face covered with several days of stubble—stared at Dhil without uttering a word.

"I need the car keys," Dhil said.

He drove past the gray building of Habibia High School. Usually bustling with romping students, the school's large courtyard stood deserted. Closed for winter vacation, the dark, shuttered complex loomed like a sleeping giant over the empty yard. A few blocks down the road, men, despite the chill and the early hour, already filled the park in front of the arched central post office. Most wore long cotton-filled chapans or ragged overcoats over their flimsy knee-length shirts and baggy pants. To protect themselves from the cold, they had wrapped their turbans over their ears, and a few covered their heads with gray or black sheepskin hats.

Some, cowering in the cold, soggy weather, hopped from one foot to the other to keep their sodden feet from freezing. Others waited in a long line, leading all the way into the building, for their turn to make a phone call to their hometowns. Soldiers, their uniforms no less frazzled than the civilians' garments, wielded long sticks to keep a semblance of order in the restless queue.

Another group of men, unable to read and write, haggled with the professional letter writers over their fee. Blankets wrapped around their legs, woolen gloves protecting their hands from the cold, the letter writers sat on low stools along the wall of the post office building and, using their knees for a surface, drafted petitions to the government for their customers or wrote messages for out-of-town visitors to their families in the provinces.

When Dhil crossed the swollen Kabul Darya, his mind trailed the river's muddy water as it surged southward to the Khyber Pass and on across Pakistan's North-West Frontier Province. After tumbling down the high mountains of southeastern Afghanistan and rushing through the steep gorges of northwestern Pakistan, the river slowed to a measured pace. The mud having settled down on the riverbed, the water shone steel-grey as it poured into the Indus.

Dhil imagined Miriam and himself floating on the water, as the Indus traversed Punjab's fertile fields and the arid terrain of Sind. Then the river drained into the Indian Ocean, emptying the two of them into the infinite and wondrous sweep of the sea.

The thought of being able to roam about with the woman he longed for, over vast stretches of land, unhindered by governments and borders, caused a liberating sensation to ooze through his body.

Turning onto the right bank of the river, he continued along the jewelry shops, still closed at this early hour. The fashionably dressed women who usually arrived in their husbands' government limousines to shop at those stores probably still lay in their warm beds. Even the roadside vendors, the penniless drifters, and the ragged beggars, who brought life to the sidewalk in front of the jewelry shops, had yet to begin their daily ordeal. Only a few pedestrians walked briskly, their shoulders hunched, their heads pulled in, their eyes focused on the ground.

Dhil parked his car as closely as he could to the entrance of Shaheen Market and walked by the market's ground floor general-merchandise stores. Some shopkeepers were already unlocking the shutters of their shops and seemed surprised at seeing Dhil.

Situated at the top of the stairs, Suleiman's overheated office was cramped with furniture. An enormous safe stood beside Suleiman's desk. Bundles of American dollars, Iranian rials, and Pakistani rupees were stacked on a table.

Suleiman rose, walked around his desk, and the two men embraced.

"It's hot in here," Dhil said, pulling up a chair opposite Suleiman. "Don't you worry about catching cold when you go outside?"

Suleiman laughed, exposing his shiny-clean dentures. "When you're seventy-six, you like it this warm and don't worry about the consequences. How about a cup of tea?"

"I'm in a hurry. I can't stay long."

"What's the rush? It's early in the morning. Government offices are closed."

"I'm going out of town."

"You'll be stuck in traffic. By the time we'll have our tea and finish our business, traffic will have cleared and you won't arrive a moment later than if you left right now."

"All right," Dhil relented. "But let's take care of business first."

"As I told you on the phone, I think you should wait a few days. The currency market's crazy right now."

"I can't wait. My local sales are down. I'm counting on higher export sales to compensate for my losses here. But that'll take several months to materialize."

I'm afraid you'll be disappointed."

"I've got no choice. I need the cash to pay my bills."

"I'll pay you forty-nine for the dollar."

"That's just one Afghani over the bank rate. I might as well go to them. With a little haggling, I might get them to give me a few afghanis more."

Suleiman smiled. "You're just saying that. I know you won't deal with the bank. It's too cumbersome. It's not reliable."

"Then give me a better rate."

The old man scratched his beard. "The dollar has been soft lately." He leaned back in his chair. "By the time your funds hit my account and I can resell the currency, only the Lord knows what the rate will be."

"Isn't that the risk you always take?"

"These are difficult times my friend." Suleiman shook his head. "Some say that firebrand cleric Khomeini will kick the Shah out of Iran. It's only a matter of time, they insist. Jimmy Carter's indecisive. The Soviets seem to be winning the Cold War. The exchange rates have never been so volatile. The rate for the dollar is especially unpredictable. I need to have a better margin than usual."

"Suleiman-sibe, you don't want to lose deals of the size I bring to you." Dhil pulled out his checkbook. "I'm ready to write the check, but I have to have two afghanis over the bank rate."

"All right," Suleiman said. "All right. For the sake of our friendship, let's divide the difference."

"Only this one time," Dhil said, extending his hand. Despite his advanced age, Suleiman's grip was firm.

Dhil put Suleiman's draft in his pocket and watched the old man place his check in the large safe beside his desk, locking it and pressing the handle twice to make sure the safe was really fastened. Then he sat back, obviously enjoying the green tea his assistant had served.

Dhil observed Suleiman who was smiling but seemed to lack his usual satisfied air. There was a marked difference in his countenance since he had seen him last. The wrinkles carved deeper in his face. His expression revealed more clearly his advanced age. His right hand, holding the teacup, shook more than usual.

"What's the matter, Ishaq?"

"I worry about my community," Suleiman said, his eyes wondering to the window and beyond to the overcast sky. "It is no longer good to be a Jew here."

Dhil thought about this for a moment. "But you, my friend, are respected here. Has anything happened?"

Ishaq didn't answer immediately. "Most of our young people leave for Israel. They see no future for themselves here." He took a sip from the tea. "We don't want to live apart from our children but don't know what would happen to us if we followed them. Life in Israel is different. It won't be easy for us older people to start new lives."

"Come on, Ishaq. You aren't ready for retirement."

A smile lit up Suleiman's face. "Oh no. Not yet."

He turned serious. "But old age is not our only problem. We also worry about what the Russians are up to. Their influence is growing here. I think they're intent on turning our country into another of their satellites. Russians are virulent Jew haters. When they come, we Jews will have to leave. Whether we like it or not."

"I'm afraid we all will have to leave when that happens," Dhil said. "That's if we manage to survive our own government."

Suleiman got up hastily and closed the door to his assistant's office. Returning behind his desk and catching his breath, he said, "Be careful, young friend. You never know who's listening. He leaned forward and tapped Dhil's hand. "Anyway, we are businessmen and should leave politics alone."

When Dhil left the city behind, the countryside opened before him and the snow-wrapped landscape rose into the misty horizon, touching the gray clouds in the far distance. Serenity had settled over the area. With its delicate clarity and soft pastel colors, the scene resembled the frail, placid landscapes of the Japanese paintings he had viewed at the Japanese embassy when the Japanese Prime Minister visited last summer.

Impervious to the slippery snow that covered the highway, Dhil pressed the accelerator, forcing his Land Rover up the winding road. The engine howled from the strain as the car struggled up the steep grade. He had made the trip so often that he drove automatically.

A few walled mud huts, the homes of mountain farmers, dotted the snow-covered slops. Otherwise, the area appeared to be free of all human activity. It felt as if he were the only soul on the move.

Without his own doing, yesterday's images began flitting through his head. The disaster at the central depot, his promise to obtain Zeb's release, and his desertion of Zeb beleaguered him. The hurt of guilt marred his senses, and he tightened his grip around the steering wheel.

He had always coveted an uncomplicated life, simply wanting to be in control of his own days—the liberty to choose his own ways, the right to live and work in security. He had never desired anything that should not have been his under any circumstances. What he wanted seemed so damned elementary, the simplest of all things. He wanted to breathe freely —no more, no less.

But it all had happened differently. Despite his struggle to keep his distance from the government, the regime's raw power had encroached upon him. No matter how hard he had tried to stay away from the system, it had run him over, flooding around him, causing him to lose his hold even on his own existence. With each passing day, he saw his life drifting further and further into an increasingly purposeless living, a way of life without dignity, a life consumed by insecurity.

He was aware of his growing inclination to avoid confrontations, to give up easily, to eagerly accommodate the whims of the bureaucrats. What he had done yesterday at the central depot summed up what his life had become. He had not fought for Zeb; he had merely felt sympathy for him. And all he had done had been to placate the director's ego and to satisfy his greed.

In the past, when frustration seized his heart and bred doubt about the direction of his life, he had at least been able to escape into memories of his childhood, a period in his life where he'd had the illusion of perfection. The farm in Baghlan had been the focal point of those fantasies and his grandfather the main character.

But lately even those precious recollections had begun to fade. When he tried to immerse himself in those visions, he could no longer see his grandfather's understanding smile, and his voice didn't sound comforting anymore. More and more, moments of anxiety and anger came up in Dhil's mind. He remembered the most upsetting episodes, pictures of torment, incidents such as his grandfather's reaction when Dhil had mentioned that he might sell their land once he inherited it.

"You cannot sell our land," his grandfather had said sharply. "This land is the essence of what we are. Our security and our dignity depend on it. Nobody in his right mind would sell his land."

"I don't want to be a farmer."

"What was your father?" his grandfather shot back. "Did his life or mine resemble that of a peasant? No, our family are respected members of the community. You will live in the city and run our business from there. It's the factories that bring us our money. But it's the land that gives us our status. Don't ever forget that."

"Okay, we are not farmers but business people," Dhil said, thinking he had gotten his grandfather's point. "But I want to be a politician." He was sure his grandfather would understand the strength of his conviction. "I won't have time to take care of the farm."

"Who are you to go into politics?" his grandfather said, his rising voice reflecting his growing annoyance. "You already have an important task awaiting you," he said, lowering the pitch of his voice. "You must build on what your father and I have created. When necessary, we buy politicians. We pay them off to keep them away from what we're doing. That's how things have worked for ages."

In the end, he had done exactly what his grandfather had predicted. He wasn't sure whether it had been his grandfather's influence—those intense gray eyes he had feared and loved at the same time—or whether society's sway had proved too overwhelming to withstand. Whatever the reason might have been, it had made him give way and lose his sense of rebellion. He had neither sold the farm, nor had he entered politics. Growing indifferent to his destination, he had let circumstance take over his life, allowing chance to lead him wherever it took him.

He thought about the men the government regularly executed for one reason or another and about those who vanished never to be seen or heard from again.

When will it be his turn? Will he be able to avoid it? He remembered what Miriam had told him before she had left for Europe to accompany her mother who needed medical treatment. "We can't hide forever," she had said. "I can't carry on with this secret hanging over our lives." Remaining quiet for a moment, she had added, "Besides, I think my father knows about us."

She would never understand, but he didn't have the boldness to take her completely into his life —not under these conditions.

And he could never bring children into a world that stood at the edge of a precipice.

Near the top of the pass, the road veered to the left and he entered Paghman. The hamlet lay deserted. The massive branches of the towering trees hunched under the snow's heavy weight. The houses appeared dark and foreboding. Some looked elegant, others merely bulky, monstrous monuments to their owners' vanity. With their shutters tightly fastened and their driveways covered with deep, pristine snow, the houses, in their seclusion, appeared mysterious and ghostlike. Wrapped in the brutal cold of a mountain winter, Paghman, a town ostensibly emptied from human presence, seemed a grotesque place to meet with one's lover.

He continued his climb toward Paghman's northern boundary. Farther up, the car broke through the clouds. Brilliant sunshine poured down from the sky and flooded the surrounding peaks which, glowing under the dazzling light, soared high up as if wanting to challenge the heavens for ascendancy. The frozen snow sparkled as it reflected the sun's heat into the amazing vastness of space.

At the edge of town, all the way up the northern slope of Paghman Mountain, Dhil turned right onto a narrow bridge. On the other side, he continued along the lane through a private enclave in a park-like setting. Century-old cypresses lined both sides of the path. Whenever he drove by them, he admired their silent majesty and envied them for their strength and permanence.

The large windowpanes of Prime Minister Khan's summer estate up the slope reflected the sunlight. The radiant rays blinded him but he could feel Miriam's presence and imagine her standing behind one of the windows, watching him drive up to the house.

He stopped the car close to the entrance and stepped out. The piercing cold hit his face like the slap of a powerful hand. Slamming the car door shut, he walked over the crusty snow toward the gateway. The harsh call of a crow shattered the absolute calm.

Through the steel bars of the gate he saw Miriam. As always, she waited on the other side of the portal, a few steps inside the compound. When she saw him, she nervously brushed her long, brown hair out of her face.

A guard swung the steel grill open, its clinking noise sounding familiar.

Miriam smiled and gave Dhil a brief kiss. They walked up the slope toward the large house, strolling through the snow-covered garden, passing by dormant trees, silent witnesses of some of their happiest moments.

Taking off her glove, she slipped her hand into his overcoat pocket. Their fingers touched, and she grabbed hold of his hand. Her palm felt gentle and warm. When they strolled by the empty pool, he remembered the warm summer night when they had made love there. It had been a long afternoon and a lazy, sleepy evening. They had left the house late at night. Shivering in the cool mountain breeze, they had run to the pool and jumped into its warm water, holding fast to one another. Inside his overcoat pocket, she tightened her grip on his hand as if having sensed what he had been thinking about.

At the top of the steps, he pulled the door open and let her enter. They walked through the hall and went into the living room. The drawn curtains dimmed the light, and he gradually took in the familiar hand-carved chairs and brass-inlaid tables, the pale blue satin covers of the armchairs, and the beige background and dark brown patterns of the rug.

Still holding his hand, Miriam led him to the couch in front of the fireplace. The ascending flames cast a reddish shimmer on the floor.

Chapter Twenty

The military contingent reassembled outside the village. Police Chief Nawaz, one officer, and two soldiers were missing. In the confusion, no one quite knew what had happened.

He should have listened to Nawaz and used force immediately, Gol reproached himself. He alone was at fault. He had made a mess of the situation by trying too hard to avoid a riot. If he had arrested the young man at once and sent him to Kunduz, he now could take the time to interrogate the villagers and identify those who had rebelled against the police the day before.

The idea of retreating crossed his mind, but he dismissed it immediately. "Let there be no misunderstanding," Secret Police Chief Dost had said. "You're leading the mission and you will be held responsible for what happens there." Gol knew there was no safe way out of these circumstances.

"We must return at once and complete our assignment," Gol said to the assembled soldiers. "Get back to your vehicles."

General Asil waited by his Volga. Gol explained his plan. "I think it best if you return to your base, General."

Asil nodded.

Once again, they surrounded the deserter's house. Police Chief Nawaz, the missing officer, and the two soldiers lay on the ground, shot dead by the angry peasants.

A number of villagers still stood close by. Seeing the soldiers return, they grabbed their children and scattered in all directions, searching for cover.

Watching the dusty chaos from inside a troop carrier, Gol ordered the machine gunner on top of the armored vehicle to open fire. Three men tumbled to the ground. When the machinegun fell silent, the villagers remained still wherever they lay or stood.

Gol jumped off the vehicle and walked over to the dead conscript's hut and kicked the door in. Inside, the mother sat in one of the hut's two rooms, hugging her two children. Her husband, covered with a cotton bedspread, lay in the far corner of the other room. Hanging from the ceiling, a dusty kerosene lamp lit the windowless chamber.

The peasant lifted his head when he heard Gol in the doorway. It seemed as if he wanted to say something but dropped his head again, staring lifelessly at Gol with eyes whose white had turned yellow.

"Your son has killed the Governor," Gol said, surprised at the ease with which he could repeat Secret Police Chief Dost's story. "I must charge you with harboring a murderer. Is there anything you wish to say in your defense?"

"You have killed my boy." The peasant spoke with difficulty, a crust of dried skin covering his lips. "It makes no difference what I say."

"If you refuse to answer my question, I will have no choice but to detain you."

"You have already shed my family's blood. Is that not enough?"

"I have no personal vendetta against you or your son. I need to find out who else was involved in your son's conspiracy. You have nothing to fear if you tell the truth." Gol felt some satisfaction with his own speech. Right there, in the presence of witnesses, the headline for tomorrow's newspapers was unfolding. Major Conspiracy Uncovered, One Officer's Diligent Work Exposes a Foreign Plot. Dost's red, chubby face would light up when he learned about the complete success of his mission. Gol pondered what Prime Minister Khan would say but the peasant's strangely soft voice interrupted his musing.

"Officer," the sick man said, wiping a tear from his sunburned face. "I have failed to defend my family. That's enough humiliation."

"You must answer my questions," Gol yelled. "Why did you fail to report your son's presence?"

"You are out to kill me, too, officer," said the peasant calmly. "You thirst for blood."

"Restrain yourself, you foolish old man."

"For too long your kind has ordered us around. Today, I cannot oblige."

"I'll hang you right here in front of your own hut if you don't cooperate."

"Officer, your guilt is great before the Almighty. Don't forget, you will be judged by your own deeds."

Gol felt his rage boil over, more at himself than at the peasant. He had allowed the villager too much latitude. The old man made a fool of him. Invoking God to mock him was simply intolerable. He pulled out his pistol and fired.

The peasant's wife rushed in from the other room. Her soaring wails filled the hut as she threw herself on her husband. Following her, the two children, weeping deafeningly, hurled themselves upon their parents.

Outside, the sun had moved up in the sky and the long shadows of soldiers fell on the small courtyard in front of the shed. Gol worried that things had been progressing too slowly. Secret Police Chief Dost's revised order called upon him to report before noon. He reminded himself that the announcement of the governor's death and the story of the crushing of the rebellion had to be released in time to be carried on the one o'clock newscast.

According to Fahd, the timing of the announcement was critical. The midday news bulletin, with its limited viewership, would serve to muffle the explosive nature of the report, giving Chief Dost time to quell any disturbances both within government ranks and among the populace. "After all," Fahd had portentously said, "many malicious people are just waiting to disrupt the government."

Considering his next move, Gol decided he didn't have enough time to conduct an investigation to find those responsible for the murder of the police chief and the other uniformed personnel.

Did it really matter who had done the actual killing? The point was to set an example. Executing a number of men would adequately serve that purpose.

To that end, he chose three men. His first choice fell on the man who had been exceptionally loudmouthed during the altercation with the conscript's mother. "Don't do their dirty work," he had yelled at the soldiers, trying to incite them to rebel against Gol's orders. "Imagine your own villages invaded. Imagine government agents destroying your families."

In choosing the other two, Gol tried to be practical. He picked up two men who had been severely wounded when Gol had ordered the villagers to be fired upon. One had sustained a stomach wound and bled profusely. He would die anyway. Gol congratulated himself on his compassion.

The three were made to stand against a hut. In a brief proclamation, Gol accused the three men of cooperating with foreign powers to destroy the country and discredit its leadership. "These men, together with our foreign enemies, have plotted to assassinate our beloved leaders. Their assault on the governor was merely the first step in their wicked plan. For their betrayal, they must die."

Charging them also with the murder of Police Chief Nawaz and the three army men, Gol ordered the soldiers to open fire.

Arriving back at the division headquarters, Gol was immediately met by Fahd who whisked him away to the offices of the Kunduz provincial government. Rushing up the steps, Fahd motioned Gol to hurry. On the third floor, he entered a room where he said he had a telephone with direct access to Secret Police Chief Dost. Closing the door, he dialed a number. "Sir," he said into the mouthpiece. "This is Fahd from Kunduz. Yes, sir, he's here." He passed the receiver on to Gol.

"It's high time." Dost clearly sounded irritated. "We were about to reschedule the announcement. What happened?"

Gol began explaining how unforeseen events had obstructed the operation and why he had been unable to bring the conscript to Kunduz alive to be hanged in public as his orders had directed him to do. He tried to explain to Dost that Nawaz's shooting of the deserter had been out of his control and his subsequent actions were justified and necessary.

"Don't give me the details now," Dost interrupted Dhil. "Just tell me what I need to know. Is the conscript dead?"

"Yes sir. He is."

"Who else was executed?"

"The conscript's father and three other men."

"What about other casualties?"

"Three villagers died when the riot had to be contained."

"What about our own people?"

"We lost four men, Police Chief Nawaz, an army officer, and two enlisted men."

"That's too many losses."

"There wasn't —"

"We can't discuss it now," Dost cut Gol off. "We will talk about it when you're back. For now, I know what I need to know. I will report to the Prime Minister and get back to you. Don't leave the office. I'll call you in a few minutes."

Gol paced the small, bare office. Obviously, Secret Police Chief Dost was unhappy with the high government casualties.

"I wouldn't worry too much," Fahd said.

Was Fahd reading his mind? "I'm sorry what did you say?"

"It's the outcome that counts," Fahd said. "Headquarters will be happy with what you have done. I've seen similar situations before. As long as the result is acceptable, the leadership in Kabul doesn't care about the rest."

When the telephone rang, Fahd answered it and immediately passed the receiver on to Gol. "Colonel," said the Secret Police Chief, "as planned, the Governor's death will be announced on the one o'clock newscast. The news release will also confirm the assassin's death and the demise of the other traitors. The Prime Minister will personally inform the King of his son's death. As you know, the King will be told that the Governor committed suicide. This will remain the unofficial private version among the top leadership. We will not announce the death of the police chief and the other uniformed personnel. That will be handled confidentially."

Gol could hear Dost's heavy breathing, but the Chief said nothing. The seconds became painfully long.

Finally Dost spoke and Gol was relieved to hear the tone was friendly. "In the fight against the enemy we cannot always expect that our plans work out exactly," the Chief said. "What counts is that we succeed in frustrating the enemy and preventing damage to the state. You have done that today. The Prime Minister is satisfied."

"Thank you, sir."

"When are you coming back?"

Gol wanted to visit his farm in nearby Baghlan but since he had not discussed it with Dost earlier, he wasn't sure whether this was the right time to do so and hesitated. "Am I needed back at once, sir?"

"Do you have something in mind, Colonel?" Dost said.

Encouraged by the warmth in Dost's voice, he asked if Dost had any objections to his desire to visit his farm.

"No," Dost said. "Go ahead and do that. Instruct General Asil to accompany you. His presence will provide you the importance now due you. But I want you to fly back tonight. We're still uncertain about the King's reaction. If we have an emergency, I would like you to be available. Oh, and tell General Asil he is the acting Governor of Kunduz until further notice. Fahd will brief you further if there are additional instructions."

Chapter Twenty-one

Miriam realized that Dhil had barely spoken since he arrived. She, too, found it difficult to talk. During the last several days of her trip through Europe, she had thought of a thousand things she wished to tell him. But far away, on another continent, among different people, she had forgotten how complicated it was to escape the constant supervision she had to endure at home. After her return, as the shackles of convention once again tightened around her soul, bitter complaints filled her mind, and she was ready to heap them upon Dhil for insisting that they keep their relationship secret. Had he proposed, the embarrassing and touchy situation with Reza Bahaadur would never have materialized.

Now, though, sitting beside him, she felt incapable of expressing her frustration. Like him, she remained still, feeling the heat of the fire warm her face, listening to the crackle of burning wood and the whooshing of the flames.

She noticed him watching her with a strangely steadfast look. She was familiar enough with his moods to realize that something raged within him. What was it that kept his mind in constant ferment? If only she understood, she could help ease his burden. She would do anything to free him from those inner struggles.

Among the things she couldn't comprehend was his insistence on keeping out of government. After all, in her own circles, men aspired after power through government and regarded bureaucratic achievement as the essence of manly fulfillment. Had he agreed to work for her father's administration, it would have made everything so much simpler. He would be a leader instead of an outsider. He would have come to know her father and, once Habib had seen for himself the diligence with which her father watched over their country, he would have come to respect him. He would appreciate her father's dedication and—surrounded, as they were, by deadly foes—recognize that only her father had the ability and strength to direct the affairs of the nation.

She looked at him, placing her hand on his cheek. He smiled shyly in return.

In many ways, Dhil was a mystery. Despite knowing him for more than four years, she hadn't yet solved the puzzle of his contradictory nature. A well-born, sensitive man with a peculiarly shy charm, he at times displayed great dignity and grace. On other occasions, he could be detached, impenetrable, prone to taking offence easily. In that condition, she could not make out what was wrong with him. Something seemed rebelling in his soul, refusing to make peace with the world.

She had to find better ways to communicate with him. In that way, she might be able to influence him. Perhaps even interest him in joining her father's government. She wanted to make him a part of the world to which she belonged. That would be the best way to protect their relationship.

The flames shimmered scarlet across his face. His faraway

look reminded her of the wedding ceremony where they had first met. Then, he had worn the same withdrawn expression, and she'd had no idea that at the end of that evening, he would turn her life upside down.

She wore the pink dress she had bought in Washington. It was during one of her mother's two visits when Miriam attended university there. Her mother had objected to the purchase, maintaining the dress was too skimpy, too clinging.

"Don't forget where you come from," her mother had said, obviously irritated with Miriam's obstinacy. "You simply can't show that much flesh at home. Besides, you're too young for it. Buy something more appropriate."

But Miriam continued to insist and, as so often before, her mother relented.

The wedding was the first time she had worn it. She stood in her parents' bedroom, examining herself in the mirror of her mother's makeup table. As she watched her reflection in the full-length mirror, she realized what her mother had meant. She was stunned herself. Despite her lankiness, the dress's tight fit accentuated her shape, making her look womanlier and much older than her real age. Perhaps her mother had been right, and she was too young for this exquisitely tucked and fitted gown. Perhaps she shouldn't display her body with that much brazenness.

Her father must have been similarly surprised. When he came in, he stood beside her and observed her image in the mirror for several long seconds. "God," he said, "you've grown up." Putting his arm around her shoulders, he added, "You're going to break some hearts tonight. But promise not to fall in love yourself. It's too early for you."

Strange, she thought. As if her father had sensed it. It had happened that same evening, and she had neither expected it nor willed it to occur.

A last-minute disagreement about the bride price had broken

out between the two families, abruptly dampening the jovial atmosphere of the festivity. Urged by relatives, the two fathers left to settle the dispute. After a substantial time elapsed, during which a somber mood spread among the guests, the two men returned.

Watching them enter the ballroom with beaming faces, the guests burst into joyous applause and the tension that had descended upon the chamber lifted. In the relaxed air that followed, the children, who had been assigned to a separate room, managed to leave their designated space, mingling with the grownups, noisily crowding the ballroom, running between the tables, turning the celebration into a rambunctious affair.

Even now, Miriam felt a surge of excitement when she remembered the moment she had noticed Dhil.

Together with her parents and a small number of friends, Miriam had been sitting at a round table. It had been a happy moment. Enjoying the gossiping and the carefree quality of the occasion, she caught sight of Dhil as he stood at the buffet table and ate his food. He seemed unperturbed by the throng around him as if he were removed from it, locked away in a different, self-enclosed world. When he was done eating, he handed his plate to one of the waiters and stepped away from the dining area.

Bumping into an acquaintance, he stopped and chatted for a while. Suddenly and without any discernible reason, he turned toward her. When their eyes met, her heart jolted violently, and as if an invisible magnetic field sucked her in, a powerful force drew her towards him. Different sensations rushed up within her—joy, anxiety, but above all confusion. At once frightened and uplifted, she realized that she was no longer the same person. In a mere flash, she had been transformed. She had opened her soul to him, and he had walked straight into her heart. At that instant, the crowd around her melted away and cleared the space for the two of them. They were all there was left of all life and all the living.

"What are you thinking about?" she said.

"I thought a lot about what you said before you left on your trip to Europe," Dhil said. "You're right. We can't go on like this any longer." He paused for a moment before continuing. "What would you do if I left and never came back?"

She was startled. "Why would you say such a thing?" The finality of his tone struck her brutally. "What has happened?"

"Nothing in particular."

"Why would you speak of leaving?"

"It's only a sense, a feeling of vulnerability, as if something bad might happen."

Without warning, she became fearful and started to tremble. She had a sensation, a sharp pain, and with it came an unbearable realization that she could lose Habib at any moment. Even though he sat motionless, she worried that if she closed her eyes, he might vanish before they opened again. Moving closer to him, she put her arms around him, hoping to bring him comfort.

He agonized over threats that had nothing to do with him and personalized conflicts as if finding pleasure in despair. She had to devise a strategy that would cleanse his soul of the rage that poisoned it. She had to pull him out of his sadness and bring him back to her where he belonged.

Gliding down from the sofa onto the floor, she pulled him along. Straddling on top of him, she placed her head on his chest. Listening to his rapidly beating heart excited her, and she pressed her mouth hard on his lips. He struggled to find an opening through her clothes to touch her while she clumsily unzipped his trousers. Miriam pushed the soft material of her garment aside, then guided him until he entered her.

Bending over him, she watched as Habib lay beside her, his eyes closed, his face peaceful—like that of a child. His breathing had slowed down and the tension in his body had relaxed.

"You worry too much," she said. "Tell me what's bothering you? Perhaps I can help."

"It's not that simple," he said, his eyes still shut. "It's not just what happens out there that worries me. It's me, too. My own weakness makes me angry. Yesterday, I promised to take care of one of my employees who had been jailed at the Ministry of Interior. Instead, I'm here. I lacked the resolve to resist seeing you."

"Your employee won't die by spending a day in police custody."

Dhil opened his eyes and looked Miriam squarely in the face. "I left that poor man in the clutches of the police, knowing full well they might beat him up. Even torture him."

"Nonsense," Miriam said.

"Bad things happen every day," he said. "And the police are behind most of it."

Miriam's pulse began to race. She felt a hot wave rush to her head. Condemning the police amounted to berating the government. And attacking the government was a direct assault on her father. "Only traitors and Communists could think that," she said, angrily. "Besides, what the police do is none of our business."

"You live a protected life," he said, his voice calm, his face expressionless. Lifting himself up on his elbows, he added, "You don't see the other side of the coin."

"How can you speak this way? Something must have happened during my absence. You've changed completely."

"Nothing has happened. I've told you before what I think. Apparently, you haven't listened."

"Don't forget, this is also your government," Miriam said. "You're rich because this government protects your interests."

"That's why I'm bothered even more," Dhil said. "I feel caught in the middle. Government leaders resent me because I disapprove of the way they do things. The people don't trust me because they see me as part of the government. I'm stuck in this predicament because I can't make up my mind one way or another."

Dhil was different from everybody else. That was partly the reason she fell in love with him. Besides, God had willed him to be that way. But now she also recognized another side of him—his weakness. Unable himself to cope with life's daily burdens, he tried to find a villain responsible for them.

She gave Dhil a fierce stare, and as she was about to lash out at him, she saw the vulnerable look in his eyes and held back. Reminding herself that her love for him stood above all else and knowing she could never let anything come between them, she emptied her mind of anger and let her feelings flow from her heart again.

She had noticed his distrust of the government a long time ago. But believing his sense of alienation had something to do with his temper, she had not imagined the possibility that he might be chewing over some other conflicts, struggles more fundamental than his disagreement with the system. At happy moments, he would be unaffected and easygoing. Only when he fell into a brooding mood, had he had dark apparitions—visions of disaster and turbulence. At those times, depression seemed to drive him to hysteria, and she avoided discussing with him anything that might trigger his fatalistic outlook.

She worried about his inclination to dissect everything. It sapped his energy. He destroyed his peace of mind by tying his personal struggle to the fate of others and seeing the government's hand behind the most routine adversities.

They sat in silence. The murky light, seeping faintly through the heavy curtains, gave the impression that dusk had already set in.

The fire burned low. Dhil rose and threw a large log into the fireplace and blew at the ashes. As the flames flared up, the intensifying heat reached her face.

Settling back beside her on the floor, Dhil pressed his body against hers. Happy that the unexpected strain between them had evaporated, she gave him a kiss. Pulling him by the hand, she said, "Come, let's go to my room."

Miriam loved her room. The intimacy within those four walls comforted her, made her happy. Feeling Dhil's body against hers within those familiar surroundings enhanced her sense of confidence.

In her youth, she had spent most of her summers in this room—the only place she could be alone, where she could hide from the constant comings and goings of all types of people who came to visit, doing nothing but sitting around in silence, mostly looking at the ground, apparently just wanting to be in her father's presence. Her room was where she could have her own private thoughts, about anything and everything, without the restraints of the maddeningly busy world of her parents.

Here she had played with her dolls. Later, as a schoolgirl, she spent the mild summer nights lying on her bed with her friends, gossiping and arguing about all sorts of things, naturally also about boys and about who was the handsomest in town.

Her friends' overnight stays became less frequent as they all grew older. Increasingly she preferred to be alone.

At about that time, sensual urges began unsettling her. And sometimes, they became insufferably forceful. As much as she resisted, she'd had to touch herself to still them.

After satisfying herself, she would be tormented by guilt, mortified by the thought that she had betrayed her parents, particularly her quiet, pure mother. At those moments—especially in the prime of summer, when dusk began its brooding dance of shadows and the mountains' jagged silhouette soared belligerently in the twilight—she would be plagued by sadness.

Before she met Dhil, her sensual fantasies had never had the features of any man she knew. They had been purely imaginary, never applying to any real person. But Dhil could have been one of those shining warriors who, in the cavernous dark of moonless nights, used to appear in her girlhood dreams and excited her with such intensity that she thought her heart would stop. She studied his lips, his well-formed ears, and his straight nose. She felt his trim body along hers and smiled.

Sometime past noon, Miriam called Zarina to bring them some food. As he had before, Dhil again voiced his misgivings about sharing their secret with Zarina.

"Don't worry," Miriam said, raising her head and looking down at him. "She's been with me since my childhood. She would never betray us." She kissed him on his lips and laughed lightheartedly. "She says I'm crazy to have fallen for you."

"Why would she say that?"

"She says you aren't the right man for me."

"Does she give a reason?"

"She doesn't want to talk about it."

The old woman laid the food tray down on the floor in front of the door to Miriam's bedroom, knocking on the door before retreating.

After giving her a moment to return to the servant's quarters, Miriam went to the living room and switched on the tape deck. Then she fetched the tray, leaving the bedroom door open, so that the music could reach them unobstructed.

"Zarina didn't let the cook prepare the meat," Miriam said, watching Dhil put a chunk of lamb in his mouth and eat it with a slice of thin naan. "She said she knew how you liked it prepared. She marinated the lamb in yogurt and garlic and broiled it on the open fire of the tandor."

"It's delicious. The bread's excellent, too."

"It's freshly baked. Zarina brought the dough along and baked the bread here." She had hardly finished her sentence, when she heard hurried steps approaching. She held her breath, listening intently. The steps came closer. Jumping out of the bed, she slammed the door shut and locked it, pressing her back against it, as if dreading that someone might kick it in.

Then she heard a faint, familiar tapping on the door. Hearing the soft knock peculiar to Zarina, Miriam sighed with relief.

"What is it?" she asked.

"Quick," she heard the old woman say from behind the door. "Turn on the TV. Governor Bahaadur has been assassinated."

"What?" Miriam said, not quite sure she had understood Zarina correctly. "Who has been assassinated?"

"It's the Governor. They've killed him."

"All right," she said, still confused, still unable to fully grasp the significance of the message. "You can go back now."

For some reason, she looked at her watch. A minute past one. Dhil jumped out of the bed, pulled up his pants, and rushed out. She put on her morning gown and joined him. He switched on the TV set. Seconds before a fuzzy image appeared, the newscaster's voice was heard, " ... According to reports, some time this morning, the assassin, disguised as a member of Governor Bahaadur's guard, entered the Governor's mansion. Governor Bahaadur was leaving his private quarters for his office when the intruder surprised him in the hallway. After committing his heinous crime, the assassin, aided by seven heavily armed helpers, fled the scene. A police detachment pursued the saboteurs and foreign agents."

The image on the monitor cleared and Reza Bahaadur's picture, framed in black, appeared on the upper left corner of the screen. The announcer continued, "The gang of traitors opened fire on the police. The security contingent returned the fire. According to police reports, all eight saboteurs died in the ensuing gun battle." The newsman looked down at the papers in front of him. "In a related news release, the office of the Prime Minister has announced that the Governor's body will be flown to Kabul for burial."

Chapter Twenty-two

Dhil stared at the television. Something was wrong. Who could possibly gain an advantage from such an attack? Not an outside group. Nor communists or religious extremists. Then it hit him. This was an act of the government itself; feeding on itself for reasons Dhil did not understand.

His brief conversation with Alam's sister yesterday came back to him. What had she said? "The Colonel left for Kunduz a short while ago." Dhil could hear her timid voice. "There is some type of an emergency."

If the emergency was yesterday, not this morning, and if Alam was involved, it all at once seemed to make sense to him. This episode was planned and executed in the Prime Minister's office, possibly by Khan himself.

Still, one thing didn't make sense. Why in the world would

Khan have his future son-in-law murdered? After all, he had arranged the betrothal. Had Miriam convinced him to change his mind? Dhil decided that was unlikely. Khan was not the sort of man who changed his mind.

It was Zeb's tormented face and his bloodstained shirt that interrupted Dhil's brooding. Zeb appeared before Dhil like a spirit and he could visualize him in a cold cell, shivering, worried, and angry. Yet, it hadn't registered until now how strangely acquiescent, almost reconciled, Zeb appeared when the police locked him up.

No matter what was behind these events, one thing was obvious. This was a dangerous time to be in police custody. Everyone, regardless of how innocent, would suffer. He knew he had to get Zeb out of the interior ministry before paranoia swept over the city. He walked back into the bedroom and gathered his clothes.

"Habib, what are you doing?" Miriam asked, following him into her chamber. She grabbed him by the arm. "Where are you going? Do you realize what this means for us?"

Dhil turned his back. "I have to go back to Kabul," He said, buttoning up his shirt, tucking it inside his pants, pulling the zipper. "I have to get my procurement manager out of the Ministry of the Interior before trouble begins."

"What do you mean by trouble?" Miriam's large eyes looked confused, surprised. "Why should your manager get into trouble for what happened in Kunduz?"

"I mean before the government begins cracking down on everyone suspected of anti-regime sentiments."

"You're being foolish," Miriam said. "Why would the police suspect somebody in Kabul of an assassination plot in Kunduz?"

"It happens all the time." Dhil put his right foot on a chair and fastened his shoelace. "They use one incident as an excuse to punish others. People they don't trust. People they want to hurt."

"Stop that." Miriam's voice rose sharply. "I know you despise my father. Stop these accusations. It's my father who leads the government, not just anybody. He is a good and just man."

"I'm sorry. You're right. I shouldn't speak that way."

"Are you saying you actually believe in that nonsense?" Miriam asked. "Do you really think the government persecutes people at random?"

"Look," Dhil said, "let's not start a fight. You should get dressed and return home. You will be missed. People will start asking questions."

"You hate my father, don't you?"

"Let's not get into that again."

"I understand." Miriam's lips quivered. "I understand." She sat on the edge of her bed. "Because of your hatred for my father, you're prepared to sacrifice our love."

"What your father does is his business," Dhil said, tying up the shoelace of his left shoe. "It has nothing to do with us."

"Don't tell me that," she said. "You know it has."

Dhil grabbed her hand. It felt soft and warm. "I have to go," he said and walked away from her, first slowly and then, as he left the bedroom, briskly. He rushed through the dimly lit living room where the fire still glowed in the fireplace. When he opened the house door, chilly air collided with him as if he had run against a brick wall and the brilliant light of the sun blinded him. Icy patches of frozen snow crushed under his steps.

The same guard who had opened the gate earlier hurried out of his small guardhouse and pushed open the portal. Hunched over and bouncing from one leg to the other, he waited for Dhil to leave.

Dhil turned and saw Miriam. Dressed in her blue morning gown, encased in rich, bright light, she stood in the doorframe and waved. He waved back with a smile, feeling the pain and sadness for having badly injured her. And now he had no time to make right. Would she forgive him?

Winding down the road that led to the Kabul-Paghman highway, however, it wasn't Miriam but Maggie Reed's face he recalled. True, there was no denying the physical attraction he felt for the American. He knew she felt it, too. But it was more. Maggie was accepting of his unpredictable moods, his dark visions. Was it depth that Maggie saw in him or was he just a crazy native to her, an exotic being that brightened her drab Afghan world.

No matter, he couldn't help comparing Miriam's angry rejection of his suspicion of government brutality and Maggie's unquestioning acceptance of his suppositions.

He wondered whether Miriam really loved him. While Maggie accepted him the way he was, Miriam constantly tried to mold him in her own vision, a vision darkened by blindness to the realities of life.

Did he love both of them? If not, whom should he love? Yes, whom could he love? A rough tremor shook him, and his inner voice accused him of disloyalty. But he knew from the first moment he had taken Maggie in his arms that he would be torn, eternally torn, between them.

As if wanting to remove the torment from his mind, Dhil shook his head, tightly squeezing the wheel and steering his thought to Miriam, to the firm flesh of her thighs and to how the mere touch of her hand aroused him. He gathered every detail of memory he had of her delicate body, wanting to make that sight indelible in his mind. But speeding through the wintry countryside, he knew that something had come to an end and the thought of Miriam lying in bed at his side suddenly seemed illusory.

Chapter Twenty-three

The hallways of the Ministry of the Interior were in a state of absolute chaos. Civilians and uniformed personnel dashed by Dhil, rushing in and out of offices, shouting and pointing. To Dhil it resembled more a pack of animals than civilized human beings.

Dhil tried grabbing one or two men gently by the arm, but they brushed him aside, not even taking time to show the usual annoyance for the interruption.

Finally, he stepped into the path of one heavyset bureaucrat with a short haircut and thick mustache. With a loud sigh, the man paused to hear him out.

After Dhil explained his concern about Zeb, the man threw up his hands in exasperation. "Don't you know what has happened?" he asked.

Dhil nodded. "I've seen the news."

"Then you should know. This is not a good time for you to be here."

"I'm worried about my employee."

"You're not the only one who's worried." The official's face looked increasingly somber. "Everybody's worried. No one knows what's going to happen next." He turned and began to walk away.

Dhil held him back. "That's exactly why I'm so anxious to get my employee out of here," he said.

The man removed Dhil's hand but stayed. "He might not be in this building anymore."

"Why? Has he been removed from here?"

"After the Governor's assassination was announced, a large number of detainees were brought here. To make room for them, most of the prisoners already here were taken to other locations. Just a short while ago, I saw two vans, packed with prisoners, leave the ministry. Your man could have been among them."

"How can I find out where he is?"

"The secret police have taken over this ministry. Go up to the sixth floor. Try your luck there." He again turned to leave but hesitated. Then, taking a step closer, he whispered, "If I were you, I'd go home and stay put. This isn't the time to ask about people who are in trouble."

Dhil watched the man disappear into an office and walked up the stairs to the sixth floor. To his surprise, it was quiet. He approached the first guard he saw. He was insistent. He must speak with an official in charge.

"The mamours are busy," the guard said. "You must wait till they're ready to see you."

"My case is urgent," Dhil persisted. "I must see someone at once."

"It's not up to me. The mamours themselves decide when they will receive petitioners. You have to wait like everyone else."

Dhil walked toward the other end of the narrow, dimly-lit corridor. Dirt, waste paper, and cigarette butts covered its green linoleum floor. Dust coated the glass pane of the small window at the end of the passageway, blocking out most of the incoming daylight.

As Dhil paced along the corridor, his focus on helping Zeb gave way to an indistinct fear, and he was seized by a compulsion to remain unnoticed, to avoid doing something that could attract the attention of the sentries guarding the many doors along the two sides of the hallway.

He shouldn't have come alone. He had contacts, knew officials who could intercede on his behalf. What would it take? A few more Afghanis. Zeb would forgive him once his ordeal was over.

He looked around. Nobody seemed to notice him, yet his sense of shame, of humiliation, was beginning to overcome him.

He saw an old wooden chair and sat down to collect himself. He didn't understand it, but in his guts he knew that the less anyone noticed him, the safer he would be.

Dhil looked at his watch. Counting the eight-hour time difference, he realized that night had spread its dark wings over the American east coast. In his mind, Dhil saw behind the reception area of Hotel Fort Meyer. Sitting there in his cubical was his friend, Anwar Haq, patiently adding income and subtracting expenses.

Haq would know what to do. He knew how to handle every situation. Nothing could throw him off balance. His smiling face and subtle manners always softened the edges of difficult moments and his pleasant voice and patient nature eroded any resistance.

Chapter Twenty-four

Like many upper- and middle-class sons from Kabul, Anwar Haq had entered government service, rising to a midlevel management position at the Ministry of Industries. He had often smoothed the way when Dhil needed import permits for spare parts and industrial oils. Once, he had even helped out when the Minister of Agricultural Products had refused to sign off on Dhil's purchase requisition for raw cotton.

But Haq wasn't around. Kabul was a long way from the suburbs of Washington where he now lived. He had left to study advanced management at the American University. And he wasn't coming back. He had said so himself when Dhil paid him a visit during his last trip to America.

After having finished up his affairs in New York, Dhil decided to take a train to Washington for a weekend excursion. Haq seemed pleased to hear from him, although he sounded a little remote. From Union Station, Dhil took a taxi to his hotel in Georgetown and then went directly to the address Haq had given him. The cab pulled up in front of a secondhand clothing store in a rundown part of Arlington. Haq's place was a tiny room upstairs, situated at the end of a narrow corridor.

He opened the door and greeted Dhil warmly. Inside, it was drab and the air was revoltingly stale. The tiny window, looking out on a neglected courtyard, had probably not been opened for some time. Next to the unmade bed, stood a wooden chair and a portable cooking plate was placed on a small table. A large television set sat near the head of the bed.

"Can't you afford a better place?" Dhil blurted out, aghast at the primitive state of Haq's accommodation. Immediately, he regretted his bad manners.

But Haq just smiled. "Don't I live better than most of our fellow Afghans in Kabul?" He picked up a tea pot, filled it with water from a small sink. "And look. Everyone has as much running water as they want. It's safe, too."

Dhil didn't know how to make up for his rudeness. "I didn't mean to—"

Haq interrupted, "Habib, don't be troubled. It's okay. This is all I can pay for with the money I make."

"I thought government employees were paid adequately on foreign assignments."

"That's what people generally think," Haq said. He shook his head. "Maybe that's why so many of us are desperate to get out and live abroad for a few years."

"I can't believe your American sponsors don't know how much a person needs to live on decently."

"My situation has nothing to do with what I get paid here."

"What do you mean?"

"The Americans pay for my expenses here," Haq explained.

"It's our government that's not paying its share. Under the agreement between the two governments, the Ministry of Industries is obligated to pay my salary to my family. It's not doing it. I'm sending money home from here."

"Why would the government withhold your salary? Have you quit your job?"

Haq laughed, exposing his big stained teeth. Deep wrinkles formed at the corners of his eyes and a graying lock of hair fell across his forehead. Dhil realized how much older he appeared than the last time they had been together. Normally Haq's demeanor was cheerful. Now even his laughter sounded shrill.

"You still don't understand how things are done back home, do you?" Haq said. "As a man in your position, you should really know better. You have to pay for what you get from the government."

"But you are an employee of the government. Isn't it different in your case?"

"That makes no difference. I wanted the grant. To get it, I had to forfeit my salary."

Dhil was embarrassed by Haq's blunt revelation. He didn't understand it but felt shame for something he had not caused and had nothing to do with. He drank his tea in silence and avoided looking at Haq.

Haq's assessment of him was accurate, Dhil had to admit. His desire to avoid government involvement had made him naïve, unable to use his obvious power to his best advantage.

One thing Dhil understood was the greed that permeated the government culture. Yet he never ceased to be amazed by the bureaucrats' inventiveness when it came to using their position to make money.

"Do you attend classes?" Dhil asked, more to overcome his discomfort than to find out what Haq did with his time.

"Fuck my classes," Haq's small eyes seemed to be glaring behind thick glasses. He took a swallow from his tea. "I've given up my studies. I sleep during the day and work at night in a small hotel as an accountant and receptionist. That leaves me with little time to study. I'll carry on this way as long as the Americans pay my stipend. I'm trying to save enough money to get my family out." He fell silent.

Finally, he looked at Dhil. "I work hard and save every penny to bring them over. But I'm also afraid of having them here."

"Why's that?"

"With all its advantages, this is a very different country. The Americans have their own culture and it's nothing like Afghanistan. But I see no alternative. Back home, things are falling apart. The Communists are pulling at us from one end, the religious fundamentalists from the other. Our government's incompetence will only aggravate the situation." He took another sip from his tea. His hand trembled when he put the cup back on the saucer. "Something has to give," he went on, his voice taut. "And when that time comes, it won't be just a rebellion against the regime. It will be civil war. Everyone against everyone. I don't want my family to be there when the slaughter begins."

"You have given up on our country, haven't you?" Dhil said, in a playful tone.

Haq ignored Dhil's effort to lighten up the mood of the conversation. "If I were you, I would get out. When the killing begins, it's going to be too late." He paused for a moment. "You won't make it out then."

A cool breeze swept over them as they waited for the taxi. Haq stood in his shabby raincoat, forlorn, his life's hopes dissipating if not having already vanished. But he also looked dignified, even heroic, and Dhil admired his determination.

As they embraced, Dhil slipped a few hundred dollars into Haq's hand and quickly climbed into the back seat and sped away, not giving Haq time to protest.

Back at the hotel, the doorman greeted him and as he entered the spacious lobby, the solid brass of the door handles, the shining marble floor, and the wood-paneled walls appeared immoderate and unseemly.

Chapter Twenty-five

Habib Dhil inhaled deeply then vehemently blew the air out. Looking both ways down that dim hall on the sixth floor at the Ministry of the Interior, he began to observe the other men standing around. Some wore rumpled suits. Others were dressed in the traditional baggy breeches with long shirts and cotton-filled chapans. A few had wrapped blankets around their shoulders, trying to protect themselves from the bone-chilling cold that emanated from the concrete walls. Almost all of them stood completely still as if they were nailed to the same spot. Only when one of the doors along the hallway opened and an administrator stepped out, they became alert and rushed to the official, imploring him to hear them out. Obviously resolved not to be drawn into a debate, the bureaucrats ignored them, pushing them aside when they came too close.

Dhil shuffled along the seemingly endless passageway and

became aware that two furious eyes were focused on him. The possibility that someone was observing him made him uneasy, and he wondered why he had attracted the stranger's attention. He tried but couldn't ignore the inexplicable fury in the man's stare. Finally, he turned around at the end of the corridor and resumed his walk in the other direction, reassuring himself that in the hall's poor illumination and limited visibility he could be mistaken.

Even while his back was turned to that man, Dhil could sense the seething fire in his gape and felt his stare piercing on the skin of his back. What had he done to this stranger?

He decided to stare back at him and force him to blink. But as he walked past him, he discovered that the man wasn't watching him at all. His despondent eyes simply stared at the nothingness of a blank wall. Relieved, Dhil dismissed his agitation as a delusion, the byproduct of his trepidation. In that bleak place, everyone was preoccupied with his own predicament, he told himself. No one gave a damn about who the others were or what had brought them there.

Walking back to the other end of the hall, Dhil felt the weariness that had gradually settled over him and paused by the small window, where the crusted glass broke the incoming light into a multitude of dim rays and the diffused illumination deepened the gangway's gloomy atmosphere.

He looked at his watch. More than an hour had passed since he had entered the ministry building. He began to doubt whether he would ever see someone in charge.

Unable to face the uncertainty of this situation, he entered, unconsciously, a world of fantasy where the dark hallway did not exist and a polite officer—standing behind a polished wooden counter, in an adequately lit room with a clean stone-covered floor—told him that Zeb's detention had been a mix-up, the erroneous product of an overzealous official.

A feeling of comfort oozed through his body and made him brighten up. He would not have to wait much longer, the officer reassured him. An official would soon turn up and sign Zeb's discharge papers. "I'm sorry for the inconvenience," the officer said. "You know how it is. Unfortunately, these deplorable misunderstandings happen at times."

The sudden movement of people rushing toward an administrator, who had just exited from one of the closed doors, jolted Dhil out of his daydream. He rebuked himself for his wishful thinking and his mood again became sullen. He realized that the longer he waited in this bleak, confining place, the more sinister life appeared to him. The sight of the bored, lethargic police officers exasperated him. For a minute, Zeb and what might happen to him appeared irrelevant, and he simply wanted to escape this wretched place and go home.

But he struggled against the temptation to give up, dismissing the notion of defeat, chiding himself not to let things take their own course. Not this time, he said to himself. This time, he would stand his ground and test whether he could shape things in his own way.

Turning abruptly, he went over to the same guard, a policeman whom he had spoken with earlier. "How much longer do I have to wait to see an official?" he asked brusquely.

"That's up to you," the officer answered, irritated. "The ministry isn't going anywhere. If you prefer to leave, you can do that and come back at a time more convenient to you."

Regretting his gruff conduct and realizing the futility of risking a confrontation, Dhil apologized.

"I understand," the policeman said, responding with surprising friendliness. "The long wait can get to you."

An awkward silence followed.

"Are you here to see one of the new prisoners?" the police officer asked at last.

"One of my employees was taken in yesterday," Dhil explained. "It was late and no charges were filed."

"Your employee may not be here," the officer said. "Most of the overnight prisoners were taken to other locations. You need to speak with the chief. He can tell you what's happened to him."

"Chief?"

"Chief of the Secret Police."

"Where can I find him?"

"He's here," the officer motioned with his head to the door he guarded, "behind this door. But he's busy now. It may take a while before you can see him."

Dhil walked back to the small window at the end of the hall. The police officer confirmed what he had earlier learned from the mustachioed man. Speculating where Zeb could be, Dhil concluded that the most likely place would be Pol-i-Charkhi Prison, a large penitentiary at Kabul's eastern outskirts.

He dreaded having to navigate around Pol-i-Charkhi's security apparatus. A prison of that size probably had had an unwieldy administration, rendering negotiation with it time-consuming and complicated.

But at least the suffocating uncertainty had been lifted. He now knew he had not waited in vain. Soon he would be able to see the Chief of the Secret Police who would listen to him and order Zeb's release. And once he left this building, he would purge his memory of this sinister place, trying to forget he had ever been here.

Soothed, he leaned against the window and closed his eyes to hold on to those calming notions a bit longer. But a sudden shuffling of steps hauled him back. Opening his eyes, he saw Nabi Dost, the Chief of the Secret Police, looking straight at him. Dhil recognized him at once. They had met at several large functions—marriages, funerals, and other such ceremonies and had even shaken hands occasionally in a receiving line. But they had never been formally introduced to each other.

Before Dhil knew what to do, the chief turned to the officer guarding his door and, pointing at Dhil, asked loudly: "Why is that gentleman here?"

Surprised by the chief's question, the policeman looked over at Dhil. "Sir," he stammered. "He's searching for his employee."

"Why would he search for his employee at the ministry?"

"I can explain," Dhil said, moving closer, planting himself right in the middle of the crowd surrounding the Chief.

Turning towards him, the Chief observed him for a moment. "Please come inside," he said and went back into his office.

Dhil followed him inside the office. It was a small room, containing a desk and three chairs. Its bare cement floor lacked carpeting but had been scrubbed clean. Three pictures hung side by side on the wall opposite the door. From one of them, Bahaadur Shah looked down with a large nose and a roguish smile. Prime Minister Khan's piercing eyes stared from the other. Despite their iciness, a flash in them resembled the way Miriam sometimes glanced at Dhil. The third photograph, the one in the middle, depicted the Bamyan Valley with its two Buddha statues. Carved into the red-stone mountain above the canyon, the gigantic Buddhas dwarfed the valley. Once their smiling faces and large, friendly eyes had watched over Bamyan's fields, poplar trees, and scattered farmhouses. Now the statues looked forsaken—their souls long extinguished, after invading Arab armies in the 10th century had mutilated their features and reduced their faces to two flat, lifeless slabs of stone.

A general sat beside Dost's desk. He looked up briefly when Dost and Dhil entered, turning his attention immediately back to his hat that he turned about with his hands.

Seating himself, Secret Police Chief Dost invited Dhil to sit down as well. Dost watched him intently, and Dhil felt increasingly uncomfortable. Without uttering a word, Dost turned to the files piled up before him. Grabbing one, he opened it and leafed through its pages.

"Did I understand you correctly?" Dost said, turning his red face toward Dhil again, his eyes expressionless. "You want to know whether your employee is here."

"I was with him when he was taken into custody yesterday."

"I don't understand the problem. What else do you need to find out?"

"I was hoping to get him released."

"Why should he be released so soon, if he was detained only yesterday? Surely, the police had a reason to arrest him. Isn't it a bit early to expect the investigation to be completed?"

"It was all a misunderstanding. My employee hasn't done anything wrong. It was too late to sort things out yesterday. I was hoping to do it now, so he could go home."

Secret Police Chief Dost took his time studying Dhil's face. "Look here," he said. His voice was brusque. His tone was obviously impatient. "We're in the midst of a crisis. We have our hands full right now."

"That's precisely why I rushed here. I thought the incident in Kunduz might lead to complications. I came to obtain Zeb's discharge before an emergency arose."

"What was that name again?" the general asked, looking up for the second time since Dhil had entered the office.

"Agha Zeb," answered Dhil, "He's the procurement manager at my mill. And my name—"

"We know who you are, Mr. Dhil," said Chief Dost. "Your grandfather was a great patriot and your father —" The general interrupted Dost, pointing to a sheet of paper, which lay on the table before him. The general drew Dost's attention to something written on it. Secret Police Chief Dost studied the document for a while. When he raised his head, his eyes had turned stone cold. "Mr. Dhil," he said, "you said the Governor's tragic death could lead to other complications. What exactly do you mean by that?"

"Nothing specific," Dhil replied. "After all, he was His Majesty's son."

"But why would you think the Governor's death could have wider consequences?" Dost scrutinized Dhil carefully, looking at him with stone-cold eyes. "Repercussions that might even affect routine criminal investigations here in Kabul? That's what you mean, isn't it?"

Dhil was on guard. Dost could very well accuse him of some crime and detain him too. Dhil became nervous his face began to heat up. Had Dost noticed his momentary lack of self-command? Dhil reminded himself to do a better job controlling his emotions.

"Are you really worried," Dost asked, "that Governor Bahaadur's tragic death could cause disruptions here in the capital?"

"Of course not," Dhil replied, keeping his voice from cracking. "I'm not implying that at all. I'm merely concerned about my employee."

"One naturally worries in such instances," Dost said, his voice softer, his manner less hostile. He looked once more at the sheet of paper the General had pointed out to him and turned his face briefly toward the General. The General's attention had returned to his hat.

"You are one of us, Dhil Sa'heb," Dost said. "I can speak with you openly." He looked pensive, taking time to talk. "What I'm going to tell you is privileged information and must stay within these walls."

"I understand," Dhil nodded, relieved that he was out of danger.

"Your employee was involved in anti-state activities."

"What?" Dhil blurted out, unable to suppress his utter disbelief. "That's impossible. There must be a misunderstanding."

"Not at all," the Secret Police Chief said matter-of-factly. "Your employee has committed treason. As a responsible employer, as someone whose wealth and status is well protected by the state, you should have observed your employee better, Mr. Dhil. Had you watched your procurement manager more closely, you could have found out about his political intrigues."

Dhil felt how his anger reached a dangerous level. The accusation against Zeb was absurd, a wicked libel, no more. Before his surging rage and revulsion could ignite a violent outburst, he told himself again to remain calm, to avoid irritating Dost. That would only hurt Zeb's chance to be released. Indeed, he had to be vigilant or he himself might get drawn in and accused of complicity.

"With all due respect, Chief Dost," Dhil said, choosing his words carefully, "I find it very difficult to believe the charge. I've known Zeb for many years. I can assure you he does not belong to any political organization."

"We have evidence of his illegal activities," Dost said with certainty. He had an aura of indestructibility and radiated health and vigor. "You will understand I can't give you concrete details."

"Is there anything I can do to prove his innocence?"

"I'm afraid I can't help you any further."

Dhil recognized the finality in Dost's tone. As far as the Chief of the Secret Police was concerned, the discussion had come to an end. Nevertheless and without much hope, Dhil asked, "May I see him?"

Dost turned his attention back to the dossier that he still held in his hand. After reading several lines, he turned to the General and asked, "What do you think, General? Should we inform this gentleman of the situation surrounding his employee?"

"Why not?" answered the General without looking up. "Let the man know what has happened. Then he can go home and we can continue with our business."

"Today we discovered an assassination plot against our country's entire political leadership," Dost said solemnly. "Your employee was an active participant in the conspiracy. A military court has found the traitors, among them your employee, guilty of treason. The executions took place earlier this afternoon."

Dumbfounded, Dhil didn't know what to say. Had he even heard correctly?

"Are you all right, Dhil Sa'heb?" Dost said.

"I'm fine."

"You look tired, Dhil Sa'heb," Dost said. "These are unstable times. It's better you go home."

Dhil got up to leave. As he walked toward the door, his grandfather's spirited face appeared before him, and he recalled the old man's words, "It's a precious gift from God to die in your own home and be buried among your forefathers."

A sense of duty gripped him. If Zeb had been denied the prerogative of dying at home, Dhil thought with a weighty measure of guilt, he should at least try to deliver his body to his family.

He turned and asked, "Chief Dost, may I know what happened to his remains?"

Dost looked at the file. "The body is at Wali Khan Military Hospital. If you wish to take it, I'll instruct the hospital to let you have it. But you must remove the body before 6 p.m. The hospital administration is under orders to bury him by dusk."

When Dhil left Dost's office, the guard outside smiled. Dhil thought he should shake hands with him to thank him for his simple kindness but realized that his hands were shaking uncontrollably. Pretending he didn't see him, Dhil walked away briskly.

Chapter Twenty-six

Before leaving for Baghlan to visit his farm, Colonel Alam Gol had a quick lunch with General Asil at the division guesthouse. As they ate, they watched the one-o'clock news and the report of the Governor's death. At the mention of Bahaadur's demise as an "act of terrorism committed by foreign agents," General Asil winced. His quick glance at Gol looked troubled.

Gol was surprised at Asil's show of discomfort. After all, as an old hand in government matters, one would expect him to recognize the necessity of government actions—measures, if viewed as isolated occurrences, might be tricky to explain but were altogether justified when considered in the larger context of the government's overall responsibilities.

General Asil's obvious misgiving occupied Gol's mind all through the meal and even later when they had departed for Baghlan. But as soon as they entered Baghlan's hilly countryside, he became oblivious to the General's irritation. The sight of the fertile land sliding by the car's window elated him. The sheep grazing on the green hills and the large, well-built farmhouses reminded him of home. A long-forgotten feeling of security emerged within him.

Turning off the paved highway, the driver continued on the dirt road that led to Gol's village. The yellow dust that had been trailing the car swooped over them when the driver stopped the automobile in front of Gol's farmhouse. After the suffocating cloud settled and the air cleared up again, Gol got out of the car and, taking a deep breath, tasted the soil's strong aroma and the pungent smell of farm animals.

The house, standing at the bottom of a gracefully sloping hill, appeared isolated. Fertile fields stretched to the horizon where distant knolls rose up, forming the natural boundary of Gol's land.

Gol depended on the farm's agricultural activities to augment his meager government salary. While prestigious and the stepping-stone to better assignments, his government job was quite removed from the public, offering him few opportunities to use it to make money. The fifty thousand afghanis he had recently received from Akbar Nouri for the land deal he had arranged for the developer had come after a frustratingly long dry stretch.

After his mother's death, there had been no pressing reason for him to come to the farm, and he had stopped visiting. The old manager, who had run the farm for years, continued to take care of it. Gol trusted him.

Returning to the farm after so many years felt strange. He recalled his mother, caring, concerned, and forever afraid of his large, overpowering father. His father's commanding image loomed before him, holding him by the shoulders with his big hands, scolding him for one misdeed or another. And, of course, no remembrance of this place would be complete without Habib Dhil, brimming with ideas, constantly speaking of his vision for the future, virtually glowing with excitement.

Gholam Ali, the farm manager came out of his house. From afar, he didn't seem to have changed much, even though his gait had slowed a bit and his stubbly beard grown a touch grayer. But up-close, Gol noticed a forlorn expression on the manager's face, his bright smile having vanished, the light in his piercing eyes dimmed to near extinction.

"Salam, Agha Jaan," the manager said. Without waiting for Gol to return his greeting, he asked, "What extraordinary occasion brings you here?" He shook Gol's hand, holding on to it for so long that Gol became uncomfortable and pulled it away.

Although he seemed friendly enough, Gol detected a suspicious look in his eyes and—as absurdly as it felt—wondered if the farm manager knew something about Kunduz. He felt an urge to say something, but before he could, the manager turned to General Asil, greeting him with excessive formality, placing his hand on his heart and bowing deeply before the general.

Neighbors and several tenant farmers arrived. Their curiosity didn't surprise Gol. He knew from his own childhood how the appearance of an automobile in this area incited interest and even now, in the 1970's, little had changed. He had, however, almost forgotten how bulky the locals looked in their big turbans, cotton-filled baggy trousers, high-heeled black boots, and ankle-length striped chapans. He knew from experience that they needed the protection that the bulky clothing provided, especially at night, when Siberia's shrieking blizzards swept over the countryside, carrying with them the piercing chill of Asia's vast tundra.

Among the farmers who had rushed to see the visitors was the village mullah. A small man with a wrinkled face, his cheeks drawn inward into his toothless mouth, he looked up at Gol, his gaze eager, wondering. "You've forgotten us," he said, air lisping through his thin lips. "You should come more often. Things aren't well here."

"Later, Imam," the farm manager said, steering the visitors in the direction of his house.

But the mullah held on to Gol's hand and said, "Two years have passed since I got my last set of clothes from my congregation. Instead of giving me one bar of soap every month, I'm now getting one every three months and —"

Pulling the mullah away, the farm manager said, "You can talk to him later. Let's go inside now."

With evident pride, the manager led them into the small side building where the manager had always lived. Before stepping inside, Gol glanced at the surroundings. Locked since his mother's death, the farmhouse looked shadowy and brooding. The door to the stables, its bright green color faded, stood open, revealing crumbling, empty stalls. It was no less desolate inside the manager's dwelling where daylight barely entered through the coarse curtains. The frazzled condition of the woolen mat on the dirt floor bore witness to the rug's old age and utter exhaustion. Even the flowered slipcover of the cushion Gol leaned on was torn and spoke of long years of neglect. As far as he could make out, the only new object in the room was the television set and the embroidered piece of cloth that covered it.

As a child, and even later as a teenager, he had spent hours in this very room without ever noticing its bare walls or its faint light. In those days, he had felt secure and happy here, listening in amazement to the manager's stories, especially about his flight from Uzbekistan. As he described Russia's relentless drive to extinguish nationalist dissent in Uzbekistan, his sunburned face became agitated and his black eyes furious. But his outrage changed to sadness when he recounted how Russia's scorched-earth policy had driven so many Uzbeks out of their country. Then Stalin had come to power and begun enforcing his agricultural communization plan. The campaign had caused widespread hunger, forcing even more Uzbeks to flee.

The farm manager had been among them. Russian soldiers had sprayed his small raft with a machinegun as he tried to cross the Amu River. His wife and five of his six children had been hit, slipping off the raft, drowning one after another right before his eyes. Only he and his youngest child, a baby boy, had survived. The agony of that long-passed moment reappeared in his eyes as he had related how he had pressed the baby against the raft, hovering over him and hoping against hope to make it to the Afghan side of the Amu River. He never understood how he made it to the other side of the river unharmed. When he set foot on Afghan soil, daylight had dawned softly on the horizon. The baby had looked at him and chuckled cheerfully, throwing his little arms all about.

All these memories and conflicting emotions made Gol weary. Except for an old man, a distant cousin of his father, who sat motionless, the peasants seemed exuberant, enjoying their tea, speaking animatedly, laughing quietly. The old cousin, his features expressionless, his fingers slowly but continually moving the pieces of his prayer beads, stared in his direction. His empty gaze and crumpled face brought pictures of decay and death to Gol's mind. Trying to avoid the aged man's stare, Gol looked down and saw the powdery dirt that had settled over him as he had exited the car. Suddenly, he felt enclosed by a cloud of dust that seemed to be everywhere. Not only had it covered his clothes, it had entered his mouth and gone into his eyes. Feeling smothered, he found himself in desperate need to breathe fresh air.

Gulping down his tea, he rose abruptly. The manager stared at him, his mouth open, embarrassment visible in his face. Without taking leave from the others, even ignoring General Asil, Gol left. Asil rushed out behind him. Following them, the manager tried hard to keep pace with his tall, massive master as he hurried away.

"We clean the house at the end of every month," the farm

manager said, motioning toward the locked-up farmhouse. "You can come whenever you wish. It is always ready to be moved into."

"I know you're doing your best," Gol said. "I'm satisfied."

"I haven't sold any of the firewood we collected this season," the manager said. "There is no room left to store more. What should I do with it?"

"Sell it," Gol said, harshly. "But now, return to your guests."

Asil and the manager watched as Gol walked away.

When Gol reached the brook that ran a little distance from the house, he finally stopped under the trees that stood along the stream. As the dilapidated stables and fading paint of the house had indicated the relentless passage of time, the serenity in the shadow of this small grove seemed to proclaim that time had stood still and nothing had changed since his childhood. There, along the rivulet, he had played for hours, dreaming of battles won, worlds conquered, and glories gained. Here, he had sat with Dhil after hours of running about. Tired, they had taken off their shoes and dipped their feet into the cool water, looking up at the treetops, listening to the mysterious rustling of the leaves high above them.

Nothing had changed here. The creek, the trees, and the dust were there as they had always been. Yet something seemed different. The quietly flowing water failed to charm him. The tranquility of the thicket no longer seemed peaceful. The memory of his childhood disturbed him. He had lost the exuberance of those sorrow-free years.

He recalled the momentous feeling of command and power that had swept over him as he had carried out his orders earlier today. That power had enabled him to remain aloof throughout the operation. But now that intensity had dissipated. Confronted by the timelessness of his surroundings, he sensed a profound weakness deep within himself and shuddered.

Chapter Twenty-seven

"I'm heading to the municipal hospital to rent a hearse," Dhil told Faizullah, his office manager, from a telephone booth outside the Ministry of the Interior. The cool air had cleared his mind a little. "I'm taking Zeb's remains to his village."

"Masoud's here," Faizullah said in a muffled voice. "He wants to know where Zeb is."

Masoud, Zeb's sixteen-year-old brother, was the only member of Zeb's family who lived in Kabul. Zeb's wife and his other relatives had stayed behind in their village, Guldara, about twenty miles north of the capital. It would have been too expensive if all of them had moved into the city. The cost of Masoud's food, books, daily bus fare, and pocket money already created a heavy burden for Zeb. Zeb's financial troubles invariably came up whenever he applied to defer his monthly payment on the loan he had received from Dhil's company.

"Have you told him what's happened?" Dhil asked.

"Should I tell him?"

"Send him to the municipal hospital. I'll meet him there and speak with him."

Masoud had not yet arrived when Dhil got to the Amir Bahaadur Shah Municipal Health Center. He waited for him inside the hall at the hospital's main entrance. After half-an-hour or so, he recognized Masoud through the glass door, getting out of the rear door of a city bus, crossing the street, hopping over puddles, dodging piles of slushy snow. As he observed Masoud walk toward the building, Dhil thought of various ways he could break the news of Zeb's passing to his brother. Still shivering from the cold, Masoud entered the hospital.

"Something terrible has happened," Dhil said, putting his arm around Masoud's shoulders.

"Has he had an accident?" Masoud asked.

"He's dead," Dhil said. "God forgive his soul."

Masoud's mouth opened slightly but no word came out. Then, after several seconds, as if the impact of the information needed time to work through his mind, his face crumpled and he began to weep.

"But how?" he finally asked, tears rolling down his cheeks.

"The secret police claim he was involved in the killing of Governor Bahaadur. They have executed him."

"But that's not true, is it?"

"No, of course not. He had nothing to do with the Governor's death."

Masoud pleaded, "Why did they kill him then?"

"It was a mistake." Dhil gave Masoud his handkerchief to wipe his tears. "He did nothing wrong. He was innocent."

"How shall I tell my mother?" Masoud shook his head, using Dhil's handkerchief to wipe off tears from his face.

"You must keep calm. You'll have to console your mother

by being strong." He let Masoud be for a while. "Let's go," he finally said. "You and I have to take him home."

Masoud nodded.

When Dhil and Masoud entered the office of the relevant employee of the municipal hospital, he was conducting his afternoon prayer in the far corner of his office. After he was done, he carefully folded the prayer rug and put it on a shelve. Then he walked barefoot over to his desk and sat down. He pulled his shoes and socks out from under his desk and put them on.

After he was done with tying his shoe strings and without even glancing at his two visitors, he took the application that Dhil placed before him and read it.

"I'm sorry about your loss," said the municipal employee, raising his lean face and adding, "May Allah bless his soul." Although a good-sized, wood-burning furnace provided adequate heat, he wore a bulky overcoat. He nervously scratched his cheek with his long fingers. "At a time like this, I wouldn't speak of money. But there is a nominal rental charge for the hearse."

"I understand," Dhil said.

The municipal employee began filling out the rental form. When he finished, he turned it around for Dhil to sign. Dhil immediately affixed his signature at the bottom.

"Did he die of an accident?" The municipal employee seemed genuinely interested.

Before Dhil could say anything, Masoud blurted out, "They killed him."

"What do you mean?"

"Those murderers executed him."

"It was a mistake," Dhil interrupted, grabbing Masoud's arm, pressing it. Although he saw how the municipal employee stiffened and realized it was too late to repair the damage, he added, "A tragic mistake."

The official, his bulky eyebrows and thick stubbles forming a dark circle around his hostile look, snatched the rental form from Dils hand. "The municipality does not provide services to enemies of the state," he said firmly, tearing the rental form up and throwing the torn pieces of paper in the wastebasket.

The official's reaction didn't surprise Dhil. Government employees routinely denied services to those who had come into conflict with the government. After all, they were often simple people themselves, frightened of the state and its brutality and would not dare extend a helping hand to someone who the authorities considered dangerous and undesirable. Somebody, they would never know who, might punish them for having aided enemies of the regime. The simplest way out was to refuse services.

Dhil asked to use the phone and the municipal employee, with obvious reluctance, agreed. Mayor Nowroz was Dhil's first thought since he had done Nowroz favors in the past. But when he called the mayor's office, he found out that neither the mayor nor any other high-level official on his staff was available to intervene.

He had no choice but to proceed to Wali Khan Military Hospital and hope that he could coax somebody there to let Zeb's body remain overnight at the hospital mortuary. By morning, he would find a solution. He knew enough people to force the municipality's hand to help transport the body. Or in the event it proved impossible to get a hearse, he could have Zeb's remains transported in a company delivery van. The vehicles were large enough to accommodate the body. Presently, the vans were out on their daily delivery routes to retail shops and clothing manufacturers. But by nightfall some would be back at the factory, and in the morning he could assign one to take Zeb's remains to his village.

Chapter Twenty-eight

The wood-fired heater in the office of the administrative manager at Wali Khan Military Hospital had broken down. Cold wind blew into the room through several broken windowpanes, sealed in makeshift fashion with brown packing paper. The duty officer—a colonel, a scrawny man of medium build, brown hair, and tired eyes—had bundled himself up in a heavy military overcoat, buttoned all the way to the neck. His hands, tucked inside woolen gloves with several holes at the fingertips, held the sheet Dhil had handed to him.

"I can't accommodate you," the colonel said, holding out the written request, motioning for Dhil to take it back.

"I promise, I'll be here first thing in the morning," Dhil insisted. "I'll pay any charges this might entail."

"Sorry," the duty officer said. "I've my orders. I can't assist you.

Besides, this hospital lacks the facility to store bodies. I couldn't keep your employee's body overnight, even if I wanted to."

The officer seemed to be a calm and reasonable person. His restrained conduct gave Dhil a glimmer of hope, and he pressed on with his request. "Colonel," he said, "it's freezing right now. It'll be even chillier during the night. There's no danger. The body won't decompose overnight."

"Be that as it may," the colonel said, straightening up in his chair. "Please understand. There's absolutely nothing I can do."

"I know you can." Dhil paused. "And money is no problem, Colonel."

"Listen to me," the colonel said, his voice rising, "I can't help you. Your man is not the only person I have to take care of. My orders are to bury all of them by 6 p.m. And that's what I will do. I can't make an exception for you. If you haven't claimed the body by then, it'll be put in the same grave with the others."

Realizing nothing more could be gained, Dhil rejoined Zeb's brother who waited outside at the top of the steps in front of the hospital.

The chill had begun to tire Dhil. A soggy mixture of snow and dirt had seeped through his shoes, causing him excruciating pain. The biting cold had cracked his lips. He constantly slid his tongue over them to moisten them and prevent them from bleeding.

As he gazed at the snow-covered land surrounding the hospital, he wondered whether he could have saved Zeb had he not gone to Paghman. Though no longer relevant, the question caused a sore upwelling of guilt in his heart. It had been his responsibility to intervene on Zeb's behalf. No matter how he looked at it, he could not find an excuse for his negligence. By ignoring Zeb, he had broken his word to him. That plain fact stirred up within him a crushing feeling of his own inadequacy and inferiority.

The only way he could try to make up for his failure was to return Zeb's remains to his family, even if he had to transport the body himself. He stood silently for a moment, then pointed to the area where the vehicle was parked and said, "Masoud, come with me."

They walked down the steps, took the Rover, and drove to the hospital mortuary, a one-story building some two hundred yards away.

Backing up his car to the mortuary entrance, he cranked down the rear window, opened the back door, and folded away the backseat.

While Massoud passively followed, Dhil pushed open the mortuary door and entered a large, rectangular chamber, poorly lit by a few bulbs hanging from uncovered electric wires. Wrapped in coarse white cloths, the dead lay on rough wooden planks along two walls and in two parallel rows in the middle of the room.

The mortuary keeper read the release order for Zeb, folded the paper, and put it in the pocket of his dirty, blood-besmirched overalls. He waved his arm across the room. "Go ahead and find the body yourself," he told Dhil, his voice dull, disinterested.

The dead were not tagged. Dhil had to walk from corpse to corpse, uncovering each person's face. Several bodies down the row, he unwrapped the first of the bloodstained linens and saw a man's features covered with blood that had flowed out of his nostrils. Lifting the cloth a bit more, he noticed that the man's chest had been torn open by a volley of bullets. He covered the mutilated corpse and realized that he could save time if he checked only those bodies that were covered with bloody shrouds, the most likely to contain victims of executions.

Dhil jolted when he recognized Zeb. Blood and dirt splattered his face. His deeply recessed eyes made the lifelessness of his features appear even more pronounced.

Before he could cover Zeb's face again, Masoud arrived at his side and took a glimpse of his brother. He fell on his knees, retching, whimpering quietly, hitting repeatedly the dusty ground with his fist.

Dhil kneeled beside him, putting his arm around his shoulders, waiting for him to calm down. After a minute or so, he started to pull the young man to his feet. "Please Masoud, we must go. It's getting late."

Masoud nodded.

They both lifted Zeb's body and carried it over to the door. The mortuary keeper stood in their way asking for the shroud.

For an instant, Dhil thought he had misunderstood. He motioned for Masoud to continue.

But the keeper persisted. "It's hospital property," he said. "I'm responsible for it."

"You don't expect me to take him out of here naked, do you?" Dhil asked, exasperated.

"What you want to do is none of my business," the mortuary keeper said. "You can do whatever you like. I'm responsible for the linen. You can't take it out of here."

A stabbing pain raced through Dhil's head. Lowering Zeb's body and letting it rest on the ground, he paused for a moment to collect himself. While he tried to decide how to respond, he observed Zeb's remains on the dusty floor, draped in a dirty, blood-drenched cloth. He noticed Masoud's colorless face, his eyes glazed, his features incredulous. And there stood the mortuary keeper—a man without any distinct features, just a man like a million others, crusts of hardened blood covering his overall.

The surprisingly strident sound of his rapidly throbbing heart brought Dhil back from his trance-like state, and he took several deep breaths. When the mortuary's stale air penetrated his lungs, the sweetish stench of cadavers made his stomach spin. Another shooting pain darted through his head, and an evil craving took possession of him. He felt an urge to inflict pain upon the keeper and to see fear in his eyes. Instead, he forced himself to control his repulsion.

His mind gradually cleared up. He offered the keeper one thousand afghanis, an amount many times the value of the linen's replacement cost. He held the money out.

"I can't take money from you," the keeper said. "The cloth is hospital property. I can't sell what's not mine."

"I'm not asking you to sell it," Dhil said. "I'm paying you to replace it."

"Well, if you put it that way." The mortuary keeper reached for the bills and stuffed them into his pocket.

Guiding the body through the Land Rover's back door, Dhil and Masoud pushed it into the car. Zeb's feet stuck out the rear window. Numb and bewildered by grief, Masoud crouched next to his dead brother.

"Hold him down," Dhil said. "Use both hands."

Driving through the darkening countryside, Dhil's head felt curiously empty. Even Maggie and Miriam, the two people usually present in his mind, remained outside his thoughts.

Chapter Twenty-nine

The tiny borough where Zeb's family lived lay at the foot of a mountain that soared high into the sky. Parking his car on the main road, Dhil turned to the backseat where Masoud cowered over his dead brother. "Go on ahead," he said. "We need help to carry him. I'll wait here."

Masoud ran down a narrow alley and within a few minutes, he returned, together with his older brother, Wahid, and several other men. They listened in silence to Dhil's explanation of what had happened. Then, Zeb's relatives, without asking a single question nor uttering one word, lifted Zeb's body out of the car, laid it on the string bedstead they had brought with them. Heaving the charpoy on their shoulders, they carried the corpse away. Dhil followed them.

When they entered the small mud-brick house, Dhil noticed the steep stairs leading up to the second floor. While the men struggled to carry the corpse up the steps, Dhil leaped forward to give them a hand. But realizing that in the constricted space he would be more of a hindrance than support, he stepped back.

At that moment, the body slid downward. Zeb's head stuck out from under the cloth cover, colliding with the face of one of the men carrying the charpoy's lower end. Obviously startled, the man lost his balance, nearly falling backward. Another man jumped up the stairs, propping him up and pulling the shroud over Zeb's face again.

Upstairs, they lifted the corpse from the string bedstead and placed it on a coarse, hand-woven mat in the middle of a small room. Taking their places around Zeb's body, the women began wailing.

The news of Zeb's death must have traveled through the village. Soon, the small house filled with people. Wahid led Dhil into an adjacent room where the men sat along the bare brick walls. Except for Masoud's brother and uncle, he didn't know any of the others present.

The village mullah arrived and, after a moment of silence, began to recite passages from the Quran. "Every soul shall have a taste of death: And only on the Day of Judgment shall you be paid your full recompense."

He stopped. Then he said, "Let's be thankful to Allah that his remains were brought back to us to be buried beside his kin. It is a sign of the Lord's benevolence towards the departed that his body is returned to his family."

"Imam," Sher Ahmad, Masoud's uncle, said, "how often have you preached to us that it is God's mercy when we die between our bed sheets?"

The Mullah didn't reply.

"And how often have you said that those whose bodies are returned to earth intact are God's favored children?" Sher

Ahmad continued, his lips razor thin, his skin leathery, burned dry by many years of hard work under the mountain sun.

"Have you seen him, Imam?" the old man's voice rose, surprising Dhil with its vigor. "They have cut him in two. Did you see the blood? Had you seen his face, you would've known from the dirt on it that he didn't die in his bed. They killed him, Imam. Now tell us. What does God say in this case?"

Unable to hide their embarrassment, the others shuffled their feet awkwardly and cleared their throats.

Except for the women's lamentation seeping through the wall, quiet held sway over the room.

The mullah took a deep breath. He spoke about the human inability to understand Allah's will. One should not, he said, expect to find all the answers to one's questions in this life.

"It's all right, Imam," one of the men said, his voice reassuringly calm. "This isn't your fault."

Eager to bring the momentary overwrought situation behind him, the mullah used the reprieve to continue reciting from the Quran.

Observing the villagers' sun-burnt faces, Dhil began to feel like an intruder. His presence among the grieving family suddenly seemed absurd and unnecessary. He got up, shook everybody's hand, and left. Masoud and Wahid walked him to the car. No one spoke, and Dhil was content that the dark of the settling night hid their faces, preventing them from looking into one another's eyes.

Chapter Thirty

Mud-brick houses shimmered cold and ghostlike in the dim moonlight. Occasionally, a flickering beam from a gas lamp seeped through the closed shutters of dingy, roadside shops, indicating glimmers of life inside.

The impoverished landscape squeezed Dhil's already destitute spirit and the day's hideous events reinforced his angst about the future. While sensing a gigantic tragedy approaching, he saw himself guarded only by the fickle generosity of a haphazard world where hatred, deceit, and destruction had increasingly overtaken daily life.

Racing through the dark countryside and amidst those unceasing impressions of hopelessness, a cold shiver shot through his body with such elemental force that he momentarily lost control over his car and had to turn sharply the steering wheel to avoid hitting one of the massive trees that lined the road. The shock of virtually seeing the last moments of his life and the satisfaction of his lightning-speed reaction in avoiding certain death triggered a vigorous sense of resolve within him. That sensation, a blend of contentment and recklessness, dashed through his mind like a thunderbolt zips across the sky, jolting his wits out of its faltering, weak-willed state.

Unexpectedly, he felt energized. Calm filled his mind. The perpetual fear that had imprisoned him most of his conscious life in a twilight world of dimming hope and mounting despair vanished, releasing his thoughts from their constant ferment.

His personal safety, his future, questions of money and property, all the things that had loomed large before him and caused him to shudder at the possibility of their loss, now appeared insignificant. Khan and Bahaadur Shah's iron-fisted rule looked like a trivial matter, unworthy of attention. Even death seemed less frightening.

He now saw the importance of time above all else. It was a commodity he had seldom given much thought about and wasted so much of. Now that he could dare face the world, he wondered whether there was enough time left to resurrect himself.

In his new found clarity, he immediately realized that he must forever leave this place, travel as far as possible from this land of his ancestors.

Should he talk with Maggie about it? For a moment an image of Maggie's face flashed before him. Would she be pleased at his announcement?

When he reached the top of the Shomali pass, the valley on the other side of the mountain opened before him. Kabul's lights glittered like a sea of shimmering stars against the black dome of the night sky.

Lit by powerful overhead lamps, the nearby Amir Bahaadur Shah Military Airfield glared brightly. A large Air Force transport plane landed as he entered the city limits. He wondered whether the aircraft carried the governor's body for the state funeral as the news bulletin had announced. Was Gol also in that plane?

Driving into Kabul, he noticed military vehicles parked at odd places. Soldiers with rifles stood at major intersections. In some areas, tanks blocked side streets. Armored troop carriers rumbled through the quiet avenues. In the absence of the usual jumble of gadis, bicyclists, and crowds, the narrow streets and sprawling bazaars appeared strange, like places he hadn't seen before.

Perhaps a state of emergency had been declared, he thought. But whatever the reason for the unusual display of military prowess might be, it didn't concern him. Khan and Bahaadur Shah and all their warped doings no longer mattered to him.

At an intersection, less than a mile from his home, a group of soldiers stopped him. He cranked down the window as two of them approached him.

"Where are you heading?" one of the soldiers asked.

"Home," Dhil replied.

"But you're not allowed to be out at this time," the soldier said.

"Why?"

"We have orders to take in anybody who violates the curfew."

"The curfew?" Dhil asked.

"Yes, the curfew."

"I didn't know about it," Dhil said. "I was busy all day and haven't listened to the radio."

"Let him go," the other soldier said. "He doesn't know anything. Let him go home."

"How do we know he's going to go home?" the first soldier asked.

"He looks like he's telling the truth," said the second soldier.

"He's right," Dhil said. "I'm on my way home."

"The first soldier looked at Dhil's Rover, then at the other soldier. "Well, I guess since you are so close, there is no—"

His was interrupted. A Russian-built Jeep approached the intersection and stopped beside Dhil's vehicle. Turning down his window, an army captain asked, "What's the matter?"

"This man claims not to know about the curfew," said the first soldier. "He says he is on his way home."

The officer grunted and thought for a few seconds. "Our orders are clear," he said. "No one is to be out after the time set for the curfew. Anyone in violation is to be immediately detained." He looked at his watch. "Arrest him," he ordered. "Send him over to the Ministry of the Interior. Let them decide whether he's telling the truth."

The two soldiers snapped to attention as the Russian Jeep drove off.

Chapter Thirty-one

As soon as Gol set foot on the tarmac, a sergeant came up to him. From the tiny red star sewn on the upper left pocket of his uniform jacket, Gol recognized him as an agent of the secret police.

"Colonel," the sergeant said, "I have orders to take you to Chief Dost immediately."

Amir Bahaadur Shah Military Airfield was on alert, its administrative buildings fully staffed, technical personnel busy in the hangars, and, under the airfield's glaring floodlights, MiG fighter planes checked and made ready for takeoff.

The sergeant's Russian Jeep left the military base and sped through deserted streets. Armed soldiers had been posted at major intersections and troop carriers rambled throughout the city.

"What's going on, Sergeant?" Gol asked.

"After Governor Bahaadur's assassination, the army occupied

the city. Wait until you see the Prime Minister's office, Colonel. It looks like a fortress."

"Is there an emergency?"

"Something must have happened. The Chief took charge of the Ministry of the Interior and the police have arrested a large number of people. To make room for the new detainees, many of those already under investigation had to be taken elsewhere."

"Where were they taken?"

The agent hesitated. The Zeel raced down the city's empty avenues. Despite the faint beam of the streetlights, Gol could see the anxiety on the agent's face.

"It's all right, Sergeant," he said. "You can talk to me. I work for the Chief, too."

"Colonel, I'm not spreading rumors. I'm merely telling you what I've heard."

"Don't worry," Gol said. "I understand."

The Sergeant still wasn't sure. "They... They were driven outside the city and executed."

The eeriness of the deserted streets and shuttered stores gripped Gol's imagination. Something big must be afoot, he thought and tried to picture today's executions. He visualized the firing squad discharging their guns again and again; the deafening blasts of their rifles roaring over the flat country; men tumbling to the ground, blood leaking through their ripped cloths, percolating through the snow-covered soil.

"What about the prisoners?" Gol inquired. "Did you hear about who was among them?"

"As I said Colonel, I didn't see them myself. I heard ministers and generals were among them."

Gol shook his head. He was quite sure. Prime Minister Khan had unleashed a struggle for power with the King. Since Secret Police Chief Dost, a close ally of the Prime Minister's, had brought the Ministry of the Interior under his control, it was probably the King's supporters who were being purged. The Governor's death had provided Khan with a pretext for mass arrests. He would use the opportunity to get rid of all those he considered dangerous or simply undesirable. At the same time, the elimination of well-known persons would serve to frighten the general population into continued submission.

Gol checked the time. He was tired. If Dost wanted to see him immediately, the purge was likely well under way, and he would have to get involved in it. Now that he had killed the King's son, he had no choice but to continue to do everything to help Khan and Chief Dost as well.

He took a deep breath. He needed to focus on one thing: Khan's victory over his enemies. That, and that alone, would guarantee Gol's own survival.

Chapter Thirty-two

Habib Dhil was suffocating. The cloth sack they had slipped over his head not only blinded him, but had severely limited his breathing. He took shallow breaths to conserve the air.

At first he had tried to protest his treatment, but a tap to the side of his head from a rifle butt encouraged him to remain quiet. He and his guards rode in silence.

The Russian Jeep came to a sharp stop. Cold air gushed inside.

"Get out," a voice commanded.

Handcuffed and blindfolded, Dhil was unable to control his movements. He nearly fell when he stepped out of the vehicle. Someone held him by the arm, steadying him until he finally stood firmly on his own two feet.

When his foot bumped against a doorstep, he understood

that he had been taken inside a building. After descending four flights of stairs, they made a turn and walked along what seemed like a long corridor. The only thing he could hear was the sound of heavy boots on the concrete floor.

They stopped, and Dhil heard a key turn and a door open with a squeaking noise. Somebody took off his handcuffs and pushed him forward. Then someone, perhaps the same person who had shoved him, pulled the hood from his head. He spun around. But before he could look at the men who had brought him to this place, the door was slammed shut and locked.

Darkness again surrounded him. The smell of mold, urine, and vomit assaulted his nostrils. He groped his way along the walls. The room was tiny, just about large enough for an average-sized person to stretch out.

Exhaustion and disorientation made his head spin, causing his body to sway back and forth. To keep himself from falling, he leaned against the wall. After a while, he sat down, the icy surface of the concrete floor pressing hard against him. His muscles ached and his limbs shook uncontrollably.

Struggling to forget his agony, he tried to think about the hours he had spent with Miriam this morning. But those moments of tortured happiness seemed to have occurred so far back in time that he couldn't recall them and he failed to even summon Miriam's face. He could only picture her standing in the doorframe, watching him walk down the slope. Instead Omar's features emerged, and he recalled how the previous night Omar had stood before him, hunched and squinting, frail and uncertain of what was expected of him.

When he first met Omar, Dhil had pitied him for the miseries the regime had inflicted upon him. Now he envied him. Omar had already experienced the horrors of arrest. He knew what it meant to be subjected to government brutality. He'd had that ordeal behind him. He had survived it. Instead it was Dhil who must worry about what lay ahead. Still, he held out hope that his arrest would be seen as just a misunderstanding.

Eventually, fatigue numbed his brain, and he drifted off. When the sharp tapping of steps on the concrete floor woke him, it took him several seconds before his thoughts could pierce the fog that had shrouded his brain and he understood his situation. The steps came closer and halted behind his cell door.

"Who is he?" someone asked.

"Some rich merchant," answered another voice. "They say he has engaged in illegal activities. The chief will conduct the interrogation himself."

With a dry metallic sound, the key turned and the door swung open. The harsh light from the passageway blinded Dhil. Several uniformed men entered his cell. He strained to see their faces. But his eyes failed to focus.

"All right," said one of the soldiers. "Let's get it over with."

They began beating him. He felt their fists against his back and their kicks against his legs. He tried to defend himself as best he could. But realizing how useless it was for him to fight back, he let himself drop to the ground and doubled over to protect himself from injury.

While the soldiers beat him, they did not utter a single word. Dhil heard only their labored breathing. Then, finally, one of the men said, "That's enough. Let's go."

They started to leave the cell, but before the last soldier walked through the door, Dhil jumped up and grabbed him from behind. With strength he didn't know he possessed, Dhil forced him to the ground, pounding him with his fists. The others rushed back and freed the soldier, who got up and kicked Dhil. Instinctively, Dhil tried to grab the man's foot to lessen the force of the kick. The tip of the soldier's boot hit the back of Dhil's left hand. The bone crackled as it splintered. The pain was excruciating.

The soldier was clearly out for revenge, but before he could hit Dhil again, an officer stepped between them. "Stop it," he shouted.

Without another word, they left, crushing the cell door shut. The key turned and the bolt slid home. Moaning with pain, Dhil cowered on the ground.

Chapter Thirty-three

"Sit down, Colonel," Dost said, as soon as Alam Gol stepped into his office. "We have a few minutes. Later we'll go to the Prime Minister. I need to discuss a number of items with him."

He took a paper from a file and handed it to Gol. "This is the list of the latest batch of detainees," he said. "Your neighbor from Baghlan is among them."

Gol immediately noticed Dhil's name on the paper. Emotions came over him like a wave—awareness of his own precarious safety, fear for the life of his friend, and, yes, concern that Dhil's situation, whatever its nature might be, could cast a shadow over him as well. The surging sensations overwhelmed his ability to think rationally, and he clung to an elusive hope that Dhil's name would no longer be on that sheet if he looked at it again. Knowing very well that he deluded himself, he nevertheless checked the log once again. Listed under the number five, the item read:

> Habib Dhil, businessman, resident of Kabul, violated curfew, refused to explain his reason for the violation, resisted arrest, directed foul and threatening language toward government leaders.

It was true then. Dhil had been arrested. What might have caused it? His affair with Miriam Khan or perhaps some other reason that Gol didn't know about?

"Are you surprised to see his name on the list?" Dost asked.

"Yes, I am." Gol handed the paper back to Dost. "Dhil's not the type to risk trouble. He probably didn't know about the curfew."

"What about his defiance of the police? And his ridiculing our leaders?"

"I can't imagine Dhil doing either of those things. He's a prudent man. He wouldn't engage in that kind of conduct." Deliberating for a second, Gol added, "Maybe he's being framed. There must be a lot of people who have a grudge against him."

"It's more likely," Dost said, "that the officers concocted some of those accusations to make the arrest appear more than it was. It's always the same," he continued, his contorted face showing his displeasure. "As soon as a purge is ordered, the officers detain everyone who crosses their path."

"Isn't it bad politics to lock up people and then let them go for lack of cause?" Gol said.

"It's the worst dim-witted politics possible," Dost said, collecting papers, putting them in a file. "But there's not much I can do about it. I have to work with the people I have. You can't ask perfection from a bunch of assholes. But to get back to your neighbor. Are you really concerned about him?"

"I know Dhil well," Gol said. "Unless there's another reason for his arrest, the charges, as they stand, are untrue. I'm sure of it." He hoped his categorical statement would influence Dost to let Dhil go.

"There is no other reason," Dost said. "In fact, he came here earlier in the afternoon."

Gol wanted to ask why Dhil had seen the Chief earlier, but said nothing.

Dost paused. "If I had wanted to detain him, that would have been the perfect opportunity." He sighed. "I know how you feel, Colonel. It isn't easy to see a friend in trouble. I'm not happy to have to deal with him either. He's not the type of person I want to detain. Certainly not at a time when we need to concentrate all our attention on those who pose a real danger." He paused again, inspecting a document. He put it inside the file. "Dhil's harmless. He might have a grudge or two against the government. But who hasn't? He has too much to lose to risk a confrontation with us."

"What about Miriam Khan?" Gol asked. "Don't you think she will give you trouble?"

Dost exposed a faint smile. "For all I know," he said, "she could burst in any moment, demanding his release. And she would get her way, too. Who am I to contradict the Prime Minister's daughter?"

"And the foreign community?" Gol asked. "He's well known among foreigners. If he disappears, they will pester us with questions about his whereabouts."

"I'm aware of Dhil's ties to the foreign community," Dost said, looking up from his papers, fixing his gaze on Gol. "My agents have frequently seen him with a young couple from the American embassy. We already have more than enough trouble with the American ambassador's constant bitching about human rights violations. Dhil's absence would only make that self-righteous motherfucker meddle more in the business of our government."

Seeing an opportunity to plead for Dhil's release, Gol said, "Why don't you let him go then? He isn't worth all the trouble. Besides, now that Governor Bahaadur is dead, the Prime Minister might even let him marry his daughter."

Dost smiled. "It's not that simple. Habib Dhil has never shown support for our government. That could make it difficult for Khan to permit their marriage. Anyway, his arrest is already on file. I can't let him go without some investigation. Precise paperwork is important. I have to cover my tracks, too."

Gol nodded his understanding. "Are you going to inform the Prime Minister of his arrest?"

"Of course I will," Dost said. "He's a hot potato. I'm not about to make a decision on him myself. The Prime Minister himself must decide what is to be done with him."

He paused, seeming to deliberate. Gol noticed that Dost appeared distracted, unable to keep his thoughts focused.

At last he continued, "If you have a specific wish for your friend, tell me now. I must know about it before I take the matter to the Prime Minister."

Gol remained quiet.

"Well?"

Gol still wavered.

"Perhaps it would help if you knew that Prime Minister Khan has a lot of respect for your father," Dost said. "He spoke fondly of him. He thought you would be as much of a patriot as your father was. With the work you did in Kunduz, you have proved him right. If you have a specific wish in Dhil's case, the Prime Minister might accommodate you."

It seemed so easy, but what if it were a trap. Gol hoped the nervousness he felt was not noticed. Perhaps this was the test of his willingness to put everything aside in the interest of his superiors, an assessment of his complete loyalty.

Gol regretted that Dost had told him about Dhil's arrest. He doubted Dost's assurance that no particular reason existed for Dhil's detention. Since Dost seemed unwilling to reveal the true motive behind Dhil's detention, Gol couldn't side with him more than he already had. He didn't want to find himself involved in something that might anger important people. It would be better not to deal with the issue at all. Nothing good could come of it.

"This is the time to speak up," Dost said. "Once I've submitted my report to the Prime Minister, I won't be able to do anything for your friend."

"I don't want you to do anything on my account. If Dhil has done something wrong, he'll have to accept the consequences. I've no business interfering in these matters."

"Fine", Dost said, grabbing the dossier he had been organizing, getting up from behind his desk. "Let's get going then."

In the deserted corridor, Gol keenly felt the emptiness. He could hear the wailing of the wind as it blew along the depleted gangway. The enigmatic whispering of air as it moved about the edges of the concrete walls reinforced his sense of guilt for refusing to come out in support of Dhil. A vague, nondescript unease besieged him.

"I wish this place were always this empty," Dost said, while they waited for the elevator. "The petitioners hanging around here all day are an eyesore." Looking around as if he were searching for something, he threw up his shoulders and went on, "But there isn't much we can do about it. It serves a purpose." When they entered the elevator, Dost continued, "It gives the people a sense that they have access to even the most sensitive of government offices. Whether their requests are granted or turned down often seems less important than just being heard. In a way, we continue our country's ancient customs, when kings held open court and received petitioners in person."

They left the ministry compound and turned toward downtown, heading to the Prime Minister's official residence, located among a cluster of government buildings.

"How did the King take the news of his son's death?" Gol asked.

"Bahaadur Shah turned ashen," Dost said. "He stared at the ground for a long time without saying anything. Then, he laughed hysterically and seemed completely out of control. He didn't believe for a second that his son had committed suicide and immediately suspected foul play."

"He didn't give the Prime Minister the benefit of the doubt?" Gol said.

Dost laughed heartily. "The two men have worked together far too long to fool each other easily."

"What happened then?" Gol asked

"Bahaadur Shah saw right through the Prime Minister's plan. He shouted, 'Now that you have murdered my son, have you come to get rid of me, too?'"

Gol was greatly alarmed at the idea of an angry and suspicious Bahaadur Shah. "And how did the Prime Minister react?"

"He didn't show any emotions, at all," Dost said. "He didn't even try to fake a little empathy."

Khan's reaction pleased Gol. It virtually foreclosed any attempt at reconciliation between the Prime Minister and the King, something Gol, for fear of his own safety, had dreaded.

Chapter Thirty-four

Although Gol had expected a certain measure of luxury in Prime Minister Khan's residence, the opulence startled him. Marble steps led to the entrance. A huge Persian rug covered the floor of the large hall behind the massive house door. Heavy furniture, antique tables, and well-crafted chairs filled up the expansive space. Tapestries and elaborately framed mirrors hung on the walls. Intimidated by his surroundings, he was unsure as to whether he should walk on the valuable rug and instead remained frozen. He decided not to move until Dost did and then do exactly as he did.

A bulky, Mongol-featured Hazara, dressed in a blue uniform-like outfit, entered the foyer from the opposite end and led them across the hall to a room several times the size of the reception area and no less extravagantly furnished.

Embarrassed by his awe at so much grandeur and by the

power it conveyed, Gol felt a familiar prick of envy. Such lav-
ishness reminded him of Dhil's house in Baghlan. The main
house of the sprawling quarters had large, airy rooms fitted
out with expensive-looking furniture. As in the Prime Minister's residence, soft rugs covered the floors in Dhil's house
and an army of servants scurried about, keeping the mansion
immaculately clean.

As he grew closer to Dhil and their visits to each other's
homes became more frequent, he gradually lost his apprehension
about the differences in their residences. Time had taken care
of those trepidations; time would take care of them once again.

He looked over at Dost to find out whether the Secret Police Chief had noticed his bewilderment. But Dost, sitting on a
deep-blue, satin-finished armchair, seemed preoccupied, leafing
through the pages of one of the dossiers he had brought along.

"You must be tired, Colonel," Dost said, without looking
up. "Why don't you sit down? This is going to be another long
night. You might as well be prepared for it."

Before Gol could accept the offer, the same Hazara servant
came in and asked them to follow him. He guided them to what
appeared to be the Prime Minister's private study.

In contrast to the exquisite room they had just left, Khan's
tiny study looked bare and neglected. Wrapped in a silken
cloth, a book, probably a Quran, lay on the only table, a small
desk made of light-colored wood, standing on four flimsy legs.
Miriam Khan's silver-framed picture stood on the same table
under the sideways-hanging, dusty shade of a lamp. At the
sight of Miriam Khan's exceptional beauty, Gol envied Dhil
and wondered whether his old friend appreciated all that life
had presented him.

The Prime Minister sat beside the table. Instead of hiding
the deep wrinkles that drooped around Khan's mouth, the
dim light accentuated them and made him appear even more

worn out. And, in view of the turmoil he had unleashed on the country after the killing of Governor Bahaadur, he understandably looked worried. Apparently, he felt the tide had not turned in his favor yet, leaving him uncertain about the future success of his plan. But Khan brightened when he saw Dost. He straightened in his worn armchair with unexpected energy.

"Your Excellency," Dost said, "Colonel Gol has just returned from Kunduz. He will be working with me closely during the coming days."

"Colonel," Khan said, "your late father was an outstanding patriot and a good friend."

"Thank you, Your Excellency. My father was an admirer of yours."

"I remember his hospitality. And shooting a bluebird. I seem to recall. Was it your rifle I used?"

"Yes," Gol said, his face growing hot. He tried frantically to suppress the disturbing feelings that rose up within him. "It was my rifle, Your Excellency."

"Is the farm still with your family?"

"Yes sir. We still own it."

"Don't sell it. Prudent people never sell their land."

"I'm not contemplating selling the farm, sir."

"You have progressed well in your work, Colonel. I am glad to have you on board."

"I am proud to serve Your Excellency."

Turning to Dost, Khan said, "Where do we stand, Dost?"

"I'm pleased to inform Your Excellency that we have successfully rounded up all anti-regime elements," Dost reported. "Except for one man, we have completed the dossiers for all detainees and have obtained written confessions from all of them."

"Who's the man who hasn't confessed?"

Dost's face flushed. With difficulty, he slid his plump hand into the side pocket of his pants, which fit tightly on his bulging waistline. Finally succeeding in pulling out a handkerchief, he wiped the sweat from his forehead. Clearing his throat twice, he said, "It's Habib Dhil, sir. The cloth manufacturer."

"Dhil? Why has he been detained?"

"He has violated the curfew," Dost said. "According to the police report, he resisted arrest and used profanities against the leadership. We also know he employs a known regime enemy and entertains intimate relations with an American couple. The husband works at the economic section of the American embassy. We believe he's a CIA agent."

Khan remained silent for a long while. Dost breathed heavily, nervously shifting about in his seat. Gol feared Khan would draw him into the discussion about Dhil's future. He didn't want to comment one way or the other.

Khan shook his head. "He's from a good family. His grandfather and his father were fine men. Dedicated to their country and family. They worked hard and left him much wealth. And it is we who make sure that what he has inherited can be his to have. What more does he want from us?" Khan fell silent. "Can you tie him to the present situation?" he finally asked.

"I'll look into it, Your Excellency," Dost said, the tension in his face easing.

"Make sure his file is well documented and he signs a confession." Khan lifted himself up from his slumping position. "What about the King? What have you found out about his plans?"

"From what we could ascertain Your Excellency," Dost answered, "he hasn't discussed his plans with anyone. Not even his closest advisers know what he's up to."

"That's not good enough," Prime Minister Khan said in a sharp tone. "We need to know his plans. He's angry and unpredictable. For the sake of peace in the country, we must prevent a drawn-out feud."

"Your Excellency," the Secret Police Chief said, "I have the King's closest advisers under lock and key. I spent most of the afternoon interrogating them. It's my impression that the King's sudden departure is not in any way linked to a plan."

"But he must be up to something," Khan insisted. "Why else would he leave his palace and retreat to his hunting lodge where I can't communicate with him?"

"He must have panicked, Your Excellency," Dost said. "Departing for his hunting lodge makes no sense."

"We can't rest on that assessment," Khan said brusquely. "He's like a wounded tiger, poised to attack anywhere, anytime."

Did Khan want to dispose of the King? But why, Gol thought. When he searched Khan's eyes for a clue, he could not read them.

"Your Excellency," Dost said, "the King's indefinite absence from his official duties will lead to a perception of political uncertainty. A situation that could lead to unrest. In the interest of the nation, we must not allow that to happen."

Prime Minister Khan's face lit up. "What do you propose we do?" he asked.

"We should send a representative to the King and appeal to him to return to his palace."

"If he refuses to come?"

Dost glanced at Gol and then back at Khan. "That's, of course, your decision, Your Excellency." He spoke slowly, choosing his words carefully. "By leaving town abruptly, the King has narrowed your options. There is either cooperation within the leadership, or there is not. For the sake of harmony, the King must return to his duties without fail. Because of Governor Bahaadur's tragic death, the potential for traitors and terrorists to incite unrest is dramatically heightened. In view of the tense political situation, it's imperative that the leadership demonstrate unity."

Dost's characterization of Governor Bahaadur's liquidation as "tragic," startled Gol. And his allusion to the presence of terrorists and traitors, when, in fact, no acts of sabotage had occurred, added to Gol's confusion. The Secret Police Chief spoke as if he were addressing a public forum where he had to conceal the true nature of government actions and explain Governor Bahaadur's death in palatable terms. How easily things could be maneuvered and put in a completely different light, Gol reminded himself. And it didn't involve any magic. It was simply a matter of manipulating words.

And so, even here where no one would ever know, the facts were being rewritten.

Listening to the simplicity with which events could be stage-managed, Gol shuddered in his core and his own vulnerability flashed through his mind. For better or worse, he now was tied to the Prime Minister and his Secret Police Chief, he thought. As long as the King lived, he would be in danger. The possibility of Amir Bahaadur Shah and Prime Minister Wali Khan reconciling would always hover over his head. Indeed, the King could, though the prospect seemed remote, prevail in this struggle.

Deciding he had to take charge to protect himself, Gol said, "Your Excellency, I am ready to assume the responsibility for bringing the King back."

"We stand at your command, sir," Dost said, jumping instantly on board.

"Colonel, you must persuade the King to return," Prime Minister Khan said. "It's essential that he comes back. Once he's here, we will be able to control the situation."

Khan grabbed the cloth-covered Quran from the small table and unwrapped it. Pulling his fountain pen out of his breast pocket, he wrote a few lines on the first page of the book. Wrapping the Quran back in its green silk cover and holding it out to Gol, he said, "Take it to the King. My message will reassure him of my loyalty and friendship." A barely recognizable smile flitted across his face. "I know the King. When he reads my message, he will come back."

The holy book! Gol thought. How could Khan choose it for a trap?

"The interest of the country must always remain our highest priority," Khan said, as if wishing to dispel any doubts that might crop up in Gol's mind. "The King is out of control and must be treated like any other person who endangers the nation's well-being. Nobody can be spared when the welfare of our country is at stake."

The Prime Minister sat quietly then looked at Gol. "Colonel, in the event the King refuses to return to the city, you must report back immediately."

"Yes, sir," Gol said, rising from his chair, saluting the Prime Minister crisply.

As he left the Prime minister's bare study, he felt reassured. He continued to be a trusted element in Khan's plan. Under the circumstances, that was the best protection he could get.

Chapter Thirty-five

In the dark, cold cell, Dhil lost all sense of time. He held his broken left hand under his right arm, hoping his body's warmth might lessen the pain.

After what seemed a desperately long period, he heard heels pound the concrete floor outside. The cell door opened and three police officers stood at the entrance. "Get up," commanded one.

His legs had become stiff and moving them required an enormous effort. He couldn't quite stand up.

"I said, get up," the officer bellowed. "It's late. We want this to be over with."

"Where are you taking me?" Dhil said, shuffling out of the cell, shielding his eyes against the glaring lights in the corridor.

"Silence," ordered the officer who led the way.

They climbed two flights of stairs and turned into another long hallway. At least the air is better, Dhil thought. In the cell, the stench of human waste had made breathing difficult. He took several deep breaths and felt a little of his depleted energy return.

They walked past a number of closed doors. Behind one of them, Dhil heard the lively buzz of an animated conversation. The smell of food, seeping through the door cracks, reached him, reminding him of how, merely hours before, Miriam had put the food tray on the bed, and they had eaten the small chunks of broiled mutton and the freshly baked naan.

Strange, he thought. How distant that scene now appeared. The privacy of that moment, the peacefulness of it, seemed to rise from the pages of a book of fiction, entirely unreal in this furtive, violent place.

Without realizing it, he must have slowed down. One of the two officers walking behind him gave him a push. "Prisoner, keep on going."

Further along, the leading officer opened a door on the left side of the corridor. They entered a large room. As in the passageway, long fluorescent tubes, mounted onto the unpainted concrete ceiling, bathed the chamber in a cold, blinding light. At the far right corner of the otherwise entirely bare space, a man in white overalls, his back to the door, stood beside a desk. The man turned toward him. It was Dr. Zia.

Dr. Zia's presence was utterly perplexing. But the physician's proximity also lessened Dhil's sense of doom and abandonment. He wanted to greet Zia, but before he could say anything, the doctor abruptly looked away.

"This is urgent, Doctor," the officer said, handing Dr. Zia the dossier he carried. "The interrogators are waiting for him."

Dr. Zia opened the file, glanced at the first page, then lifted his head and looked straight at Dhil, a hostile expression frozen on his features. Dhil thought he understood. The doctor wanted him to conceal the fact that they knew each other.

"Take off your jacket, prisoner," Dr. Zia said, "and open your shirt."

Unable to use his left hand, Dhil was slow complying.

"Hurry up," Dr. Zia commanded in a nervous, impatient voice. "I don't have time to waste."

"I'm trying. I can't move my left hand. I think it's broken."

Dr. Zia grabbed his left hand and pulled at it. Dhil groaned as a sharp pain thrust all the way up to his head. The room began spinning.

"How did this happen?" Dr. Zia asked.

"He broke it when we jailed him," the police officer said, shrugging.

"Was this necessary?" Dr. Zia asked, his features tightening. Without waiting for an answer, he continued, "You know very well that excessive force is not to be applied at that stage. You people better observe the rules. Otherwise, I'll be forced to file a complaint. The interrogation begins after the medical examination."

"The prisoner attacked uniformed personnel," the police officer said. "The guard struck back in self-defense. We're not responsible for the prisoner's injury."

"No matter how it occurred," Zia said sharply. "I'm telling you for the last time. Don't let it happen again. After I'm done with them, you can do whatever you like."

Dr. Zia placed his stethoscope on Dhil's chest. For a split second, the physician's glance met Dhil's eyes again, and Dhil thought Zia wanted to say something. But he didn't. While listening to Dhil's lungs, he said to the policeman, "Write this down, officer."

Sitting down, the officer took out a black fountain pen from the inner pocket of his uniform jacket, unscrewed the cover, and said, "I'm ready, doctor."

"The prisoner's pulse points to excessive physical fatigue," the physician dictated. "His heartbeat is irregular, indicating a low level of resistance. Recommendations: No electrical shocks are to be administered. No severe beating or other extreme physical stress is to be applied. The prisoner is not to be subjected to prolonged sleeplessness." Going to the desk, he snatched the sheet from the policeman's hand and signed it. "Take the prisoner out, Officer," he said brusquely.

Dumbfounded by Dr. Zia's collaboration with the secret police, Dhil didn't even try to look back as he was led out of the room. The thought that Zia—his own tenant, the well-respected physician, the benefactor to the city's needy patients—would agree to work with the secret police was simply bewildering.

He must have compromised himself in some way, Dhil thought. What could he possibly have done that the police knew about and used to coerce him into cooperating? Then, considering the unbridled power of the regime, Zia might regard his collaboration with the secret police a necessary and legitimate strategy to survive.

The three officers led Dhil through the virtually endless corridor. The clinking sound of their boots on the concrete floor echoed torturously in Dhil's ears. His broken hand throbbed painfully and the cold penetrated his flesh.

At last, the guards led him into another room on the same floor, a room also filled with too much light. Two military officers sat behind a large table, a single chair placed opposite them. When Dhil entered, the two men, their tired faces unshaven, watched him.

One of them began reading the file that the police officer had placed before them.

"Be seated," the other officer told Dhil. His uniform jacket was a size or two too big for his diminutive upper body. While he aimed his gaze at Dhil, his tiny right hand nervously scratched his cheek. "Why are you here?" he asked.

"I haven't the slightest idea," Dhil replied.

"There must be some reason for your arrest. Just tell us what it is and don't try to play games."

"I was out of town," Dhil said. "When I returned earlier in the evening, soldiers stopped me. They accused me of having violated the curfew. I didn't know a curfew existed. An army officer ordered the soldiers to detain me."

"You want us to believe you're here for no reason at all? You claim to be innocent. Is that correct?"

"Yes, that's correct."

The officer leaned forward. Tiny red veins crisscrossed the white of his eyes. His stubble had begun to turn gray around his mouth and on his chin. "Don't try to mislead us," he said. "Inform us of your misdeeds of your own free will. Otherwise, we will have to make you confess."

"I'm not trying to mislead you," Dhil said, laboring to remain calm and trying to keep his voice steady. "What I told you is what has happened. Beyond that, I don't know why I'm here."

"Let him be," said the second officer, the one who had been reading the file. "He's a waste of time. If we press him too hard, he might—"

The door swung open. Secret Police Chief Dost, accompanied by a number of civilians and military personnel, entered the room.

The two officers jumped up from their seats. Everybody stood at a distance while the Chief walked around the table and sat down on one of the two chairs the officers had vacated.

A spark of hope flashed through Dhil's mind. Dost knew that Dhil had been busy transporting Zeb's body to his village. He would understand why Dhil couldn't have known about the curfew and release him promptly.

Chapter Thirty-six

Amir Bahaadur Shah's hunting lodge sat outside the city on the crest of a knoll at the intersection of the road to Paghman and the Salang highway.

The motor of Gol's Russian Zeel whined as the vehicle labored up the twisting road toward the cottage on the top of the hill. Near the peak, a detachment of Bahaadur Shah's Royal Guard blocked the road.

He sensed how his heartbeat quickened and could hear the hammering inside his chest. He lowered the windowpane and frigid air swooped over him. His nostrils prickled as the dry, cold air entered his nose. And when he exhaled, his breath froze into a misty vapor.

Low clouds hid the moon and the stars. In the darkness, he could not make out how many men had surrounded his Zeel, hearing only the muffled, almost rhythmic, thump-thump of their feet hitting the frozen ground as they, trying to keep warm, hopped from one foot onto the other.

One of them, a woolen scarf covering most of his face, stepped forward and aimed a powerful flashlight into Gol's face. It blinded him with the stream of its glaring light. Instinctively, he pulled back.

The guard opened the car door and, pointing his Kalashnikov at Gol, ordered him to get out and surrender his weapon.

Gol's mind worked at a rapid pace. He estimated his chances for survival if it came to a confrontation. Outnumbered and armed only with a pistol, defiance made no sense. Anyway, his orders precluded him from resisting.

As instructed, he handed over his handgun to the guard and began to walk the rest of the way to the lodge, still a good distance up the steep hill.

Taking small steps and trying to avoid falling on the slippery road, he climbed slowly. The cold numbed his face and the chill air painfully bore into his lungs as it penetrated his body through his frozen nasal passages.

At the top of the knoll, where the path led to a large courtyard, two more guards, their automatic weapons aimed at Gol, blocked the way.

"What brings you here?" the taller one asked.

"I carry a message from the Prime Minister. It's for the King."

"Give it to me," the guard said, extending his gloved hand. "I'll take it to His Majesty."

"I have orders to deliver it personally."

"My order is to let no one inside."

Gol rubbed his frozen ears. He hated the guard for the delay he caused. Gol tried to act calmly and reasonably, hoping his voice would match his movements. "Why don't you report my arrival to the King? Let His Majesty himself decide whether he wishes to receive me or not."

"His Majesty knows you're here." The sentry's frozen lips moved stiffly as he spoke. "He was informed the moment you drove up the hill. The choice is yours. You can either wait here all night, or let me take the message to His Majesty."

This was the King's territory and his men had the say here, Gol thought. Besides, they had the guns. Pulling the Quran out of his overcoat pocket, Gol presented it to the sentry. In correct military tradition, the guard saluted the holy book before he took it.

"Where's the message?" he asked.

"It's inside the Holy Book," Gol said. "Ask the King to check the first page."

The guard kissed the Quran and, holding it with both hands, carried it inside.

Hardly a minute or two had elapsed when Gol saw Amir Bahaadur Shah's tall, lanky frame in the doorway. Stepping out from the house's lit interior, the King walked toward him and, as he came closer, extended his hand. Gol rushed forward and kissed the King's outstretched hand. Bahaadur Shah's weak grip reminded him of his son's feeble handshake. But, while Governor Bahaadur's hand had been cold and lifeless, his father's gave off the warmth of a throbbing life.

"Who sent you here, Colonel?"

"The Prime Minister, Your Majesty."

"Were you present when he wrote his message to me?"

"I was there, sir. Standing a few meters from the Prime Minister."

Bahaadur Shah began to walk, his shoulders stooped, his head bent, his tall frame slightly swaying with each halting step. After several feet, he turned and strode back, repeating the exercise several times. Finally, he stood still for a minute or so. "Get the cars," he ordered. "Let's go back."

"Your Majesty," Gol said, as the sentry stepped away.

"What is it?"

"Could you please instruct your guards to give my pistol and car keys back to me?"

The light at the side of the door shone on Bahaadur Shah's face. He came close and asked, "Colonel, do you know whether the Governor's body has been brought to Kabul?"

A shiver raced down Gol's spine. Bahaadur Shah's unexpected question shook him and the King's steady gaze seemed to burn through his skull. Gol felt exposed but quickly composed himself. It was ridiculous to think that the King knew anything about Gol's role in his son's death, he decided. The King's need for information was understandable. Having come to this isolated place, where he didn't even have access to a telephone, he had shut himself off from what was happening outside. Naturally, he would want to know what had happened to his son's remains.

Nevertheless, Gol didn't want to appear too knowledgeable about the Governor's whereabouts. "As far as I know, Your Majesty," he said, "the Governor was due to be flown to the capital earlier this evening. But I don't know whether he has actually arrived."

"Did anyone tell you where he will lie in state?"

"No, sir."

"Do you know where the Prime Minister is tonight?"

"When I set out to bring you his message, sir, the Prime Minister left his private quarters to return to his office. One of his aides said the Prime Minister would wait for you there."

"That's where we will go then," Bahaadur Shah said. Turning to the husky sentry, he added, "Give the Colonel his pistol and car keys."

Gol followed the fleet of vehicles carrying Amir Bahaadur Shah and his entourage. He smiled. So far, his mission had advanced flawlessly. Khan's highly symbolic act had worked.

Sending somebody the Quran signified a powerful message of good faith. Gol had only heard of a few instances where people had used it to show their honorable intentions. And, indeed, Gol couldn't remember anyone having written a message on one of the Quran's pages. Unquestionably, Khan's deed represented the highest manifestation of his loyalty.

Khan's message intrigued Gol. What might the Prime Minister have written to the King? As he'd left Khan's residence, he'd considered reading the message. But once he had been on his way to the hunting lodge, he had put the message out of his mind, focusing all his thoughts on what might happen when he faced the King. Now he regretted his omission and wished he had read it. However, this was not the moment to think about that, he reminded himself. He needed to concentrate on his next step. He had not received any instructions about how to handle things after he brought the King back to Kabul.

Though Khan had said that once Bahaadur Shah returned the situation could be brought under control, he had not elaborated on his plan, leaving it to Gol to improvise.

Chapter Thirty-seven

Secret Police Chief Dost put the red folder he carried on the table and grabbed the blue folder, the one the two officers had left behind. Opening it, he skimmed through the immaculately typed pages. He returned to the first page and pored over it. After reading a few sentences, he stopped seeing the words, his eyes merely gliding over the lines. He knew what the pages contained. All the information presented in Dhil's dossier was the meticulous product of Dost's own foresight, his very own lucid and succinct style, the fruit of his clear and concise mind.

He sighed. It had been a tumultuous day, unpredictable and wrought with dangers. He was glad he wasn't still in his official, sixth-floor office. It was there, during political emergencies, that he had to make decisions on the spot, increasing exponentially the risk of overlooking important details. Afterwards, he always worried whether he had made the right choices or had unwittingly acted against the interests of one powerful person or another. The fear of falling into disgrace had been keeping him in perpetual trepidation of the future. Recently, he had been regularly having nightmares of himself being beaten and tortured.

The only place where he could shake off that ever-present anguish was in these basement chambers. Here, deep down below the building of the Ministry of the Interior, different standards prevailed. Within these underground chambers, he felt truly safe. The naked walls, the dazzlingly white lights of neon tubes, the hard wooden chairs, and bare tables reflected the unembellished nature of power. In this rough environment, he could make judgments as circumstances demanded. During these late-night encounters, he didn't have to bother with making compromises or concessions. In these nightly sessions, he could unreservedly unleash the might of his office to maintain law and order. Here, he pursued an objective of the utmost simplicity: Survival of the state. No more. No less.

He put the dossier aside and studied Habib Dhil and felt a measure of satisfaction. The contempt he had seen in Dhil's face earlier in the day had vanished. He now had him in his grasp, and Dhil knew it and feared him. He could see it in his wide, unbelieving eyes, the same eyes that had hungrily slid over the firm flesh of Miriam Khan's thighs and voluptuously observed her boyish ass. Once while masturbating one night, he had imagined himself forcing his stiff penis into Miriam Khan's anus. As she cried out in pain, Dost ejaculated with such joy that he gasped in anguish and pleasure, lying for a long time without the slightest movement, holding on to his limp penis, feeling his semen drip slowly from his jutting belly onto the mattress.

An atmosphere of nervous excitement surrounded him and a reassuring ease swept over him. Now, he could do with Dhil as he wished.

On a certain level, he thought, he sympathized with Dhil. In a way, they were cut from the same cloth. They were loners, two lonely souls walking down the randomly lethal path of life, both afraid of a violent death, even more of the hazard of living in a system where power was unbridled and the will of a few the law. And both had done their best to survive it—he in his way, Dhil in his. As he stared at Dhil's distressed countenance, Dost couldn't stop himself from smiling.

Chapter Thirty-eight

Three tanks blocked the entrance to the complex housing the Prime Minister's office, one parked on each side of the street, the third placed right in front of the entrance. Two high-powered lamps, mounted on top of the heavy concrete pillars on both sides of the broad gateway, lit up the scene. Bunched together to protect themselves from the cold, soldiers stood about, observing the column of vehicles that had arrived.

The duty officer—a slender, gray-haired colonel with a nervous twitch at the corner of his left eye—refused to clear the passage. Only Amir Bahaadur Shah and Colonel Gol could enter the grounds, he said. He had orders to let no one else go inside.

The King showed no anger and did not object to the officer's intention to separate him from his guards. His features appeared relaxed, unconcerned about his safety. He had an air of indifference, as if he were inclined to let events take their course.

Had his son's death dulled his awareness, Gol wondered, or was it Khan's message and the symbolism behind it that had soothed him?

"Your Majesty," Gol said, stepping forward. "I would be honored to drive you into the compound and escort you directly to the Prime Minister."

One of the King's guards, a burly man apparently particularly devoted to Bahaadur Shah, planted himself in front of the King. His eyes blazing, his hands clenched into fists, he said, "Your Majesty, I don't trust the situation. I strongly suggest that you not enter the compound alone."

The street had been cleared of the snow that had fallen the day before. The pavement shimmered black under the two bright lights. The sound of a running engine came from a troop carrier that had been parked in a distance from the entrance and the illuminated area.

"It's all right," the King said, his voice impassive. "There's nothing to worry about. Now return to your men."

Bahaadur Shah ordered the duty officer to have his soldiers move the tank. He turned to Gol. "Let's go, Colonel."

The tank's engine roared. Thick plumes of smoke burst from its exhaust pipe as it moved to clear the way for the King's Limousine. Holding one hand on his nose to prevent the tank's exhaust fumes from entering his lungs, Gol opened the rear door of the automobile for the King.

Once the King had entered the car, Gol hurriedly squeezed his massive frame behind the steering wheel and the front seat. In his haste to move on, he nervously searched for the electric switch to slide the driver's seat backward and to push his squeezed body enough away from the steering wheel to be able to drive. When he couldn't immediately locate the switch, his face turned hot, and he broke out in a sweat. But then, after a few seconds of frantic exploring, he found the button and, adjusting the seat, took off with screeching tires.

As he stopped the car in front of Khan's office, one of several army officers, who stood at the foot of the steps leading to the building, came forward and opened the door for Bahaadur Shah.

Bahaadur Shah climbed out. Gol saw the Quran on the rear seat where the king had been sitting. "Your Majesty," he called out after Bahaadur Shah, "would you like to take the Holy Book with you, sir?"

"Leave it in the car," Bahaadur Shah said. "I'll take it later."

Followed by Gol, Bahaadur Shah mounted the steps to Khan's second-floor office.

Meeting them in the hall, Captain Assad, Prime Minister Khan's secretary, saluted Bahaadur Shah and opened the door to Khan's office.

As it closed behind them, Khan got up abruptly and rushed in front of his desk. "Your criminal game of betrayal has been exposed," he shouted at Bahaadur Shah.

"What did you say?" Bahaadur Shah asked, startled.

"You heard me," Khan replied, shaking with anger. "I said your game has been discovered."

"Are you suggesting I am capable of treason?" Bahaadur Shah said, standing tall, looking down at Khan.

"Yes," Khan said. "That's exactly what I'm accusing you of."

"If you entertain such monstrous suspicions, you should have the courage to explain yourself." Bahaadur Shah's lips were trembling.

"I'm acting in the interest of the state," Khan said. His tone was quiet, almost conversational. "I don't have to justify myself before a criminal."

"I, I've always had the best interest of our country in mind," Bahaadur Shah said, his certitude crumbling.

"You disgust me," Khan said without a trace of emotion on his face or in his voice. "You are a nobody. Without me, you wouldn't have survived a week."

"My son," Bahaadur Shah said, looking for a moment at Gol and then back at Khan. "You killed him, didn't you?"

"Your son," Khan screamed, his face suddenly turning into an angry frown. "He was a traitor like you. A disgusting faggot."

"And your daughter is a whore," Bahaadur Shah yelled back. "Ask anyone. Ask this colonel."

"What's a son to you, you motherfucker?" Khan said. "You've a collection of them from your many whores. How many bastards have you fathered over the years?"

Gol pressed against the wall, as far from the two squabbling men as possible. He very much wanted to leave this place.

Khan grabbed the dagger that lay on his desk. He held it in both hands. The dark red ruby on top of its handle glistened under the light. Both men seemed transfixed by the reflection.

Khan's mind flashed back almost a quarter of a century, and he was certain Bahaadur Shah was remembering the same defining moment in their lives.

Chapter Thirty-nine

1954

Wali Khan wiped the fog from the inside of the wind-shield with the back of his hand. "Damn weather," he said to Amir Bahaadur, who was slouched in the seat beside him. Squinting to see through the dismal rain, Khan maneuvered his Zeel through the chaotic traffic of Kabul's commercial district. His face suddenly lit up as the high walls of the King's palace loomed up beside them. Nodding in the direction of the palace, he said, "In a few days, we'll be running the place. I can't wait to see this son of a bitch rot like a street dog."

Amir Bahaadur frowned. "I've got a bad feeling about it. I'm afraid something might go wrong."

Wali Khan glared at Bahaadur. "When the King's dead, you'll feel better."

Bahaadur shook his head. "It's reckless; the King's too powerful. We'll never make it."

"Bullshit!" Khan exploded. "The King's powerful as long as he's alive. Once he's gone, nobody will care about him."

"He's changed." Bahaadur was vacillating again. "He's an old man now. He won't touch us as long as we pretend to be kissing his ass."

"He's changed, all right," Khan shouted. He tightened his grip around the steering wheel. Lowering his voice, he continued, "He no longer gives a shit about the army. Now that Khrushchev is firmly in control, we finally have our chance. The Russians will give us equipment and training, too. Think of it, Amir. You and me in control of a modern, strong army. Instead the King, his majesty, fucks his whores, smokes his opium, and worries about old Joe Stalin coming back from the dead. He'll never allow their help."

"I just think we should put our plans on hold for a while."

"What the fuck is the matter with you? You know damn well it's too late to stop things. Too many people are involved. If we delay, somebody could have second thoughts and start talking. We can't take that risk."

"I've always followed you wherever you wanted us to go. But this is different. This time, I smell the stench of death. Please, let's postpone it. Let's think it over once more."

Khan laughed. "The only stench is from you shitting in your pants again." He shook his head. "We must act now. This is a perfect opportunity. We can't let it pass by. Once the bastard's eliminated, everything will be over. We will take charge of the army. With the army behind us, the country will be ours, too."

"What about his lackeys?" Bahaadur's resistance to Khan's resolve was already crumbling. "How do we know they'll go along with us?"

"What can they do in the middle of nowhere? Once we

take over the guard, they'll have to go along with us." Khan concentrated on the traffic, then glanced at Bahaadur before continuing. "When all's done, you can tell your creditors to go to hell. You won't ever have to fear Ghazi when you fuck his daughter. In fact, he'll personally bring her to you. Nobody will dare touch you."

Bahaadur dropped his head. He resigned to the fact that they would use the occasion of the King's hunting party in the plains outside Kandahar to assassinate him. Khan was probably right. Too many people had been involved in the preparation of the undertaking. Delaying the execution of their plans would indeed be unwise, probably outright dangerous. Silently, Bahaadur nodded his agreement.

"Remember," Khan said. "The key is to take immediate control of the Guards. Once the commandant is implicated, we will move and take charge of the situation."

The sun dropped slowly at the far-off edge of the plain, drenching the evening sky red. Darkness descended gradually on the camp. The King, seated at a low table under the open sky, pushed his plate away and wiped his mouth with a napkin. He raised his heavy body from the soft cushions and invited his companions to join him in evening prayers. Afterwards, he shook hands with his guests and set out for his quarters. General Naim, the commandant of the King's Guard, joined him. His upper body inclined, his hands locked behind him, Naim, walking a step behind the King, asked, "Your Majesty, may I have the honor of accompanying you to your tent?"

"That's not necessary, General," the King replied, motioning Naim to stay behind.

As the King walked away, his ministers and generals and the tribal maliks scattered about. Their bellies were bloated from having indulged too freely in the brown rice, the barbecued

lamb, and the aromatic gazelle meat from the two animals
the hunting party had shot earlier in the day. They walked
about the camp in small groups before they, too, proceeded
to their designated tents and, one after the other, retired for
the night.

Pots and pans clanged and crockery clacked as the servants,
murmuring, washed up. Gradually, the noises died down and
quiet settled in.

Shortly after midnight, Khan and Bahaadur prowled toward
the King's tent. Gripping Bahaadur's arm, Khan whispered, "The
day's chase has tired him. He'll be sound asleep and won't hear
anything. Everything will be all right."

"I hope you're right," Bahaadur said, pulling his arm free.

"Have you checked your pistol?" Khan whispered. "You
haven't forgotten to attach the silencer?"

"Of course not," answered Bahaadur. He sounded surly.
"Don't you think I can do anything right?"

"Show me the silencer."

"It's attached." Bahaadur said impatiently and raised his
hand to display the pistol he was holding.

"When you see the guard, don't hesitate. Shoot him immediately."

There was only one sentry guarding the King's tent. To show
his sense of friendship and trust to his government ministers,
military leaders, and tribal maliks, the King had wanted to dis-
pense altogether with the soldiers guarding his tent. But General Naim had insisted that there be at least one sentry posted.

The sentry—leaning on his rifle, his head nodding on his
chest—was jolted out of his slumber as Colonel Amir Bahaadur,
General Naim's Deputy, suddenly appeared before him. He
rushed to straighten himself and saluted his superior.

Bahaadur felt the cold metal of his pistol in his hand. He
had to exert an enormous amount of energy to raise the weapon,

which suddenly felt tremendously heavy. His forehead wet with cold sweat, he ultimately hoisted the gun, almost touching the sentry when he fired. The sentry collapsed with a muffled thud and sprawled on his back. Bahaadur's head spun. Khan gripped his arm and shook him.

Bahaadur collected himself. Feeling weak and wobbly, he craned his long neck from side to side, listening intently for any sound that might spell disaster.

Khan tightened his grip around the hilt of the knife he was holding in his right hand. He entered the spacious quarters, noiselessly closing in on the sleeping King. For a moment, he stood beside the bed and looked down at the heavyset man he hated. As he listened to the King's regular breathing, his own heart pumped wildly. He got down on his knees and thrust the sharp, narrow blade into the King's heart. The King lifted his hands briefly; his feet quivered momentarily; he died.

Khan rubbed his hands in a washing motion. They were dry. Not a drop of blood had sullied them. He lingered for a few seconds. Then, leaving the knife inside the King's chest, he rose and joined Bahaadur outside the tent.

"It's done," he whispered.

"Did you make sure he's dead?" Bahaadur asked.

"Shut up. Don't be stupid.

"I was just asking."

"Let's finish the job."

They grabbed the dead sentry under his arms and pulled him to the back of the tent, leaving him lying on the hard earth, his face turned up toward the star-filled sky.

Daylight broke out faintly over the foggy countryside. The camp came to life again. The bread maker heated up the temporary mud brick oven dug in the ground, its walls covered with clay. The smell of freshly baked bread spread over the camp as the baker pulled the first pieces of the flat naan out of the tandoor. The cooks put kettles on top of the oven to make tea for breakfast.

Government ministers, generals, and the King's guests stumbled sleepily out of their tents and went over to the well to perform their ablutions before sunrise prayers. Each took a pitcher, which a soldier had already filled with water.

A piercing cry came from the King's tent. Everyone froze. Then, dropping their pitchers, the men dashed to the tent.

Babbling, his words unintelligible, his face terror-stricken, the King's personal servant staggered out of the tent. Nobody dared to go inside.

This was the moment Khan had been waiting for. Disregarding any constraints of rank and age, he pushed several men aside, among them Abdul Akim, the minister of the interior, who stood frozen on the spot, his mouth gaping, his big brown eyes bulging. Khan lifted the tent's doorway curtain and entered, motioning the others to follow him. Inside, a gold ewer lay on the red carpet, where the attendant had dropped it. Water had spilled onto the carpet and was pooling beside the King's camp bed. The King lay on his back, his fat stomach bulging. Khan knelt beside him and put his ear to his chest. He slowly got up.

"The King's dead," he said, shaking his head. "May his soul be at peace."

The men, packed tightly inside the tent, cried out and jabbered in confusion. After a few minutes, their jabbering stopped, and they calmed down. Their eyes wide open, they pushed and shoved to scrutinize the body. They wanted to see for themselves whether the King was really dead.

Khan pulled the knife out from the King's chest and raised the bloodstained blade. A large ruby at the head of the knife's hilt glistened darkly.

"Who can identify the owner of this dagger?" he asked the crowd, looking hard into one face after another.

Realizing the dagger's similarity to his own, General Naim rushed forward and snatched it from Khan's hand. He turned pale. Then, panic distorting his features, he dropped it.

"Is it yours?" Khan asked the commandant.

"Somebody must have stolen it from my tent," the general stammered. His eyes wandered from face to face.

Horrified at the possibility that, by an evil twist of events, one of them could be implicated, the assembled men stood by silently and stared at General Naim.

"Did you hear the commandant?" Khan asked. "He's not denying ownership of the murder weapon."

"This is a tragic situation," said Malik Osman. "Nobody wishes General Naim ill. But, under the circumstances, we must know where he was last night."

"This is an evil plot," Naim cried out. "I'm being framed. I had nothing to do with this."

"The commandant is obviously refusing to tell us where he was last night," said Malik Osman. "In view of the gravity of the situation, I propose that the general be temporarily relieved of his duties. Until we know more about his role in this treacherous act, Deputy Commandant Amir Bahaadur should take charge of the King's Guard."

"The respected malik is right," hollered another tribal leader. "Let's secure the commandant before he can cause more harm."

"Don't listen to them," Naim pleaded. "This is a conspiracy. Ask the sentry who was assigned to guard the King's quarters last night. He'll tell you that I had nothing to do with his Majesty's death."

Bahaadur ordered the King's Guard to assemble outside. When the unit leader reported a sentry absent, Bahaadur formed a search party, instructing it to fan out and look for the missing man. In minutes, the body was discovered. Lifting him by his feet and shoulders, four soldiers carried the dead sentry before the King's shelter.

"General Naim knew that this man could not contradict his claim," said Malik Osman, raising his eyebrows, stroking his graying beard with his large hand.

"Deputy Commandant Bahaadur," somebody called out. "Do your duty. Detain the murderer."

"Seize him," Bahaadur ordered the guards. "Bring a rope and tie him."

Several soldiers threw the commandant to the carpet. They bound his hands and feet with a long piece of cord that one of them had brought. Bahaadur stuffed a piece of cloth into the general's mouth to smother his earsplitting screams. Bound and gagged, the general grunted and vehemently shook his head as he was carried out of the dead King's tent.

"Dear brothers," Khan addressed the assembly. "There seems no doubt who the killer is. But Allah, the All-Knowing, is watching. We shouldn't judge General Naim in a hurry. We must make an attempt to find more evidence. If anybody knows something that could help us find the truth, speak up now."

"I do, Colonel." A young cadet, a student training with the King's Guard, stepped forward. He was short and chubby with a reddish face. His shrewd eyes twinkled behind round glasses.

Khan's head snapped around, looking at Bahaadur.

Bahaadur broke into a sweat. He stared aghast at the cadet, then glanced at Khan, shook his head, shrugged almost imperceptibly.

Khan's mouth dried up. He took a deep breath. "What can you tell us, Cadet?"

"Last night, I saw the commandant walk toward the King's tent."

Khan's fists unclenched. Buoyed by this unexpected validation of his plan, he dashed to the cadet and clapped his hand on the young man's shoulder. "Here's a brave patriot who's not afraid to tell the truth," he called out.

Turning back to the cadet, he said, "Repeat what you just said, Cadet. Introduce yourself first. Then restate your testimony. Speak clearly so that everyone can hear you."

"My name's Nabi Dost," the cadet said with a strong voice. "I was visiting the latrine late last night. On my way back to my cot, I saw the commandant. He was going toward the King's tent."

"Are you sure, Cadet Dost?" asked Khan.

"Yes, Colonel. I am."

A murmur arose among the gathering of elders and government leaders. Huddled together, they whispered and gesticulated nervously.

"I wonder why the commandant wanted to kill the King," said one of the maliks. "In whose pay might he be?"

"This calls for an investigation," observed Minister Akim, widening his eyes and scratching his head. "Only an inquiry can solve the puzzle."

"But an investigation would take a long time," remarked Malik Osman. "It could create suspicion and spite between the tribes. We must be careful to avoid rancor. Animosity could lead to murder and even annihilation within our own ranks."

Khan's gaze glided over each distressed face. The men were exchanging worried looks. The situation seemed ripe for a swift solution. "Brothers," he said, deciding to push on. "In the interest of peace in our beloved country, I propose that we bring the perpetrator to justice. As the respected malik just said, delays will result in rumors. Gossip will spread like wildfire and incite groundless allegations. Inevitably, hostilities will follow. Swift justice is the only answer in this most lamentable situation. This isn't a case in need of an inquest. We've got the murder weapon. We've got an eyewitness. We don't need anything more to establish the truth."

"I support Colonel Khan's recommendation," Malik Osman joined in. "It was God's design that most government leaders and the distinguished maliks of many tribes are present here at this tragic day. Allah, in his wisdom, wished all of us to witness for ourselves this calamity and to observe that this heinous crime is not the result of a conspiracy. There are no indications that one clan has tried to gain advantage over the others. No government leader has attempted to take power for himself. This senseless murder is simply the deed of one despicable individual."

"They're right," another malik called out. "Let's execute the traitor."

"In God's name, let's do it," the others yelled.

Bahaadur, followed by several soldiers, rushed to the tent, where General Naim was tied up. Pulling at the rope that bound the general's hands and feet, the recruits towed the suspect out again, dragging him over the rocky earth.

Khan and the other men came out from the King's tent to observe the spectacle. Bahaadur hurriedly formed a firing squad. Naim, his face covered with dust, his eyes bulging, lay on the ground. Eight soldiers aimed their guns at him.

Bahaadur hesitated and looked over to Khan. Khan's face was dead serious.

"Fire!"

The guns' deafening reports rumbled through the broad plain, and the smell of burnt powder filled the air. The general jerked under the impact of the bullets. His limbs tugged violently at the rope. Then he quivered and, just as he released his last breath, blood gushed out of his nose. His eyes were locked in a stare of incomprehension.

Accustomed to a leisurely pace when conducting business

themselves, the tribal leaders were overwhelmed by the dizzying speed of the present proceeding and the general's swift execution.

Khan knew this was not the time to hesitate. "Distinguished friends," he said. "By guiding us to find the murderer, Allah, in his mercy, has spared us another calamity. But our task is not yet complete. It's God's will that we not separate before we have chosen our next leader."

"Distinguished ministers and generals, honored maliks," Bahaadur his voice cracking, his eyes avoiding contact with the assembled men, picked up the thread. "Colonel Khan sees far ahead and recognizes the dangers awaiting us. Departing from here before we've installed our next leader will cause uncertainties and may lead to unrest. If we fail to act promptly, a crisis will be inevitable. We must avoid a fratricidal war at all cost."

"After all," Khan said, "Ataullah Shah has no heir."

"No legal heir."

"What was that Minister Akim?" asked Khan.

"I was just pointing out that His Majesty does have a son."

"The bastard?" someone shouted. "His mother isn't even Pashtun."

Minister Akim was resolute. "Even so, my point is that we're moving too far ahead. The succession can't be decided in the absence of several maliks and cabinet ministers. They must be consulted before a decision can be taken."

"But a majority of our elders, maliks, generals, and ministers are present," Khan countered. "I see no reason to postpone this important decision. The sooner we've chosen our new leader, the better it is for the country."

"He's right," somebody from the crowd hollered. "Let's choose our next leader, before the succession becomes a problem."

"This is a very big step you're—"

Before Minister Akim could repeat his objection, somebody

cried out, "Shut up, old man. We don't need to listen to you. You're responsible for security. And this is the result."

"Friends," another person said. "The minister has served the country well. He deserves our respect."

Khan was pleased with the confusion. "Dear friends," he said, raising his hand, in which he was holding a Quran. "God Almighty is watching us. He commands us to be brave, not to shy away from our responsibility. He impels us to rise to the occasion and solve the leadership question now."

Khan pointed to Bahaadur. "I believe our next king is—right here among us. Amir Bahaadur."

There was much murmuring but little open disagreement. Bahaadur, not expecting Kahn's maneuver, tried to hide his surprise.

Khan pushed on, "The respected leaders assembled here will agree with me that our brother Bahaadur comes from the finest family. Indeed, centuries ago they were once the rulers of us all. He will command the respect of everyone.

"How about the military?" someone called out. "And how about the merchants, the bazaar traders?"

Khan smiled at the crowd and, keeping his voice low, said, "My esteemed brothers, we cannot please every single person. And who among our women will be pleased unless it is you who is chosen to rule?"

Everyone laughed.

Khan looked around. "Indeed, my brothers, there are high-ranking military leaders among us. Do they object?"

No one spoke.

"As for the merchants and bazaar traders," Khan said, "they should be informed. Out of respect. One is Haroun Dhil, the cloth maker. A powerful man, yes, but a close friend of Amir Bahaadur's father. He has influence among merchants. He's an ally. We can rely on him to explain things on our behalf."

"I must interrupt," said Minister Akim. "The King has spoken to me on more than one occasion of his gratitude for the loyalty that the Bahaadur family had always shown him. And how Amir Bahaadur was destined to be a great leader."

Khan looked at Akim and thought the Minister must have made a calculation that his government career was over. Now he was concerned about his safety and that of his family. And Khan said, "Minister Akim is a wise man. We should listen to his opinion."

"Thank you, my friend," Akim said. "Let's all join together under the leadership of our dear brother, Amir Bahaadur."

"Yes, I agree," Malik Osman seconded.

"So be it, then," Akim concurred. "In the name of Allah, The Merciful, Amir Bahaadur will be our next King."

"Thank you, brothers," Bahaadur Shah said, a nervous smile on his face. His eyes began to water. "I accept this heavy burden. And, in my first official act, I'm installing my dear brother Wali Khan as prime minister."

The throng broke out in spontaneous applause. The maliks, the generals, and the bureaucrats joyously hailed their new leaders.

After every man present had congratulated them both and paid homage to them, Khan announced, "Dear friends, we must leave for the capital immediately. Much remains to be done. We must arrange a fitting funeral for our slain leader. And prepare for the installation of our new King."

The caravan prepared to depart. Bahaadur Shah and Khan would ride back to Kabul in separate vehicles. They lingered for a moment, but neither could find anything to say. Finally, they grabbed each other by the arms and embraced.

Chapter Forty

Khan took his eyes away from the ruby on top of the knife's grip. For a moment, he looked as if the anger had left him. But then, without warning, the two men moved toward each other. Khan raised the knife and rammed it into Bahaadur Shah when the King collided with him. Bahaadur Shah, his eyes protruding oddly, gave a short sputtering sound.

Khan tried to pull out the knife but it didn't budge. As he struggled with the weapon, his entire body shook from the exertion. "Help," he shouted, turning his head toward Gol. "What are you waiting for? Help."

Gol took the dagger's grip and pulled with all his weight. Bahaadur Shah screamed as the blade came out of his body with a swishing sound. Blood and feces burst out of his punctured bowel.

Still on his feet, still clutching Khan's chubby neck, Bahaadur Shah pulled Khan closer, trying to strangle him.

"Do something," Khan said to Gol, his face covered with blood and excrement. "Use the knife. Stab him."

Gol drove the smudgy knife into Bahaadur Shah's side, just below his ribs. The blade pierced Bahaadur Shah's soft midriff, sliding unhindered all the way to the hilt. Bahaadur Shah cried out. Warm blood poured over Gol's hand. He pulled back, extracting the dagger.

Bahaadur Shah let go of Khan's neck and hurled himself at Gol, grabbing him in a desperate last effort. When Gol thrust the blade into him again, his features convulsed and his grip slackened.

Jumping to the side, Gol let Bahaadur Shah fall to the floor and, close to vomiting, ran out of Khan's office. As he staggered into the bathroom at the end of the foyer, he heard Khan's shrill voice. "Close the door," he hollered. "Close the damned door."

Gol opened the faucet, dipping his hands into the sink, letting the icy water run over them.

When he looked in the mirror, he stared at the face of a stranger. Bit by bit, his features took on the shape of the renegade soldier's sick father in the village outside Kunduz. Even the white of his eyes had turned yellow.

"Don't forget, you will be judged by your own deeds," he heard Amir Bahaadur Shah's voice call to him from behind. He spun around. There was nobody. He was alone.

Wiping flecks of blood and feces from his uniform, Gol thought about his father and his undisputed obedience to the two ruling families. He wondered whether they had used his father for similar assignments. If asked to kill, would his father have refused, risking his own life rather than acquiescing?

The door flew open and Captain Assad stormed in. "Chief

Dost's on the phone," he said, struggling to catch his breath. "He wants to speak with you."

Straightening himself to a stiff, ramrod posture, Gol said, "Tell him I'll call him right back."

Minutes later, Assad returned. "You don't need to call the Chief from here," he said, now breathing normally, his voice collected. "He wants you to go straight to the Ministry of Defense and call him from there."

On his way out, Gol walked past Khan's office. The door to the office was closed. No one stirred in the hallway and a peculiar sense of abandonment filled his mind. He rushed outside and got into his vehicle and hurried out of the Prime Minister's office complex.

At home, he changed his uniform for a fresh one, dumping the sullied clothes in the trash. Then he headed for the Ministry of Defense. "Idiot," he muttered as a fast-moving personnel carrier nearly forced him off the road.

Soldiers had cordoned off downtown—the site of the King's palace, Khan's office, and most other important government installations.

At the checkpoint, an officer approached Gol's Zeel. He turned down his window, "I'm on my way to the Ministry of Defense," he said. "I'm in a rush. I'm on an important assignment."

"Aren't' we all, Colonel?" the officer, a colonel himself, remarked. "Only authorized personnel can pass through. I have to call Chief Dost's office to clear you."

Except for military vehicles, the streets in downtown were deserted. Tanks guarded government buildings and major intersections. Soldiers, trying to keep warm, stood in small groups around open fires.

Unable to prevent the images of the past hours entering his

mind, Gol perceived the spectacle around him only vaguely. Scenes of the recent past moved before his mind's eye: Khan, sitting in his small, bare study, his face ashen, his heavyset body drooped in the worn armchair, writing his message to Bahaadur Shah in the Quran; Bahaadur Shah, standing in front of the unyielding duty officer outside the Prime Minister's compound, impassively letting events take their course.

Gol's mind replayed in minute detail the King's dogged but doomed struggle to survive. He saw once more how Bahaadur Shah's strength had gradually dissipated, how his will to fight faded, and how the glow of life eventually left his eyes, and he wondered why Bahaadur Shah had walked straight into his death. What had the Prime Minister written to him that had persuaded Bahaadur Shah to trust him?

Passing by the Prime Minister's complex and sensing a compelling urge to read the message, he decided to retrieve the Quran from Bahaadur Shah's limousine and made a U-turn.

The King's guards were gone. The same three tanks still barricaded the entrance to the Prime Minister's office buildings. But the security contingent now included more guards and several additional armored vehicles. Recognizing Gol, the duty officer instructed the tank commander, whose tank blocked the gate, to clear the way.

As Gol approached the central structure housing the Prime Minister's office, he saw cleaning people going inside. Soldiers carried out a rolled-up rug, several chairs, and a couch.

Bahaadur Shah's limousine stood at the same place Gol had parked it. The Quran still lay on the car's backseat. Quickly, he opened the door and took it.

Chapter Forty-one

Secret Police Chief Dost's stare made Dhil uncomfortable. But he felt reassured when a shadow of a smile darted across Dost's face. Surely the Secret Police Chief had realized the error the police had made.

"Dhil-sibe," Dost said, his fat cheeks shining crimson, his small eyes glimmering. "This is the second time we meet today. What brings you here this time?"

"I wish I knew," Dhil said, trying to settle his arm in a comfortable position. "Anyway, what I say makes no difference. Perhaps you could tell me why your people have locked me up in an icy cell? Why am I being treated in a way even a criminal shouldn't?"

"You're here for reasons of state security," Dost said. His eyes suddenly turned hostile.

Dost's alarming accusation and remorseless stare jolted Dhil. He straightened reflexively. "You can't be serious!"

"I'm quite serious," Dost said, lighting a cigarette, inhaling deeply. "You're charged with having conspired against the state." Smoke came out of his mouth in small puffs as he spoke.

"That's absurd," Dhil said.

"I believe you had a role in the assassination of the Governor of Kunduz," Dost said, his voice flat and even.

"That's a grotesque lie," Dhil said, anger rising in him. "What do you want from me?"

Dost checked out a page in the file before him and took another drag from his cigarette. "I've obtained information that you recently received a large sum of money from a foreign source."

This is ridiculous, Dhil thought. He struggled to keep his voice calm. "I do business with foreign firms. You know that. I receive money from abroad regularly. I get paid for the goods I export."

"People like you always have an eloquent answer for every question," Dost said. "Your foreign masters have trained you well. But in your case, too many things come together. You probably want me to believe it's all coincidental."

"What are you talking about?" Dhil asked. "I have a right to know what I'm accused of."

Dost raised his right hand and bent his fingers. "First," he said, opening his thumb, "one of your employees was arrested and found guilty of anti-regime activities." He lifted his index finger. "Second, in violation of government directives, a known anti-regime activist, a convicted criminal, is presently in your employment." Now he raised his middle finger. "Third, you maintain a highly suspicious contact with a man from the economic section of the American embassy." Then, he freed his ring finger and stared at Dhil with cold eyes. "And, as I have already mentioned, just a few days ago, you received a large sum from abroad."

"I do not deny having hired a former political prisoner,"

Dhil said. "His employment in my company has nothing to do with his past. And, as I explained earlier in the afternoon, my procurement manager did not belong to a political party. He fell victim to a misunderstanding. He should have —"

"Are you telling me your employee was executed without cause?"

Dhil could feel an electrifying intensity drilling into him from Dost's steely eyes.

Dost tilted forward in his chair. "Are you accusing the government of murder?"

Dhil dropped his gaze, but immediately regretted not having withstood Dost's challenging stare. He looked up again and found the Secret Police Chief's stare still fixed on him. A predator, Dhil thought, hypnotizing his prey. Chastising himself for having been the first to drop his eyes, he oscillated between hating Dost and thinking him superior to himself. He closed his undamaged hand into a fist and pressed it together until his knuckles hurt and his fingers became numb. The exertion vented his anger and he calmed down. He would be more careful with what he said and had to find a way to contain the primal malice of this evil man. He made sure his voice remained free of any contentiousness. "I'm not accusing you of anything. All I want is to go home and forget this nightmare ever happened."

"The more you cooperate the easier this will be for you," Dost said calmly. "No matter what you think of us, we're only interested in finding the truth. Don't let your anger make you deny facts."

"I know nothing that could be of interest to you."

Dost turned to his men. Raising his hand, he said, "Gentlemen, here's a paragon of virtue. He wants us to believe he's a simpleminded fool." Dost smiled when he turned back to Dhil but his voice had become ice cold when he continued, "Dhil Sa'heb, the trick's too cheap to impress me."

"I did not know about the curfew."

"What about your liaison with Prime Minister Khan's daughter? Is that also an innocent association? Nothing more than a simple romance? Or were you using her to secure state secrets?"

The mention of Miriam startled Dhil. So, they knew all along. "That is nonsense. You know that."

"Don't try to deny your guilt, Dhil Sa'heb. I know how you abused Miriam Khan's trust. Unaware of your treacherous intentions, she passed state secrets on to you, which you delivered to your foreign masters."

Dhil felt a compulsion to smash Dost's head on the concrete floor and scatter his ugly brain all over the room. He was hardly able to speak. "Listening to you makes me sick."

Dost jumped from his chair, propelling himself across the table and slapping Dhil. "You are accused of sedition," he shouted, spit spewing from his mouth, "and you have the gall to say that I make you sick. Who do you think you are?" Breathing heavily, he opened the pink folder and took out a sheet of paper, striking it down in front of Dhil. "Sign it," he said.

Dhil pulled the sheet closer and read:

> I, Habib Dhil, herewith confess to being an agent of a foreign power. Further, I admit to having bribed military and civilian personnel in an effort to subvert the country's leadership.

Dhil grasped that his situation was much worse than he had anticipated. Dost's accusation made that brutally clear. But as hopeless as his situation looked, he refused to give up. Signing that paper meant forfeiting his life, and that he was not prepared to accept. He noticed that his breathing had become irregular, and he tried to control it. He'd have to stay calm, he told himself. He'd have to counter Dost's assault with intelligence.

"Why do you wish to destroy me?" he said. "Do I, for some reason, frighten you so much that you wish to see me dead?"

"You should've considered the consequences before you engaged in treason," Dost said. Then, bending over the table and looking at Dhil with a stern gaze, he continued, "Don't you know that I struggle day and night for the survival of our state and the preservation of law and order? Nobody can hide from me. I've even watched you in your lover's den in Paghman. Zarina, the old woman, has reported to me your each and every move."

"You are an evil man, Dost," Dhil said, dumbfounded by the madness that had been going on behind his back.

Secret Police Chief Dost tried to punch Dhil. But Dhil managed to grab Dost's arm with his good hand. Pulling Dost toward him, he spat in Dost's face.

Somebody seized Dhil from behind and Dost freed himself from Dhil's grip. A military man handed Dost a handkerchief. He wiped the saliva from his face. "Let him be."

The person who had been holding Dhil released him.

Slowly and gradually, the ambiguity in his mind receded and he recognized the gravity of his situation. He looked at the sheet of paper Dost had put before him. He comprehended the deadly trap that Dost had set for him. Now he knew firsthand how the Secret Police Chief persuaded his prisoners to confess.

It was his turn. He understood that. Circumstance had assigned him the role of the vanquished in the ruler's game and the time had arrived to endure whatever he must to complete his commission. But the task would not end with his death. Afterward, they would continue the game without him. Others would come along the same path and assume the role that was currently his to play. They would fight as hard as they could and, in the end, quietly submit to their fate. The attempt at conquest would never end. Only the players would change.

Tears welled in Dhil's eyes. He didn't try to hide them.

Looking at the sheet, he attempted to read those two fateful sentences once more. But his tear-filled eyes failed him. That he couldn't read the neatly written lines didn't matter. Once the government had them printed in the newspapers, they would sum up his life's work to the public—a man who had taken money from a foreign power, somebody who had betrayed his own people for personal gain.

"If I sign this paper," he said, "won't I sign my life away?"

"It depends," Dost said, still breathing heavily. He took off his glasses and wiped them clean. "What happens in the future depends on how willing you are to cooperate."

Dost smiled. He sounded friendly, concerned. "Sign the document, Shaghele Dhil. Telling the truth is always the right thing to do."

Dhil was surprised at the formal term of address. He looked around and recognized the two army officers who had conducted the interrogation before Dost had arrived. They stood to the right of Dost, leaning against the wall, observing him with tired eyes. On the other side of the large chamber, the group of men who had arrived with Dost—some from the military, others in civilian clothes—stood by the door, watching him without expression. They seemed to be whispering, trying to tell him something. Dhil focused on the men's murmuring voices and thought he heard them say he had no chance to find a way out and should surrender and sign the confession.

He agreed and decided to initial the statement, putting at last an end to his nightmare. He instantly discovered a moment of peace and felt a heavy burden lifting from him. But unexpectedly and forcefully, a strong desire to resist also reawakened in him. He thought of the terminally ill and how, despite their utter despair, they never lost hope and always expected a remedy. Their fear of death and thirst for life made them yearn for a cure until death's black cloak wrapped them in darkness.

Dhil, too, waited for a miracle, an event that would distract his tormentors and let him slip through their fingers.

So far, he had survived this ordeal. But he needed more time. With time grinding on, anything could happen. The door could open at any moment, Miriam rushing into the room, demanding his immediate release. He had no doubt that he would survive if he delayed signing the confession and decided to use any subterfuge to gain time.

"May I go to the bathroom?" he asked. "I have to relieve myself."

"Let's do it," the Secret Police Chief called out.

Somebody struck Dhil from behind. The blow threw him forward. His chin hit the tabletop. His lower lip got caught between his teeth as the blow forced his mouth shut. He tasted the salty flavor of his own blood.

"Pull his pants down," Dost instructed.

One of the men yanked the chair from under Dhil. He fell hard on the cement floor. They pushed him down to the ground, unzipped his pants, and pulled on his trouser legs. He screamed as a hard object was forced up his anus. When the electric current surged through his body, he lost consciousness.

He still lay on the ground when he came to. Grabbing the table leg with his good hand, he lifted himself and pulled up his pants. Using his good hand, he moved the chair that the police officers had pulled out from under him back to its place at the table and sat down. As he picked up the pen, his hand trembled, and he wondered why. No trace of fear preoccupied him. Death no longer terrified him. A mood of animation touched his senses and he felt like laughing aloud.

Chapter Forty-two

Colonel Alam Gol sat at the large table in the Ministry of Defense's ninth-floor conference room. As Chief Dost had instructed, he had been on the phone all night, keeping in contact with military commanders, watching out for signs of disturbances.

The Holy Quran, its green silk cover shimmering, rested before him. Several times, he had wanted to open it and read Khan's message to Bahaadur Shah but for no clear reason hesitated, ending up caressing the cover with his fingers, as if the smooth, silken sensation would somehow reveal some hidden truth. Finally, he had given up and gone back to dialing military installations, feeling out the mood of army commanders around the country, assuring them of Khan's friendship and loyalty to the uniformed forces.

At long last, daylight broke through. His eyes burned, his mouth was dry, but he was relieved that the night had passed quietly. He got up, stretched his tired limbs and walked to the window.

Cloaked in mist and low clouds, the morning beyond loomed somberly. Feeling cold and worn out, he asked the sergeant on duty to bring him a cup of tea.

Holding the cup with both hands, he sipped from the hot beverage, letting the heat seep through his palms and pour into his entire body.

Carefully, he put the teacup back on the saucer and took a deep breath, grabbing the Quran and unwrapping it. He opened the book and read:

> My dearest brother, let us leave anger and hate behind. Let us unite at this calamitous moment to deliver the remains of our beloved son to earth's eternal shelter. Let us join in prayer to Allah for the soul of our dear child. Let us use this most tragic instance to merge once again in friendship and true brotherhood.

Gol closed the Holy Book. He attempted to pick up the teacup again, but it rattled furiously against the saucer. All along it had been Khan's cold-blooded plot. Effortlessly, the Prime Minister had used him to get rid of both the younger and the older Bahaadur.

Earlier, Gol had assured himself that Khan's triumph would mean his own security. Now he wasn't so sure, wondering if Khan appreciated his dedication. While he mulled over his safety, one of the two black telephones on the table rang.

"Colonel, there is a man here," said the sergeant on duty at the entrance downstairs. "He insists on seeing you."

Whoever wanted to see him, he thought, either had a missing relative or found himself in trouble and needed help. Judging the situation still too unclear, Gol deemed it unwise to intercede with government departments on anyone's behalf. "Tell him to go away," he said and hung up.

The phone rang again. "Colonel," the sergeant said, "he will not leave. He says he must speak with you. Should I arrest him?"

Despite the gravity of all that had happened, the sergeant's enthusiasm amused Gol. "Before we do that, Sergeant," he said, "let's find out his name, shall we?"

"Please hold a moment, Colonel."

The sergeant returned. "Colonel, his name is Hadi Omar."

Omar, Hadi Omar. The name seemed familiar. Gradually, Gol remembered the face behind the name. Three years before, during the election in Paktia province, Omar had confronted the government by running for parliament as an independent against the government-supported candidate, posing an unusual challenge to the authorities, giving them no choice but to strike back.

The day before election day, Omar had been addressing a large gathering in Khost, the capital of Paktia Province. Gol, then a captain, was one of several government agents who, disguised as peasants, had been ordered to circulate among the crowd. Their mission consisted of identifying those in the gathering who displayed anger toward the regime and controlling the mob should it erupt into violence once Omar was apprehended.

In the end, nothing happened. Things unfolded with such speed that the illiterate country folks didn't fathom what had transpired. All of a sudden, the military contingent arrived. As unexpectedly as it had turned up, it vanished just as swiftly, leaving behind a gaping crowd, startled in utter amazement. The speed and efficiency with which the operation had been carried out had dazed the congregated. And, by the time the throng realized that the troops had taken Omar away, it was too late to do anything about it. After a brief, chaotic expression of their frustration, the people scattered and went their ways.

Gol had been close enough to Omar to notice the expression of incredulity on his face when the military vehicles had unexpectedly arrived. The soldiers stormed the stage, shoving Omar to the ground, pressing his face against the planks. In a matter of seconds he had been handcuffed and thrown onto the flatbed of one of the trucks. Then the vehicles had careened off, leaving behind a billowing wall of dust.

Gol wondered how Omar had managed to survive. Not many of Khan's opponents were lucky enough to leave jail alive.

"What does he want?" Gol asked the sergeant.

"He didn't say, Colonel."

"Then ask him."

A moment later the sergeant was back. "He says it's about Habib Dhil."

Gol cringed. Dhil's face had appeared before him many times during the night. He had tried not to think about what might transpire inside the concrete halls deep beneath the Ministry of the Interior, repeating to himself that it had nothing to do with him. But a profound sense of culpability persisted in his mind, resisting his efforts to blot it out.

"Send him up," Gol said.

Omar wasn't a physically big man, but had made an energetic, almost menacing impression on Gol as he had watched him address the crowd on that dusty day in Khost. Today, when he walked into the conference room, Gol was surprised to see a timid person with sickly features and an unsteady gait.

"What do you want?" Gol said without introduction.

"Mrs. Dhil, Habib Dhil's mother, has sent me." Omar's voice sounded as feeble as his physical presence appeared frail. "She would like to see you. It's urgent. It's about her son."

Gol remained quiet for a few seconds. "I've got to make a few phone calls. Wait outside."

Gol waited until Omar had left the room, then placed a call to Secret Police Chief Dost.

"He isn't in his office," his secretary said.

"Do you know where I could find him?"

"He didn't tell me where he was going. He might have gone to the Prime Minister."

Gol called Captain Assad, the Prime Minister's personal assistant.

"He's with the Prime Minister," Assad said.

"Can I speak with him?" Gol asked. "It's important."

"The Prime Minister has ordered not to be interrupted."

"Shit." Gol slammed the phone down.

He picked up the receiver again. Dialing Mrs. Dhil's number, he wondered what she would want from him. She probably wished to find out why her son had vanished and what had happened to him. But he didn't know that himself. He had only the most sinister hunch.

Nobody answered Mrs. Dhil's telephone.

Feeling he had no choice, he left the ministry together with Omar to visit Meena Dhil. He would have to face Dhil's mother sometime. As her son's friend, he would be involved in one way or another.

"Tell me, Mr. Omar," Gol said, his eyes on the road, watching out for tanks, troop carriers, and other military vehicles. "How do you know Mrs. Dhil?"

"I really don't. I work for her son. She called the office manager and asked for help in locating you. The office manager instructed me to assist her."

"Do you know Mr. Dhil well?"

"He's a busy man. I've had no opportunity to get to know him well."

"Why was he outside after the curfew? Do you know what he was doing yesterday evening?"

"He had gone out of town. He probably didn't know about the curfew. They must have arrested him on his way back."

"Mr. Omar," Gol said, veering sharply to the other side of the street to avoid hitting some carelessly marching soldiers. "Weren't you sentenced to ten years?"

"I was released early because of my bad health."

"Why did Dhil hire you? Isn't there a ban on your employment?"

Omar didn't respond.

"I'm not asking in an official capacity," Gol said. "I'm merely curious."

"I really don't know, Colonel." Omar was clearly reluctant to speak. "Dr. Zia, the physician who's treating me, interceded on my behalf. Mr. Dhil has a good heart, Colonel."

A good heart, Gol thought. Was that heart still pumping warm blood through Dhil's veins or had the bullets from a firing squad ripped it to bits?

Chapter Forty-three

No wonder Dhil's mother hadn't answered her phone. When he entered the foyer of the house, he saw the torn wire stuck out of the broken wall socket. Chunks of white plaster lay on the ground, severed from the wall where the police had ripped out the telephone line.

Meena Dhil's hair was grayer than the last time Gol had seen her and the wrinkles on her face cut deeper into her skin. In spite of her age, her resemblance to Dhil was striking. She rose when Gol entered, embracing him and kissing him on both cheeks. Waving away the servant who had shown Gol in, she beckoned Gol to sit beside her.

"Alam," she said, taking his hand. "Habib didn't return home last night. Do you know where he could possibly be?"

"I wouldn't worry too much," he said, his body heat rising. "He might have been forced to stay away because of the curfew."

"How can I not worry with all that's going on?" she said, her expression openly reflecting the anguish she felt. "He hasn't even called his office."

"The phones are down," Gol said, looking at the ground.

"I don't know what to think. You don't believe he could be involved in last night's dreadful business, do you?"

"Habib's careful," Gol said, worrying that his voice might fail him. "He never interferes in politics."

"But why did the police come last night and rip out our telephone line?"

"That probably was a routine precautionary act," Gol said. "Until everyone is accounted for."

Visibly reassured, Meena Dhil smiled. "Habib frequently talks about you," she said, sitting upright, calm, and dignified. "He always says you're his best friend."

Gol looked straight ahead.

"Do you remember the years in Baghlan?" she asked.

Her eyes, so much like Habib's, seemed hollow, revealing a vast empty space. They made Gol restless, reminding him of the dead soldier's mother in the village outside Kunduz. As she had cowered inside her hut, holding tightly to her two children, she also had eyes as hollow and bottomless as the sea.

"Those were wonderful times, Mrs. Dhil," Gol said, tears coming to his eyes.

The visit to Habib's office came to his mind and he wondered whether Dhil would have ever broken up with Miriam Khan. Gol had no idea what was going on in the mind of the Prime Minister, or in the mind of Chief Dost, for that matter. Who, but God, could be sure what might have happened if he had come to the aid of his friend? He felt his teeth grinding against each other. He should have warned him, Gol thought.

Meena Dhil grabbed Gol's hand. It felt hot, almost scalding

to him. A cold sweat began to form on his forehead. He freed his hand from Meena Dhil's grip.

Mrs. Dhil didn't seem to notice. "I always worried when the two of you went on your long outings on horseback," she said, a fleeting smile crossing her face. She paused. "Your mother, may she be in paradise, used to reassure me. She would say, 'Don't worry so much. They're young men. They know how to take care of themselves.'"

Gol hungered to listen to her and be reminded of those sweet, long-forgotten times. But her calm tone also tormented him. Her remarks stirred up a vile awareness and he felt as if a cancerous tumor devoured him from within. He moved to rise, but Meena Dhil grasped his arm firmly and held him back.

"Alam," she said, "please help me find my son. Should, God forbid, the worst have happened, I want to take him to Baghlan and bury him next to his father and grandfather."

At that moment, Gol ceased to resist the idea that Dhil could be dead and acknowledged that he might be gone forever, never to return. Only then did he picture Dhil's lacerated body, lying among a pile of bleeding corpses, a bulldozer pushing them into a freshly dug pit.

He recalled how bleak Baghlan's tranquility had seemed whenever Dhil went back to Kabul, and how the whispering winds had terrified him when he rode out alone. Now, he could feel the same desolation sweeping over him. He felt a tear on his cheek and wiped it off quickly.

Last night, when he had left to take Khan's message to Bahaadur Shah, Gol clearly remembered Khan's order to Dost. "Make sure his file is well-documented and he signs a confession." Gol knew what that meant. Along with the surging feelings of grief and shame, the fear for his own safety resurfaced. Once again, he asked himself whether Khan and his Secret Police Chief, now that he had done his part, planned to liquidate him.

He had abandoned his friend for fear of angering Khan. What guarantee did he have that Khan would not kill him too?

Otherwise, why had Dost, when describing Governor Bahaadur's death, used the terms "treason" and "tragedy?" What form of torture would they use to extract his confession? And what would be his crime? Fomenting revolt by assassinating the King's son?

It didn't matter. He had murdered his friend. He was sure of it. And he would pay for his crime.`

"Will you promise me, Alam?" Meena Dhil interrupted Gol's thoughts. "Whatever might have happened, I want my son back."

Gol nodded.

She pointed to the open Quran on the table. "And while I await your news, I will continue to rely on the words of Allah and my faith in his benevolence."

Gol glanced at the word on the page. A passage appeared and began climbing straight up to his face: "And do not plead on behalf of those who act unfaithfully to their souls; surely Allah does not love him who is treacherous, sinful." He was not a man of prayer, but more than once through the night, Gol had considered reaching out to God to ask him to ease his torment.

Now he knew he could not be saved.

"Promise me," Meena Dhil again asked.

Gol focused on the old woman. "Yes, Khanom Dhil," he said. "I promise." He rose, straightening his uniform jacket. "I'll see to it right away," he said as he walked toward the door. He needed to get outside to the cold air.

Relieved to see that Omar was nowhere around, Alam Gol climbed behind the wheel, eager to fulfill his promise to Dhil's mother. Not quite sure where he should begin, Gol headed back to downtown Kabul.

His first thought was to go directly to Chief Dost and ask

him to order Dhil's release, dead or alive. He closed his eyes, trying to suppress the truth of his friend's fate.

In a moment of clarity, he saw that Dost himself was a mere tool of the Prime Minister. Who was he to make such life and death decisions on his own. He had passed off the responsibility for Dhil to his boss, Prime Minister Khan.

He remembered Governor Bahaadur's words. "Everything revolves around us." No doubt, Dost was subject to the same authority. No, there was no other way. Khan himself had to order Dhil's release.

What if he declined? The question flashed in Gol's mind. He could see Khan—his head shaking, his face furious, "Families of traitors and criminals have no rights. His body will be disposed of like the rest. There will be no exceptions." Gol imagined Khan remaining silent for a moment and then adding, "Get out of my sight. I never want to see you again."

Gol's anger flared up even more as he recalled his father's submissiveness toward Khan and how he had made a fool of himself by rushing to pick up the little bluebird. That memory ripped his heart more than anything else. He gave out a loud howl and smashed his fist on the steering wheel.

The windshield began to fog with a film that the wipers could not wipe away. He pulled to the side of the deserted road. Outside was no better. Gol could only make out the outlines of trees along the road.

He felt something tug around his neck. It was a rope. A voice behind him called out his name. "Does the condemned have anything to say before sentence is carried out?"

"Wait! Wait! I need..." His plea sounded muffled.

"Very well then," The voice said.

Without warning, Gol felt the rope tighten. Unable to breathe, he dropped to his knees.

He wasn't sure how long he remained on the ground. His

breathing had returned to normal. The thick mist had vanished, everything looked clear again. He must be exhausted, he thought. He took a deep breath to reassure himself, returned to his vehicle and headed directly to the Prime Minister's office.

Stomping on the brake pedal, he barely avoided crashing against the small building that housed his office. After he had parked in his usual place and got out of the car, he closed his eyes for an instant, trying to empty his mind of the horrifying images that harassed him. Then, he set out to walk the short distance to the Prime Minister's office complex.

Chapter Forty-four

Colonel Alam Gol's mind filled with arguments that he would employ to secure the release of his friend. He would simply not accept anything less.

As he passed by the row of rosebushes in the garden, he recalled the scent of the flowers in the full bloom of the season. In the summer, whenever he had sought relief from the oppressive heat in the shadow of the majestic willow trees, a soft breeze had carried the sweet fragrance of the roses over to him. But now the rosebushes stuck their naked branches out from the frozen ground and the trees, without their rustling foliage, remained silent in the frigid winter day.

He climbed the steps and walked down the spacious hall outside Khan's office. Captain Assad rose to salute him.

"Do you want to see the Prime Minister?" the youthful-looking officer asked.

"Yes."

"Is he expecting you?"

"I must see him. It's urgent."

"Chief Dost's with him. Why don't you have a seat? As soon as the Chief leaves, I'll let the Prime Minister know you are here." Captain Assad smiled shyly. "Colonel, would you please hand me your pistol?"

"What did you say?" Gol asked, incredulous.

"You must surrender your weapon," Captain Assad said. "It's a new order."

"Does it apply to me, too?"

"It covers everybody," Captain Assad explained. "I'm not allowed to make exceptions." His broad smile exposed his unevenly grown teeth, his hand was outstretched to receive Gol's pistol.

Colonel Gol was shocked that this Captain would openly mock him, laugh at him without any regard to his rank.

Without any signal, Assad, the furniture, even the surrounding walls disappeared from his vision. Instead, it became the place where he would be arrested, forced to the ground, executed on the spot.

"Colonel," Captain Assad said, "your weapon, please."

"Am I under arrest?"

"Arrest, sir?" Assad laughed again. "Colonel, you don't look very well. We've all had a long night. Why don't you get some rest and come back. I'll let the Prime Minister know you were here."

Gol nodded, stood still for a moment, then hurled the full weight of his enormous body at Assad. The captain tumbled backward, crashing to the floor, pulling a chair down with him.

Alarmed by the noise, two guards came running up the stairs. Gol grabbed the captain's pa-pasha from the top of his desk and pulled the trigger. The hail of bullets brought down the guards. Another salvo tore up Assad, who had been struggling to get back on his feet.

Abruptly, quiet returned to the spacious hall. Gol heard Khan's voice on the intercom. "What's going on, Assad? Where are those shots coming from?"

Gol saw Assad and the two soldiers lying on the ground. The captain's eyes stared at the ceiling, his mouth wide open as if wanting to cry out a warning.

"It's Colonel Gol, Your Excellency," he heard himself speak. "There has been an altercation. But everything's under control now."

"Gol? What are you doing here? What were those shots about?"

"Everything's all right, Your Excellency, but I must talk to you, sir."

A revolver in hand, Khan cautiously opened his office door. Peeking out into the hall, he observed the bodies and then, seeing Gol, he leaped back.

Before Khan could slam the door shut, Gol smashed his heavy body into it, thrusting it wide open.

"Colonel?" Khan gasped, staring at Gol.

Gol fired. The bullets smashed Wali Khan's head, scattering pieces of his skull all over the room.

Feeling completely drained, Gol laid the pa-pasha down and sat in Khan's armchair. Once, he thought, Khan had turned his father into a groveling figure. Well, at last, Khan had paid for that humiliation. The incident with the bluebird began fading from his memory and already seemed far away, belonging to a dark but trivial chapter of his life, a chapter unworthy of revisiting from now on.

A comforting calm settled over him. He watched how air blew through the shattered windowpanes and pushed the curtains in a playful game of pressure and resistance. His thoughts traveled to the serene village of his youth in Baghlan, to those years of innocence, a time so entirely removed from the viciousness and corruption that held sway over Kabul.

In his imagination, he heard the faint tune of a shepherd's flute drifting from the hills surrounding the village and saw goats and sheep grazing on the green, gentle slopes. He remembered watching his neighbors walk by his house on their way to the mosque for Friday prayers, wearing large turbans, embroidered shirts, and gold-threaded red vests, their faces carefree, their lean frames moving with an agile gait. He smelled the pleasant scent of Baghlan's rich soil and recalled that sunny, quiet day his father had shown him how to plant a tree. The act of inserting the sapling into the ground in their orchard had given him a sense of permanence and his father's company made him feel secure and protected.

Sometimes, after an exhausting day of roaming about in the fields, he would stand under the refreshing shade of a grove of beeches, their smooth gray trunks rising straight up, their leaves shining a brilliant gold under the soft autumn sun. As he looked out over the gently sloping hills that stretched into the far distance, the vastness of the land and the sheer infinity of the sky revived his spent energy and inspired him to continue his wandering in search of that indefinable thing, something he himself couldn't understand, something that was perhaps no more than a mere idea.

He began listening to the wind, slowly realizing that it was not a breeze at all, but heavy breathing coming from the far-left corner of the office. Secret Police Chief Dost was watching him. Dost's face was red and sweaty, his gaze marked by shock.

Dost stepped toward the center of the office, resting his eyes on the gaping hole in Khan's head. He turned. "Is there anything you want me to do, Colonel?"

Gol remained quiet.

The telephone on Khan's desk rang. Dost lifted the receiver. "One moment." He covered the mouthpiece with his hand. "It's Miriam Khan. She wants to speak with her father."

Gol didn't respond.

"The Prime Minister is busy. He would like to call you back."

Dost replaced the receiver. "Look, Colonel, we can't allow events to roll over us. We have to do something. I propose we join hands and put things back together."

Gol looked at Khan, lying on the floor, half of his skull and his left eye blown off, a large pool of blood had already formed around his head. His right eye stared at him. Gol saw the image of the small bluebird in Khan's iris. Convinced that that image would never cause him shame again, he smiled. "Have this body removed."

Dost dialed a number. "It's the Chief." He looked away from Gol. "Listen carefully." His voice conveyed outrage. "There has been a monstrous plot to overthrow the government. The Prime Minister has been assassinated. I'm sure the investigation will reveal that the scheme was led by the Russians."

Dost glanced at Gol. The Colonel sat motionless, his eyes following the pattern of the slowly moving curtains.

"Only the actions of one brave officer have saved our country," Dost said, speaking with great emphasis. "Send an ambulance to remove Prime Minister Khan's body. We will make arrangements for a state funeral later."

He paused. "We don't yet know the extent of the treason. Put our own security forces on alert. Order Unit 1 to replace the guard at the Prime Minister's office. Send Unit 2 to take control of the main telephone exchange. Suspend all unauthorized long-distance calls. Instruct our agents in the provinces to assume command of their local police." After deliberating for a moment, he continued, "Stay where you are. I'll call you back with more instructions." Replacing the telephone receiver, he asked Gol, "Is there anything else you would like me to do, Colonel?"

Gol did not answer.

"Colonel," Dost said, "are you listening? We are in mortal danger. We have to do something before things get out of hand."

Gol's features remained unchanged.

"Wake up, Colonel," Dost said, his voice rising. He pulled a handkerchief from his pocket and began wiping the sweat off his face. Hearing the sound of his own breathing, he said, "We must act now, Colonel." When Gol still did not respond, he picked up the receiver and dialed his office again. "Put Khan's family under house arrest. Disconnect their phones. They're not to see or speak with anyone. Round up all cabinet ministers and the chief of the national police."

"Miriam Khan," Gol said, speaking up at last. He fixed on her lively eyes and beautiful face from the picture on the table in her father's small study.

"Pardon, Colonel?" Dost said, looking over to Gol.

"Miriam Khan," Gol repeated. "She must be protected."

"As you wish, Colonel," Dost said. Shouting into the mouthpiece, he ordered, "Nothing is to happen to the Prime Minister's family. I mean nothing. No injuries. No accidents. Understood?" He hung up.

"This is a dangerous time," he said to Gol. "The communists and religious fanatics may try to take advantage of the situation. We must do something to counteract any moves they might make."

Dost began to pace across the office. "Well, what do you think?" he asked, his voice growing evermore frantic. "What should we do?"

Gol remained silent. He was back in Baghlan, riding Tawoos, his favorite horse. The wind blew in his face, as the horse galloped over the dried-up bed of a canyon. The sound of Tawoos' hoofs echoed back from the slopes, filling the air and soaring upwards along the steep grades towards the clear sky.

The canyon's sharp edges softened and the mountains receded in the background. As the gorge widened, Baghlan's rolling country opened up before him. He wasn't alone. To his right, slightly behind him, another horse followed. Its rider wore a smile as wide as his own. He shouted, "Alam, how lucky we are." Gol nodded. Yes, Habib, yes.

Habib!

The memory wrenched Gol from his musing. He opened his eyes, the sound of the winds again reduced to Dost's heavy breathing.

"Find Habib Dhil," Gol said resolutely. He smiled at the thought of his friend soon being back in the arms of Miriam Khan. "Let his mother know everything is okay."

"Colonel, I... you realize ..." Dost looked at Gol, unsure what to say. "Let's get things in order first," Dost finally said.

"You know, he's my best friend." Gol looked past the window's broken panes, into the void.

"Yes, I realize that," Dost said. "But let's return to our problem. One short-term solution would be to set the religious fanatics against the communists. I could have one of the religious leaders killed and spread the word that it was a terrorist act committed by the Communists. That would put them at each other's throat for a while. And we would gain time to organize ourselves. What do you think?"

Gol shrugged.

Dost picked up the phone. "It's the Chief again. Order Unit 3 to liquidate Imam Abdul Qadir. It must appear like a terrorist act committed by the Communists. Make sure the news of Communist involvement gets out immediately. This project has priority and must be completed today. Don't forget to send a detachment to the central printing house. Order the presses stopped. There will be no newspapers this afternoon. Order all TV and radio transmissions interrupted. Until further instructions, have them play martial music, alternating with recitations from the Quran."

Chapter Forty-five

Habib Dhil's back rested against the wall of the windowless van and his head bounced against the sheet metal with a rhythmic bump. The pain in his broken left hand had intensified.

Too battered to care, he had not counted the people who shared the ride with him. Except for the engine noise and the thump thump of his head hitting the van's wall, silence prevailed in the cabin.

After what seemed like an hour-long drive, the van came to a sudden stop. When it drove off again, it made a sharp turn, throwing the passengers all about. Someone crushed against Dhil's broken hand. He couldn't help groaning aloud as an intense pain raced through his arm.

As the vehicle stopped again, muffled voices came from outside and steps approached the rear of the van. Someone pushed aside the bolt that secured the door wings. As the door

swung open, bright light flooded into the cabin. A soldier ordered everyone out.

Blinking, stumbling, Dhil climbed down. The solidly frozen
ground felt hard under his feet and the chilly, fragrant air stung
his lungs.

Military men moved about in haste. Names were called out
and people dragged away. Shots rang out and a breeze carried
the pungent odor of burned gunpowder.

Upon hearing his name being called, soldiers grabbed Dhil
firmly by his arms and dragged him to the center of a bright
spot, upon which all the lights seemed to have been focused.
At the edge of that illuminated circle, a row of uniformed men
stood side by side, their guns trained on him.

"Is this it?" he whispered to himself. "How can God allow
this to happen?"

He looked up. Suddenly, an all-embracing quiet settled upon
him, broken only momentarily by a gust of strong wind blow-
ing away a layer of recently fallen snow. The silence descended
swiftly once more, insulating him from everything beyond the
reach of the brilliant spotlights.

That stillness brought Dhil comfort and helped him free
himself from the fear of death. The knowledge that a terrifying
darkness would soon swallow up his being could not disturb the
peaceful state his mind had attained. The immaculate serenity
filling his mind and the unblemished solitude surrounding him
helped him see things with an unusual clarity. He recognized
the truth of his life in all of its frightening concreteness. In spite
of his doubts and fears, he had all the while presumed he could
control his existence. He now stood as an unqualified failure.
His rage had been in vain, the result of his fear. And fear had
robbed him of his courage. His fevered mind had precipitated
an endless search for a life of his own. Finally, that exploration
had failed, denying him a life of grace and dignity. He couldn't

even claim that all that had happened had been a diabolical trap set for him by fate. He knew that everything that had happened in his life, he had willed it himself—not by his actions, but by his inaction, simply by default.

Knowing he had reached the end made him forget the pain of his damaged hand and battered body. The hopelessness of his position brought him a degree of satisfaction. He felt unburdened, even animated. A faint smile moved across his face. There had been so much he had failed to understand.

Had he done evil things in his life? He knew he had on numerous occasions entertained wicked thoughts and wondered whether he could purge himself from them. He hoped that his inner protest, his intention to do it right, would free his spirit from guilt.

The spotlights blinded him, and he turned toward the sky. The heavens were invisible—far, far away. From the obscure haze above him, Maggie's fresh, youthful features emerged. He followed her graceful movements, observing the slightly freckled skin of her bare arms. He remembered that warm night in Baghlan and only now, for the first time, realized that they had not uttered a single word from the moment she had slipped under the bedcover until the click of the door when she closed it behind her. She had always been very concerned about Charles finding out about them. Yet, that night, she had sneaked out of their room and come to his. While they had remained silent, she seemed, with her hands, to want to communicate something to him. She had let her hand slide over his face several times, as if wanting to acquaint herself with its shape.

Why had she risked coming to him? Perhaps the holy man had let her see into the future, and she knew about his impending death. That must have been the reason why she had silently joined him in his bed, one more time offering him her warm body, her soft skin, her tender kiss. But why had she avoided looking at him the next day?

He still mulled over Maggie in Baghlan that summer night, when Miriam's pale face appeared before him. She sat in front of the fireplace in the house in Paghman. Although, he felt her slender figure press against his, she seemed distant, not really a part of his world. As burning wood crackled and flames swayed playfully, she slowly drifted away behind a darkening mist. Would she ever realize the truth of her father's evil?

Then his grandfather came into view. His eyes moved about feverishly. His accusing voice seemed to descend from far, far above. "Son," he called, shattering the all-enclosing stillness. "Didn't I tell you? They won't even return your remains to be buried beside me. We both will suffer from the separation. I wish, my son —"

Dhil couldn't hear the rest of what his grandfather tried to tell him. An enormous flash blinded him. Powerful blows ripped through his chest. He felt a terrible pain and...

Chapter Forty-six

1980

Col. Barry McCormick, USA, Ret., had seen action in WWII, Korea and Vietnam. Now he spent his days quietly as the daytime receptionist at Hotel Fort Myer in Arlington, Virginia.

At exactly 8:55 am, he entered the lobby. You could set your watch by it, Anwar Haq, the small hotel's nighttime receptionist and accountant, always noted.

"Good morning, Anwar," McCormick said, approaching the reception counter.

"Good morning, Barry." Haq left the small area behind the front desk, deciding to have another cup of coffee before driving home to get some sleep.

"Have you heard from your family?" McCormick asked.

"I haven't received a word in more than a month," Haq said, feeling the hot fluid restoring a trace of his depleted energy. "I'm beginning to worry."

"No news is good news," McCormick said, moving behind the reception counter. "From what I read in the papers, the fighting's in the countryside. They're safe in Kabul. It's possibly the mail. It's not functioning because of the war."

"You're probably right," Haq said. He appreciated McCormick's reassurance.

Immediately after the Communists had toppled Colonel Alam Gol's short-lived government and the Red Army moved into Afghanistan, Haq had sent money to his wife, Fatima, telling her to take their two children and come to the States. Even the tightfisted Jeffrey Martin, the proprietor of Hotel Fort Meyer, had shown his approval at Haq's plan by promising to give him a raise once his family arrived.

Fatima had confirmed applying for passports. She had even visited Farid Komrani, the new minister of industries and a former classmate of Haq's. Komrani had remembered him fondly, she had written, and promised to intervene with the authorities on her behalf.

As Haq was about to leave, he heard the phone ring. McCormick called him back. "It's for you," he said. "It's the Afghan embassy," he whispered.

Haq took the handset. A female voice at the other end said the Ambassador wished to speak with him. Haq wondered what the Ambassador—a member of the Communist Party, somebody he didn't know—wanted from him.

"At last," the Ambassador said. "We've been trying to reach you since yesterday."

"I wasn't home last night," Haq said, surprised by the youthfulness of the Ambassador's voice.

"We got your work number from one of your acquaintances. But let me tell you why I'm calling. His Excellency Farid Komrani, the minister of industries, is in town. He would like to see you. He'll be at the embassy for lunch. It would be nice if you could join us."

Although tired and wishing nothing more than to go straight to bed, Haq accepted the Ambassador's invitation. Komrani had promised Fatima to help her obtain exit papers. This would be an opportunity to find out what was going on.

"Is it safe for you to go in there?" McCormick asked, when Haq told him about the Ambassador's invitation. "Who knows what those sons-of-bitches are capable of."

Haq hesitated. Suddenly, he wasn't sure about going to the embassy.

"Don't worry," McCormick said quickly. "At least I know about it. If you aren't back by this evening, I'll inform the authorities."

Haq parked his car on Wyoming Avenue, Northwest, a short distance from the embassy. He remained seated behind the wheel, wondering how he should react if the minister discussed politics. Haq disliked the Communists and had always feared the possibility of Communist rule in his country. Obviously, Komrani was a member of the Communist Party and most likely approved of the Soviet invasion. In any case, under no circumstance could he afford to displease him. At the same time, he didn't want to express blank approval of the situation either. That could appear insincere and might reveal his true feelings. He must discover a midpoint between the two extremes.

After straining his mind for a minute or so to find an appropriate response, he realized the futility of the effort. He had not dealt with his country's new leaders and wasn't sure how they were disposed. Since they had seized power, he had avoided visiting the embassy—not because he particularly favored the previous regimes, but simply because the Communists, in the

short span of their rule, had proved themselves to be the cruel-
est of all.

He searched all sorts of newspapers and pored over every
report that appeared about the situation in Afghanistan, reading
with horror about the execution of tens of thousands of bureaucrats, businessmen, landlords, and other so-called "enemies of
the people."

A businessman, who had fled the country, made it to the U.S.
and whom Haq had met at a friend's house, had even claimed
that several of the new embassy employees were professional
killers, dispatched to assassinate known anti-communists in the
small Afghan expatriate community in the Washington, D.C. area.

Although he didn't believe that even the Communists would go
that far, he had thought it prudent to keep away from the embassy.

Trying to anticipate what would happen inside the embassy
was futile. He couldn't control how things would unfold. He
simply had to muddle along and hope not to offend Komrani.

He locked his car and walked the short distance to the embassy compound. It was a quiet neighborhood. Very few people
moved about and only an occasional car drove by. The noise
from the busy parts of the city sounded muted as if coming
from far away.

The grass in front of the pretty, well-kept townhouses looked
fresh. Under the sun's warm rays, life had returned to the trees
and leaves had started sprouting from their buds. Pouring down
on his face, the sun's gentle light restored his energy and lifted
his spirits.

He remembered the time when he and Komrani had gone
to school together. Komrani, a coltish youngster, had always
been game for a good prank. Later, after graduating from high
school, he had joined the military and Haq lost contact with him.

He couldn't have turned into a monster simply because he
had joined the Communist Party, Haq thought. That observation

reassured him somewhat. Stopping in front of the embassy building, he took a deep breath from the fresh spring air and rang the
doorbell.

A thick cloud of cigarette smoke enveloped the Ambassador and Minister Komrani. They stood in the middle of the
large, formal living room and seemed to be having an enjoyable conversation. Komrani laughed loudly at something the
Ambassador said to him.

"Salaam, Haq Sa'heb," the Ambassador said when he noticed
him. "Come in." He took a step toward Haq, greeting him with
a friendly handshake.

The Ambassador didn't look much more than twenty-five,
Haq estimated.

Komrani, his face beaming, his look as carefree as it had
been when they were high school students, embraced Haq and
kissed him on both cheeks. He looked him in the eyes for several seconds, his smile growing broader. At last, he said, "How
have you been, old friend?"

In the face of Komrani's unexpected cordiality, Haq didn't
quite know how to respond and remained silent.

"Come, Haq-sibe, join us for a drink," the Ambassador said,
pressing a glass into Haq's hand and pouring the drink. "This
is Stolichnaya, the best vodka available. Comrade Dobrynin,
the Soviet Ambassador, sent a case over just the other day."

Tired, his stomach empty, Haq flinched when he took a sip.
Barely able to swallow the liquor, he worried he would throw up
if he had to finish it and was relieved when the butler opened
the door and announced that lunch was served. Haq set his
glass down beside a turquoise-colored vase and followed the
other two into the adjoining chamber.

Through four large windows, sunlight shone into the dining room. With its high ceiling, the sizable dining table, and

the huge Persian rug, the room exuded an aura of grace and spaciousness. The fine china and the heavy crystal vase in the center of the table added to the air of refinement.

"Some time back," Komrani said, "Khanoum Haq came to my office. She said you wanted her and the children to join you here."

"It's been more than two years since I left my family behind," Haq said. "I want them to see me before they forget that I exist."

"I want the truth, my friend." Komrani's face turned serious. "Don't forget, we were classmates. I wouldn't do anything to harm your family."

"I don't know what you mean."

"You've decided not to return home. Haven't you?"

Haq hesitated.

"We know you've given up your schooling," the Ambassador interjected. "It was some time ago, I understand."

"That's beside the point, Comrade Ambassador," Komrani said, his voice had taken on a stern tone. "Look," he said, speaking to Haq again, the nervous pitch in his voice having vanished. "If you want me to help your family get out of the country, I'll arrange it. But why don't you go back home yourself?"

"I've no plans to return to Kabul," Haq said. "I've a job here. It's not an occupation I've trained for. But it's a job that enables me to feed my family. What would I do if I went back? As a former official without party affiliation, I would be denied work. I might even be thrown in jail."

"Let that be my problem," Komrani said. "I will protect you." His voice took on a decisive, almost sharp tone. "You realize you're here under a government training program. You're still an employee of the Ministry of Industries. I'm your superior and could insist on your immediate return. But I'm not here to give you orders. The simple fact is we need people like you."

Suddenly, Haq saw himself confronted with a situation he had not envisioned. He had never imagined that Komrani would ask him to return to Kabul. He worried that whatever he now said might destroy his plans. If he tried to placate Komrani and promised to go back, the Minister could prevent his family's departure once he realized Haq was not returning after all. And if he refused outright, Komrani would probably see to it that his family never joined him in America.

"You haven't touched your food, Mr. Haq," the Ambassador said, gulping down his vodka and looking at Haq with glassy eyes. A fine layer of sweat covered his youthful face. "Listen to Comrade Komrani. He has your best interests in mind."

Haq looked down at his plate. The Ambassador was right. Although, the pilau—pressure-cooked in meat sauce, saffron, and thin strips of orange peel—tasted delicious, he had eaten very little.

Komrani leaned back, took in as much air as his lungs could accommodate, then exhaled slowly. Leaning forward again and focusing his gaze on Haq, he said, "You must look at what's happening in our country from a global perspective." The agitated sound in his voice revealed his impatience. "Together with the Soviet Union, we're embarking on a venture of global scale. In ten years, the world will be very different from what it is today. Major changes will occur. And we will be right at the center of it.

"Haq, my friend," Komrani shifted in his chair. Unlike before, he looked relaxed and untroubled. "Our foremost goal is the rapid industrialization of our country. The main channel for those activities will be the Ministry of Industries. I would like you to come back home and participate in this great effort."

"There are foreign troops in the country," Haq said. "The government's bogged down by a raging civil war. That will make normal economic activity difficult, if not impossible."

"That's American propaganda," Komrani shouted, his face flushing. He cleared his throat. "This is exactly how our enemies want you to see things. Ours is not a civil war. We're fighting capitalism and imperialism. We've no choice but to fight to the bitter end.

"Look, Haq," Komrani's voice calmed down. "I'm an air force officer. I can fly a MiG, but I don't know anything about running a bureaucracy. We need people like you. We need administrators to run the civilian part of the government so that people like me can join the battle. Haq, I want you to be my deputy. We will be the architects of our country's industrialization."

"Comrade Komrani's right," the Ambassador said. "The Colonel's demise was the last gasp of feudal rule in our country. With the help of our Soviet allies, we'll bring dramatic changes to our area."

"This is no time to abandon your country," Komrani said. He narrowed his eyes and stared at the crystal vase in the center of the table. The vase's solid round base, its elegantly furrowed stem, its wide concave opening seemed to have mesmerized him. He grabbed it, heaved it high above his head, and hurled it to the floor. It burst into a thousand tiny pieces. Glass splinters flew everywhere.

Alarmed by the sound, the butler rushed in.

"Get out," the Ambassador shouted at the butler. "You can clean up after we leave." He turned to Komrani, his voice mellow. "Comrade Minister, I hated that piece. It reminded me of my degenerate predecessors."

Komrani and the Ambassador laughed loudly. Haq grabbed the glass of vodka that the butler had put before him and gulped down the fluid. The alcohol burned his throat. It all became clear to him. If he wanted to see his family again, he had to accept Komrani's offer and return to Kabul. Komrani had already made plans for him. He would become deputy minister of industries for the Communist government of Afghanistan.

Chapter Forty-seven

2001

Maggie Reed lost track of how many times she had made the short trip from her home to the immigration office in Arlington. She went randomly through old files of Afghan citizens seeking asylum in the U.S., absorbing the tales of destitution, reading the bureaucratic language of immigration officers justifying their rejection or, in a few cases, their approval of the applications.

Browsing through the file of a man by the name of Anwar Haq, she was about to put it back on the pile of other folders she had already studied, when she saw Dhil's name.

Haq had asked for political asylum for himself, his wife, Fatima, and their daughter, Sheila. The application had been rejected on grounds that Haq had been a high official of the Afghan Communist government and his sponsor could not

be found as the applicant had failed to mention an address
for him.

There it was. Maggie stared at the words "Habib Dhil,"
written in a clear, neat handwriting. Under the heading "Relations," Haq had added, "Personal friend."

She had been willing to make another trip to Pakistan, but
now she had direction. Perhaps this Anwar Haq knew where
Habib could be found or what had happened to him. She
needed closure, the peace of mind that came from knowing.
She couldn't continue living with this uncertainty, an ambiguity that had made her imagine Habib enduring indescribable
horrors and unspeakable cruelties, scenes that terrified her and
hurt her beyond endurance.

According to the file, Haq lived in Camp 37 outside Peshawar. She knew that sprawling tent city, a place teeming with
hopelessly destitute people. She had been there on several
occasions, distributing medicines and interviewing potential
candidates for resettlement. During those visits, she had come
to admire the stoic perseverance of the Afghans. While clinging
to a tribal culture and indubitably submitting to what their mullahs told them was the word of God had kept them mired in
biblical times, their way of life had also given them the stamina
to endure the miserable refugee existence in Pakistan, itself a
basket case of near hopeless poverty.

Chapter Forty-eight

On this morning, Anwar Haq found the latrines exceptionally filthy. The pits had not been emptied for quite some time and overflowed. People had begun using the area around the drop holes. Excrement covered even the mud-brick steps that led up to the holes. Hovering permanently over the entire camp, the stench was particularly insufferable up close.

Haq's stomach churned. He refused to use the toilets and kept on going. Shuddering with revulsion, he clenched his hands. Civil war back in Afghanistan would probably last forever. He would never make it back home and instead die here, in this damn camp, living off handouts, cheated out of a meaningful life.

He walked north toward the bare mountains looming off in the distance. The Pakistani guards hadn't bothered to secure that side of the camp. Anyone who wished to return to Afghanistan could do so freely. But no one did. Nothing could induce Haq to go back, no matter how homesick he was. No sane person would brave the brutal mountains simply to return to mayhem and anarchy.

He wandered on until he left the sea of tents behind. About a half mile from the countless shelters and their innumerable occupants, he dropped his pants in the middle of a wide-open field and defecated over the parched ground.

When he returned, Fatima had raised the olive-colored tarpaulin at both ends of their tent and rolled up the three mattresses, folded the bedsheets, and neatly stacked them, one upon the other, on the battered metal suitcase that held their belongings.

Despite all they had endured, his wife had never complained. She always tried to make do with whatever they had, without nagging, without expressing disappointment in his failure to provide better for her and their daughter.

"Fatima," he said, "I'm going into town. I'll be looking for work and won't be back for lunch."

"Do you have to go?" Fatima asked with a hint of irritation. "I must go to the distribution center. Today's our turn to pick up our ration. We shouldn't leave Sheila alone. She's despondent again."

Never before had she objected to his occasional outings to Peshawar. Why would she today? Did she no longer believe his stories about his search for a job? "She's twenty-two for heaven's sake," he said. "Spending a day alone won't hurt her."

"When will you be back?"

What was the matter with her? Why did she want to know when he would return? "It could be late." He deliberately remained vague. "I might not find a ride and have to walk back."

Before he emptied his first cup of tea, she departed for the distribution center. He wondered why she had left so early. It couldn't be to beat the crowd. No matter how timely she arrived at the distribution center, there would invariably be a long line.

And then he realized that she often stayed on after the distribution center closed down, explaining it away by saying she congregated with the other women and swapped supplies with them. Lately, she had also been bringing fresh bread from one of the bakeries that had cropped up in the camp. Just last week, she brought cheese, fresh oranges, and canned beans. The week before that, she came back with a dozen eggs and ten bananas, claiming to have gotten them in exchange for half of their flour ration.

Haq prayed she hadn't been foolish enough to touch their reserve. That little money was all they had. They needed to hold on to it for emergencies.

He turned to his daughter. As always, Sheila crouched in her corner, her head bent, her expression sullen, her large, brown eyes focused on the ground.

"Your mother's off to the distribution center," he said. "I'm leaving to look for work. You'll be alone for lunch. Will you make yourself tea and eat some of the bread?"

Sheila did not raise her head. She never did. She never looked at him anymore. She never looked at anybody.

"Sheila, do you hear me?" She stared at the ground. She won't make tea for herself, Haq thought. She won't eat the bread. She would sink into that coma-like sleep until her mother returned and jolted her out of it. Perhaps he should stay and take care of her.

For a moment he wavered and couldn't decide what to do. But then he resolved to go. He had already told Fatima he would be going into town. He must remain firm. If he gave in once, he would have to give in always. Even in this godforsaken place he was the husband and she his wife. Besides, he had to maintain the charade that he looked for work.

He watched his daughter for a few minutes. Finally, he rose and left. He strolled through the crowded campsite. Men sat in circles, talking, drinking tea from tin cups. Women cast long, gnarled shadows as they moved about inside their tents. Others, their long black chadors covering them all the way to the ground, crouched outside their shelters, washing dishes or kneading dough or making small fires to cook.

Further along, he ran into General Ayoub. Haq was horrified to see how this once athletic man had shriveled. He recalled how Ayoub used to display his muscular body, wrapping it in well-tailored, tight-fitting uniforms. Now the general's shoulders were hunched, his face unshaven, his eyes lifeless. Instinctively, Haq touched his own face and looked at the skin of his hands for signs of premature aging.

"My tent's around the corner," Ayoub said, offering him a weak handshake. "Come, let's have a cup of tea."

"I'm off to Peshawar," Haq said. "I've a job prospect. I'm already running late for the interview."

"You're lucky." Ayoub scratched his stubbly chin. "I've forgotten how it feels to make money." His languid eyes looked into the distance. Turning back to Haq, he went on, "But let's see each other soon. I would like to hear your views on what's happening and what you think about America's threat to invade our country."

"Yes, let's get together." Haq said and, embarrassed at having lied about the job, hurried to get away from Ayoub.

When he reached the gate with its large wooden sign that read Camp 37, he raised his hand to the soldiers in greeting. The bony Pakistani guards let him proceed. They didn't bother to ask him where he went. They knew his routine. They understood that he had to get out of the camp once in a while, to walk the streets of Peshawar, to mingle with people, normal people, people with their own homes, their own trades, their own lives. And there was no risk of his disappearing. Over the years, he had established a track record. Besides, he had a wife and daughter in the camp. He wouldn't do anything to bring trouble upon them.

Haq enjoyed his walk along the highway to Peshawar. Soon the thickening traffic would spread about the fetid odor of petrol and the ascending sun would relentlessly burn the earth. But for now, the air was clean and the breeze fresh. And all along his long trek to town, he felt a mysterious sense of anticipation. Auspicious whispers came from his heart and spoke of a person of means who would recognize him for the educated man he was and help him get out of the camp and find a job, work befitting his abilities, suitable to his background.

Every day he would cling to the hope that finally, after this long wait, Habib Dhil would find him and pull him out of this never-ending misery. Surely Dhil would reward him for the extraordinary friendship and loyalty Haq had shown. But the years had deadened his faith. He didn't know where Dhil was or how to contact him.

For a moment, he thought of Dhil and remembered his elegantly tailored suits and serious demeanor. He wondered what had happened to his textile mills and his farm up north in Baghlan.

When Dhil had visited him in his place in Arlington before turmoil had swallowed their lives, Haq had had a distinct feeling that Dhil was holding back. He had been pensive and uncertain. What had he been afraid of? Could he have sensed the catastrophe hovering over their heads?

A few months after his return to Kabul, he found out that Dhil's house had been assigned to the chief of staff of the military forces. Did Dhil know, or even care, about all that he had lost?

Haq didn't inquire about Dhil's whereabouts. In wartime

Kabul, no one ever asked about those who had left or disappeared.

It had been a lifetime since their last meeting in Arlington. What could he have been doing all these years? He smiled to himself. Dhil was probably in America, making more money than ever.

By the time he reached the city, shops and businesses had opened. Amid masses of disheveled shoppers, he trudged past pharmacies, spice shops, neon-lit restaurants, and stores packed with bolts of brightly colored materials. He breathed the stench of urine, rotting animal intestines, and decomposing vegetables and slowly worked his way through the crowded streets and headed to Mirza Sharif's kebab stall at the corner of Railway Road and Kissa Khani Bazaar.

He enjoyed watching the hustle and bustle around Sharif's stand. He liked betting against himself about which of Sharif's patrons would devour their meals in haste and which would take time to enjoy their food in leisure. Besides, despite Sharif's bitching that he shouldn't hang about his stall, the Kebabi would, in the end, let him have the leftovers.

He had just arrived at Sharif's stand when two Land Cruisers, filled with Afghan Mujaheddin, raced into the crossing. Horns blaring, the two cars ran the red light, causing a rickshaw to slam against a bus and forcing a mother to grab her child and dash for their lives.

"Fuck your wives, Afghan bastards," a pedestrian yelled.

Haq was not surprised. The townspeople had long since ceased to be friendly to the refugees. They had turned rude, even hostile to the Afghans among them. He didn't blame them. The Pakistanis were no longer sure whether they could still call the city their own. Peshawar's attractive colonial character had vanished. With two million Afghan refugees dwelling around the city, the supply situation had deteriorated and shortages abounded. Although Communist rule in Kabul had long since collapsed, waves of refugees from war-ravaged Afghanistan still flooded in, making a precarious situation worse.

"Here, brother." Sharif held out a skewer of freshly grilled kebab. "Eat this and then go away. The lunch crowd will be here any minute. I don't want you to stand in the way."

Sharif's slight didn't insult Haq. It wasn't personal. That was how refugees were generally treated. Over the years, Sharif's demand for him to stay away had become as habitual as his own persistent lounging around Sharif's stall.

Haq took the brochette and pulled off a piece of meat, putting it in his mouth, eating it slowly, carefully sampling the garlic, the hot chilly, and the black pepper. It was tasty but dry and chewy. What can you expect from buffalo meat, he asked himself rhetorically. The peasants sold the animals to the butchers only after they grew too old to work in the fields. No amount of seasoning could soften the tough flesh from those aged, emaciated beasts.

He put another morsel in his mouth, pressing the meat between his teeth and squeezing a little juice out of it. His eyes moved to the stack of freshly baked chapatis. He would give anything for just one of those thin slices of crisp, warm bread.

The veins on Sharif's muscular arm protruded from the strain as he fanned the fire. With quick, regular motions of his other hand, he grabbed the skewers one by one, turning them continuously over the glowing embers. "Hey, brother," he called out, squinting at Haq with teary eyes through the billowing smoke. "Step to the side, will you? You're blocking the way. How often do I have to tell you?"

Haq moved a small distance away from Sharif's stand and leaned against the waist-high brick wall that ran alongside the dusty sidewalk. He wondered whether Sheila would eat her lunch.

Guilt pierced his heart. He felt remorseful eating meat when Sheila had nothing but bread and tea. It pained him to watch her slip away, slowly, pointlessly, inescapably. But it pained him even more that he couldn't do anything about it.

If only Yousuf were alive. Maybe together they would have found a way out of here. He could still see the pride on his son's face when he had put on his new uniform and left the house. Sometimes, he wished God had let him die instead of Yousuf. But then he imagined his son wasting away in the camp, among the sprawling assembly of tents on a barren plateau of dust and rocks under Pakistan's merciless sun, his weakening body too languid to shoo away the flies. Then, he was almost glad Yousuf was gone and had been spared their humiliation.

He wished he could find a way out, to go back to America. He should have stuck by his original plan, he thought. He should have sat tight and arranged for his family to join him in the U.S.

Everything would have been so simple. He knew from other Afghans who had made it to the U.S. how easy it was to obtain stay permits. Immigration authorities were lenient in processing Afghan nationals fleeing the calamity the Communists had brought over their country.

If he hadn't returned to Kabul, Yousuf would still be alive. Sheila would be going to college, and Fatima, instead of waiting in line for meager handouts, would be shopping at a neighborhood supermarket. Had panic made him give way to Komrani's pressure?

Would Komrani have let his family leave the country if he had refused to return home? The question had become an obsession. Haq recognized the futility of it, but he couldn't help posing it to himself again and again.

Once he had gone back, he could have fled the country as millions of others did during those war years. Yet, he had stayed on. He was ashamed to admit it, but it was true: He had lacked the courage to face the unknown. He had become dependent on the comforts of the large house the state had provided him with. And it had felt good when the chauffeur drove him to work in that bulky, black Zil limousine. And yes, there was the salary. While it didn't amount to much, not enough to brag about, it had, at the end of each desolate month, arrived unfailingly. And the money's power to lessen the daily inconveniences of wartime living had kept the hope alive.

Haq remembered how deepening warfare had wrecked Komrani's overblown plans for the country's industrialization. The civil war had rapidly isolated the government from the countryside. One after another, projects had to be abandoned. Construction of factories, power plants, roads, bridges, and irrigation systems had come to a complete halt. Joining millions of ordinary citizens, thousands of government employees, including hundreds from his own ministry, had fled to Pakistan, Iran, Europe, or America. He recalled how each day, when he entered the ministry he found the halls more deserted than the day before. But, as if paralyzed by a force beyond his control, he had waited—waited patiently for the Day of Reckoning. The wait had been long and brutal. And, at the end, the final collapse had not brought relief. It had been the beginning of another Armageddon.

Chapter Forty-nine

Maggie Reed stood behind a window along the shopping arcade overlooking the driveway to the main entrance of the hotel Marriot in Islamabad. She waited for Charles, her ex-husband, and Clare, his current wife, to arrive. She hadn't seen Charles since he had been made American ambassador to Pakistan. She was eager to see how the two now handled themselves. After all, Pakistan depended heavily on American financial largess and military supplies and, in this first year of the twenty-first century, a time when American might had emerged unchallenged and loomed portentously, the American ambassador in Pakistan represented the modern version of ancient Rome's mighty proconsuls.

Except for the unusual spectacle of a chauffeur-driven stretch limousine and the retinue of several vehicles packed with bodyguards, Charles himself appeared to be the sunny-faced, carefree person he had always been. Stepping out of the car, he gave the sentry, who had been keeping the door open for him, a friendly slap on the back and waved toward the other guards who immediately surrounded him, turning their heads from side to side, looking out exaggeratedly, even theatrically, for potential sources of danger. Small and slim, Clare looked more like a child than a grown woman beside Charles's tall frame as they stepped into the hotel and walked over to the reception desk.

When Maggie approached them, she heard Charles say to the receptionist behind the oval-shaped counter, "Room 201, please." Charles' voice had not changed at all. Its familiarity surprised Maggie. Despite the eleven years that had passed since their divorce, Charles sounded as if they had never separated.

Before the receptionist could lift the receiver to make the call, Maggie put her hand on Charles's shoulder. His habitual open smile lit up his face when he turned. He seemed genuinely pleased to see her. Even Clare didn't seem to be troubled by Maggie's sudden appearance in Islamabad. She looked quite elegant and obviously took good care of herself, Maggie thought. Her lean body gave her an almost youthful look and her outfit's dark blue color contrasted well with her unusually light skin. Under the recessed ceiling lights, her hair exhibited a healthy shine.

"Here you are," Charles said, still smiling brightly, his eyes revealing a tiny measure of discomfort.

"It's good of you to have called," Clare added, brushing her cheek against Maggie's in a brief but friendly hug.

"Is it all right if we go to the embassy?" Charles said. "We'll have dinner at the residence."

"I wanted to take you two out," Maggie said.

"I can't go to public places," Charles eyes twinkled as if Maggie's simple disposition had amused him.

"Are you telling me the almighty American ambassador isn't allowed to go to a restaurant?"

"Maggie!" Charles laughed his usual carefree laughter. "You don't change, do you? Still anti-authoritarian. Still suspicious of government."

Chapter Fifty

Anwar Haq returned to Sharif's stall and put the brochette on top of the other used skewers. The Kebabi stood behind his deserted stand. The day's lunch business had been brisk. The used skewers lay in a big pile on the long table. Sharif had run out of kebab. Only some chunks of charred meat and a few chapatis remained.

Haq observed how meticulously Sharif checked the fire, making sure it was out. Then the Kebabi began pulling a long cloth over his stall. Haq stepped forward, grabbed the other end of the cover and helped Sharif spread it over his counter.

"Take the food," Sharif said.

Haq almost jumped to snatch the morsels of burned kebab and the remaining chapatis but stopped himself. There was no need to show too much eagerness, he admonished himself. He took his time with the food, wrapping it slowly in a sheet of oil-stained paper. When he looked up to thank Sharif, the Kebabi had jumped over the brick wall to urinate.

Haq set out on his way back. He passed by the large, elegant store where rich Pakistanis and foreigners, mainly Americans and Europeans, bought their furniture. As had become his habit, he stopped to admire the splendid pieces in the display window, all of solid teakwood and exquisitely hand carved. The desk with the dark polish caught his fancy especially. He visualized himself sitting behind it, reading papers, signing correspondence. Had he had the money to shop at the store, he would buy the dining table and six of the chairs with the black leather seat covers. His thoughts drifted off, and he could see his dinner guests seated at the two sides of the table with Fatima and himself sitting at either end.

That vision lasted only for a moment. Fatima's searching eyes appeared before him, making that sweet illusion dissipate, reminding him that he had to have a story ready to tell her, one that would assuage her curiosity and answer her inquisitive questions about what exactly he had done all day long. That realization brought him back to the brutality of his existence.

It was getting ever harder to come up with a credible account. Yet, once again, the sketch of a plot came to him. He would tell Fatima that the owner of a large furniture store had introduced him to his supplier's sales manager. The supplier needed a shop foreman, and the sales manager had promised to propose him for the job.

After he had made up the story, his mind relaxed and he continued on his way back to the camp. Finally, he left the noisy town behind and strode along the highway. Overloaded trucks, decrepit buses, and battered cars clogged the road. The smell of diesel and petrol pervaded the air. The pavement, burning under the sun's pitiless heat, spewed fire like an infuriated dragon.

He remembered the sense of expectation he'd had in the

morning and felt cheated. Here he was, at the end of another idle day, abandoned as before, anonymous to the countless eyes he had met, wandering back along the same highway to the confinement of Camp 37.

When he arrived at the camp, it was early in the evening. The soldiers sent him inside the guardhouse where the officer was reading a copy of the English-language paper *Dawn*. The military man tossed the newspaper onto his desk. Haq stepped forward and put down his small package. While the sentry inspected the bundle, Haq scanned the headline: "War Imminent as Taliban Reject U.S. Demands."

After the officer examined his parcel, he frisked him for weapons, then motioned him to move on.

Haq picked up the food, wrapped it again in the greasy paper, and left the guardhouse. As he strolled through the gate, he saw a tall, broad-shouldered man standing beside a taxi, talking to the guards. In his clean, white shirt, his smoothly ironed pants, and shiny, brown shoes, he looked out of place among the raggedy crowd shuffling in and out of the camp.

From where Haq approached the scene, he could see only a part of the man's face. But something about him appeared familiar. The way he cocked his head and moved his hands while he spoke reminded Haq of somebody he knew. But he wasn't sure who. He moved closer and changed his position to have a better view.

Yakoubi, he thought. Zalmay Yakoubi. He hadn't seen Yakoubi for many years and wasn't sure whether it really was him. When he moved closer and heard the man's voice, he knew for certain. Yakoubi had put on weight. His hair was receding and a touch grayer. Haq tapped him on the shoulder.

Yakoubi turned around and remained frozen for a moment. "Haq? Is it really you, old friend?"

"It's me all right."

"What are you doing in this dump?"

"This dump's my home." Haq's face turned hot. He hoped Yakoubi didn't notice him blush.

"Why didn't you go to America or Europe?"

"I left too late. The world is fed up with us. No country wants us."

"Bullshit. There's always a way, if you want to."

"There's nothing I can do. I'm stuck in this hellhole. What about you, Yakoubi? Where do you live?"

"I've settled in America."

Some people always come out on top, Haq thought. "What brings you to this god-forsaken place?"

"I'm visiting relatives. I'm arranging for them to join me in Los Angeles."

"How do you intend to do that? If there's a way, I would like to know about it."

"I could introduce you to the people who're arranging the trip for my folks. They could help you. It'll cost you eight to ten thousand dollars per head. But they can organize it. The passports. The visas. The tickets. The whole package."

Haq's heart sank. For a moment, he'd had a glimmer of hope. "That's way beyond me. I haven't got that kind of money."

"Are you telling me you didn't get any of your money out?"

"That's what I'm telling you."

"You can't get something for nothing. If you want to settle in America, you'll have to cough up the money."

"Are your relatives here in this camp?" He changed the subject, trying to hide his disappointment.

"They live in Peshawar. I've rented a house for them."

"What are you doing here, then?"

Yakoubi's eyes twinkled. A roguish smile flitted across his face. "Don't you know what's going on in this camp?"

Haq shook his head. "I've no idea what you're talking about."

"A pimp operates here. He has a thriving business."

"I haven't heard a word about him. How did you find out?"

"From this taxi driver." With a movement of his chin, Yakoubi indicated the waiting taxi. "His stand is in front of the Palace Hotel, where I'm staying. He knows several whorehouses. You can choose between Pakistani and Afghan women. The Afghans are refugees from good families. They're refined and clean, but cost more. That's what I wanted, so he brought me here."

"Was she up to your expectation?"

"I liked her. I could see she wasn't a professional hooker. She was tense. She refused to take me in her mouth. She said her lips were cracked."

Wanting to change the subject, Haq asked, "So, how's life in California?"

"It was rough at first. I entered America illegally. It took time to get my green card. But now, I have my own restaurant and make good money."

Yakoubi paused. "It's a pity. I've always wanted to start a second restaurant, but I didn't have anybody to run it. I mean, somebody I could trust. Had you been in Los Angeles, you could have run it for me."

Haq remembered the anticipation he had felt on the way to Peshawar. This had to be the benefactor his heart had promised would appear. True, he didn't particularly like Yakoubi who was somewhat of a shady character, always on the move, constantly speaking of big business deals, inevitably flaunting his money. Under ordinary circumstances, he wouldn't want to be associated with him. But these weren't normal times. This was a unique opportunity. There might never be another one. Besides, Yakoubi obviously was a winner. An affiliation with him could not fail.

"Why don't you lend me the money to go to America? As

about his other commitment. Did Yakoubi's curtness mean to prepare him for a brush-off?

No matter. Tonight, for the first time, he didn't feel dejected when he strode through the congested camp. He no longer counted himself among its inhabitants. In his mind, he had already left this hellish place. Soon, he thought, he would be freed from Pakistan's punishing heat. He could see the three of them in a plane, sitting side by side, flying over the Atlantic and across America toward the mild California weather, the houses with running water, the stores full of food. But now that dream still seemed elusory.

He shook his head and decided he would not give up easily. Tomorrow, he would pressure Yakoubi to advance him the money. Yakoubi needed him, he reassured himself, and, despite his doubts, he decided to tell Fatima about his meeting with Yakoubi.

The smell of hot food greeted him when he entered their shelter. Sheila slept on her mattress, a blanket pulled over her. Fatima sat beside the lamp, reading a magazine. She looked up and smiled.

"Fatima," he said, as soon as he sat down beside her. "You won't believe what's happened."

Fatima motioned toward their daughter, putting a finger to her mouth, signaling him to be quiet.

"I must talk to you," he persisted. "It's important."

"Later." Fatima's features were firm. "After you've had your dinner."

She lifted the lid of their one pot and took out a large chunk of meat, putting it on a plate and adding some sauce to it. She set the plate in front of him and handed him one whole slice of a flat bread from among several pieces wrapped in clean brown paper.

He unpacked his own bundle and offered her the chapatis

and the morsels of kebab. She took the packet from him and covered the food again.

"I've already eaten," she murmured. "We'll eat this tomorrow."

He broke off a piece of the bread, dipped it in the sauce, and ate it, savoring the juice of fresh meat. He had forgotten how delicious lamb could taste. He tore off a second piece of bread. Pressing it on the lamb, he separated the meat into smaller bits.

"Where did you get it?" he asked. "You didn't spend from our reserve, did you?"

"No, I didn't." Her voice was soft. She brought her face close to his. Her eyes shone brightly in the fluttering light of the gas lamp. Her hair was tidier than usual. He put his hand on her thigh.

She smiled, then took his hand in hers and pressed it. "Eat your meal," she whispered. After a pause, she added, "Don't worry. The money isn't from our savings. I sold the cooking oil I got today. I didn't need it. We have enough left from last week's ration."

When he finished eating, she removed the plate and set a tin cup before him. She took off the thick cotton cloth that covered the kettle and poured him tea. Before she could return to her place, he took her face in his hands and pressed his mouth on hers.

"What are you doing?" she said, half laughing, half admonishing. "You're hurting my lips."

"What's wrong with them?"

"They're dry. I had to wait for hours in the sun."

"You haven't complained before."

"My lips are cracked. They hurt when you kiss me."

Her lips were cracked. Perverse images flashed through his mind. It took him several seconds before he could tame the madness that exploded within his head.

He lifted his mattress, unfolded it, and lay down.

"Don't you want to drink your tea?" Sheila asked.

He didn't answer.

"Didn't you want to tell me something?"

"Tomorrow."

"What's the matter?"

"Nothing." He covered himself with a blanket.

She carried the water pitcher and the plate outside and washed the dish. When she came back, she cleared a space, spread her mattress, and extinguished the lamp. She lay down and pressed her back against him. She undid the drawstring of his pants and took him in her hand.

He pulled away.

"What is it?" she asked, watching the outline of his profile. As he remained silent, she continued, "Unlike you, I've had a busy day. I've no energy for a fit. If you have something to say, say it."

Haq's eyelids began to twitch. The pounding inside his skull accelerated as he imagined her with Yakoubi. While that picture hovered before his mind's eye, he recalled how Yakoubi, without even getting out of the car, had cancelled their luncheon appointment. He wasn't going to give Haq any money to go to America. He will spend a little time with him and then send him empty-handed back to this miserable place. Haq cringed. "I walked all the way to that fucking town and back in search of a damn job," he said.

"Don't give me that shit," Fatima interrupted. "You know and I know that there is no job. You devised this game to get away from the misery of this place once in a while. And I played along. I played along for your sake. I wanted you to spend some time for yourself. To forget Sheila's depression. Not to have to see me for a day. So don't tell me you went to town because something important waited for you there." She turned away from him, resting her head on her pillow.

He remembered the moment she had slipped his wedding ring onto his finger, how she had looked deep into his eyes and whispered, "I will be yours forever." Clenching his hands, he said, "You have never done anything for my sake, you bitch."

"Shut up. You're waking Sheila."

"Don't tell me to shut up, you slut." He felt how his hand searched for the knife he kept beside him when he went to sleep.

"What did you say?"

"I know what you've been doing in my absence, you whore."

She turned and slapped him.

The throbbing in his head intensified. A cursed vision reappeared before him. Only now it was even more explicit than before. He could clearly see her lying naked on the floor, her feet raised in the air, Yakoubi's huge body between her spreading legs. Haq grabbed the dagger and pulled it out of its sheath. He lifted his upper body and grasped her shoulder, forcing her onto her back. He mounted her. When he put his hand on her chest, he felt the rapid thumping of her heart.

"What are you doing?" she said, trying to push him away.

He tightened his grip around the knife's hilt and raised his hand.

At that moment, she lifted her head and came close to his face. Despite the darkness, he could clearly see the white in her eyes and sensed the panic in them. She didn't shout, she didn't speak, she simply stared at him.

He let go of her and rose. He felt exhausted. His limbs heavy, his head still spinning, he swayed and staggered when he left the tent. Outside, nobody was around. No lights glimmered in the neighboring tents. Night had engulfed the camp.

He realized he was still holding on to the knife. He threw it away and headed north, toward the peaks that loomed grimly against the ebony sky.

Chapter Fifty-one

Maggie Reed had stayed too long at the ambassador's residence. By the time the embassy car dropped her off at the hotel, it was past midnight.

Despite the late hour, she paid her hotel bill. She wanted to be out early so that she could catch one of the first buses. Early in the morning, traffic would be light and she would avoid the heat of the sun for most of the three-to-four hour drive to Peshawar.

Charles had offered to send an embassy car to take her to the bus station and she had been tempted to accept the offer, but then declined it. Notwithstanding the genuine expressions of cordiality that Charles and Clare had shown her, she didn't want to impose. She had been going her own way all these years, and she had been happier for it. There was no need to change that.

Instead she reserved a car from the hotel. It cost more than what a taxi would have charged, but knowing the driver worked for the hotel made her feel safer and that justified the additional expense.

Up in her room, she packed and took a quick shower.

The touch of warm water on her skin felt good. While brushing her teeth, she looked at her image in the mirror and compared her face with Clare's fresh appearance. The hammering of time had obviously taken its toll, but strangely, at that moment, she felt more vigorous than she had in a long time.

After years of traveling to this poor country, she felt as if she had reached a turning point of her own. She wasn't yet sure where this change came from or would lead to, but she hoped that something good might come of it. She thought of the physical hardship she had endured during her many visits to Peshawar and the financial strain she had accepted to pay for the trips and wondered whether she would have done any of it had it not been for her irrepressible need to try to find Habib Dhil.

None of her friends understood it and wondered why she would devote so much energy to a man who had vanished from the face of the earth and made no attempt whatsoever to contact her. Even Dhil himself had warned her not to get too close. Being born in Afghanistan, he had said, didn't bode well for a happy life. "I'm stuck with what I am," he once said. "You don't have to get caught up in the same trap." But falling in love hadn't been her conscious choice. She wondered why her friends couldn't understand that. Didn't anyone fall in love anymore?

Besides, her longing for Dhil hadn't been in vain. All the displaced families she had helped resettle in the U.S., all the medicine she had distributed to local hospitals over the years, the cash donations and the tons of old clothing she had given to the refugees, all those activities would probably not have taken place without the love she felt for Habib Dhil.

The bus driver packed about forty people in his twenty-five-seat bus and left the station with a loud prayer in Arabic. Squeezed between the hard wall of the bus and the bony, reeking body of an elderly man, Maggie looked out the window into the solid darkness that still cloaked the city.

The dirty, oddly dressed mass of people surrounding her and the tedious music blaring from the radio reminded her of the Star Wars movies and the bizarre places Luke Skywalker and his assertive princess passed through and the peculiar creatures they encountered.

The sun was about to rise at the edge of the horizon when the driver stopped the bus beside a row of mud-hut dwellings and announced that he would perform his morning prayers and anyone wanting to join him should do so.

Up to that point, Maggie had been able to find relief from the smell that emanated from her seatmate by keeping the window open. But now that the early-morning breeze shoved the stench of excrement and urine from the outside into the standing vehicle, she shut the window. Through the dirty pane, she watched how the driver squatted to relieve himself beside the overflowing pile of feces in front of an open toilet and performed his ablutions with what seemed the stale water of what once had been a small stream. Then, together with several of his patrons, he prayed at the roadside. Their dark silhouettes against the gigantic background of the crimson sky made those few men appear at once peculiar and lonely—chillingly lonely—and incited in her an odd sense of hostility.

She wondered, as she had during her previous trips, what went through the mind of the people here. Surely, the desire to cleanse oneself reflected an apparently deep-seated sense of purity. But the filthy water the driver had used to wash himself, the omnipresent stench of excrement and urine, and the pungent smell of the people stood in stark contrast to that seemingly fervent religious devotion to cleanliness. The same incongruity seemed to exist within the people's sense of morality. While they displayed a strict adherence to religious rituals, they did not hesitate to lie, to take bribes, and to be cruel to one another.

The sun had just risen gloriously at the faraway rim of a flat, fertile farmland, when the driver started his engine, turned his radio on, and began the rest of the journey with a loud exclamation of *Allah-u-Akbar*.

Chapter Fifty-two

The cramped conditions in the bus had made Maggie's limbs stiff and climbing out was painful. To regain her equilibrium, she walked several times up and down in front of the bus station in downtown Peshawar. Then, she took a taxi and drove to Green Hotel where the receptionist, whom she knew from earlier visits, greeted her with a friendly grin. When she asked whether she could have a room, he distorted his features in a gesture of exasperation and said, "You can have the whole hotel. After September 11 everyone left. Nobody comes to visit now."

The feel of the empty hotel lobby and the eerily vacant gangway leading to her room triggered in Maggie a slight sense of panic. Ignoring her promise to Charles to involve the American Consulate in locating Anwar Haq, she resolved to go her own way. Engaging American officials would merely lead to complications and loss of time. She also resolved not

to roam about Peshawar's dilapidated but still enticing bazaars
and would begin immediately with the search for Haq and his
family.

Anyway, the town had ceased appealing to her. Peshawar's
crowded alleys and the bearded men in their knee-long shirts
and baggy trousers had lost their novelty. The city had become
a sad and mysterious place.

Over the years, the segregation of the sexes had gradually
been perfected to a degree that women had become almost
invisible. One could still see a few Western women roaming
about. But, if they wanted to avoid taunts, for them, too, long
dresses and head cover had become indispensable.

Even the jewelry market, a place Maggie had visited each
time she came to town, no longer tempted her. Touching the
gold and admiring the delicately molded pieces of jewelry on
overloaded display trays had once taken her back into the distant past, and she had felt a sense of exhilaration, imagining
herself walking through the narrow lanes of an ancient town,
surrounded by people long gone. That special feeling had been
absent the last time she walked along the shops in the jewelry
market. This trip she didn't even bother.

The taxi driver stopped at the gate to Camp 37 and, turning
to Maggie, asked whether he should wait for her.

"Yes," Maggie said. "Please do."

"Will you be long, mem Sa'heb?"

"Don't worry," Maggie said. "Wait for me. I'll pay you when
we're back at the hotel."

The officer on duty had dozed off on a string bed inside the
guardhouse. A tin plate, crusted with food; a spoon; a fork; a
tin cup, half-filled with black tea; and a crumpled copy of *Dawn*
cluttered the desk. While the officer, his aversion for having been
inconvenienced marring his features, got up and occupied the seat

behind the desk, Maggie checked the paper's date. Yesterday's headline read: "War Imminent as Taliban Reject U.S. Demands."

Something caught the officer's attention as he examined the file Maggie had given him. Suddenly he put his head forward and stared at a page.

"Why do you want to see Anwar Haq?" he asked, looking at Maggie with great curiosity.

"I would like to discuss his file with him. The immigration department couldn't locate his sponsor. Maybe I can help him get his asylum approved."

"You've come too late."

"What do you mean?"

"Anwar Haq has disappeared. His wife has reported him missing."

"When did that happen?"

"His wife came in earlier today asking about him. According to her, he left yesterday evening."

"Didn't he tell her where he was going?"

The officer shook his head. "He must have left through the backside of the camp. He's probably on his way to Afghanistan."

"Why would he want to return to Afghanistan? There could be a war any day now."

"Maybe he belongs to the Taliban and wants to fight with them."

What little Maggie knew of Haq from his file, it seemed very unlikely he was associated with such radicals as the Taliban. The way Haq had described his life, he came across as a modest person, someone without great ideological proclivity. He certainly wasn't a religious fanatic. "I can't believe it," she said.

"You never know with these people," the officer said. "Afghans are a strange breed."

"Can I visit his wife?"

The officer looked out the open window. "Akram," he called out. "Come here."

Akram, a young Pakistani soldier, came in and saluted the officer.

"Take Mem Sa'heb to that woman whose husband has disappeared."

When they stood before Haq's tent, Maggie gave the soldier twenty Pakistani rupees and motioned him to leave. She waited until the man disappeared behind a row of shelters then lifted the loosely hanging piece of the canvas and looked inside the tent.

Inside, the older of the two women sat in the right rear corner. The younger lay on a thin mattress, her eyes staring upward, her slim hands covering her chest, the tips of her long fingers touching.

"Bebakhshed," Maggie said. "May I come in?"

Fatima Haq looked up. She had been crying. "Please," she said, wiping tears off her face with a white handkerchief. She made a move to get up but Maggie motioned her to remain seated. Sheila gazed at the top of the tent without making the slightest movement. She either hadn't noticed that Maggie had entered their tent or remained disinterested in what transpired around her. Fatima began crying again. They sat silently for a while.

"Do you know where your husband might have gone?" Maggie asked.

Without looking at Maggie, Fatima shook her head.

"Is it all right if we speak in English?" Maggie said. "I'm afraid my Dari isn't good at all."

Using the white handkerchief, Fatima wiped the tears from her eyes and face. "I used to teach English at high school," she said in correct but heavily-accented English. "But my English isn't very good either."

"Is he coming back?" Maggie said.

Fatima began to cry again. She shook her head. When she had collected herself, she said, "He's not coming back."

"Are you sure?"

"Yes."

"Did he leave to help the Taliban?"

"No," Fatima said, shaking her head. "It was personal. Between him and me."

Silence settled between them again.

Maggie took a moment to observe the younger woman. She was beautiful, but looked more like a spirit than a human being. "Is your daughter always this way?" Maggie said. "I mean withdrawn."

"She's very sad." Fatima looked over to Sheila. "She has been for many years."

"Do you know Habib Dhil?" Maggie asked.

"I... well, no. I never met him, but he was a friend of my husband's. Why do you ask?"

Fatima's sudden nervousness surprised Maggie. "In your application for asylum your husband mentions him as sponsor. Did he know where Dhil was then?"

"My husband said he had disappeared. And that maybe he had gone to America or Europe." Fatima glanced at Sheila. "Have you come to find him?"

Maggie thought she detected a trace of worry in Fatima'a expression. "I always search for him when I am in Pakistan."

Fatima gazed into the small space of their dwelling. She remained still for a while. "Many people have disappeared," she then said. "Their relatives and friends continue to look for them. Sometimes, I think they chase ghosts."

Maggie felt a stinging pain around her heart and a slight dizziness in her head. She turned her face away from Fatima.

"Did you know Habib Dhil well?" Fatima asked.

"I loved him," Maggie said.

"This war has destroyed too many lives," Fatima said. She sounded tired.

"What are your plans now that your husband has left you?" asked Maggie.

"How can I have plans?" Fatima said, without looking at Maggie. "How can I even live? My husband has left." Tears began to run down her face. "We have no country. We have no money. Even if we had money, we don't have passports to go to another country. We don't exist to the rest of the world. But we do exist. That's our tragedy."

"Would you come to the United States?"

"That was Anwar's dream. My dream. We have been waiting for that opportunity for many years. I've given up on it."

"Do you want me to try? I'll sponsor you."

"Will you?" Fatima asked timidly.

Maggie smiled. "I'll come back tomorrow. We must redo some of your paperwork. Your file needs to be updated."

The next morning, Maggie arrived promptly at nine. Fatima was waiting. "Sheila, I'll be right here," she said, pushing Maggie gently outside. She looked worried. "Miss Reed. Maggie. Thank you for your wonderful offer. But maybe it would be best if we did not try to go to America."

Maggie was stunned. "But why?"

"It's because of Sheila. She's all I have and..."

"She'll be happy in America. You'll see."

"Yes, I'm sure," Fatima said. "But what if we... we both cannot go?"

"Of course you can," Maggie protested. "What reason could there possibly be?"

Fatima lowered her eyes and stared at her feet.

"She is not my daughter. That is, I did not carry her into this world. My husband brought her home when she was a little girl."

"Where is her mother? What happened?"

"Anwar said it was best if I didn't know too much. It might

be dangerous. Sheila was such a lovely little girl. It didn't matter. I just wanted to take care of her."

"So you don't know who the mother is then?"

"That was years ago. I found out at some point. I heard she died sometime after giving Sheila to my husband. Sheila's mother is Wali Khan's daughter, Miriam."

"The Prime Minister? He's been dead for more than twenty years."

"Today, even in this camp there are people who would seek revenge against his granddaughter." Fatima paused. "If they knew…"

Maggie was undeterred. "I don't think that matters anymore. But we will just keep it as our secret. Hardly anyone has any documents. Everything will be fine."

Maggie expected that Fatima would be relieved, happy. Instead her expression was one of reluctance, as though she wanted to be contended, but couldn't.

"What is it Fatima?"

"Yesterday, when you said…"

"Yes. What did I say?"

"About Habib Dhil," she blurted. "The reason Miriam Khan contacted my husband was because of Dhil."

Maggie was confused. "I don't understand. What does…"

Fatima wiped her face with the white handkerchief she had been twisting. "My apologies. I am not being clear."

"Clear about what?" Maggie said.

"Habib Dhil is Sheila's father," Fatima whispered.

Maggie stood in the morning heat as the tears began to well up in her eyes. The faint queasiness she had been feeling intensified. Her head began turning faster. She sat down on the ground, burying her face in her hands. She sensed Habib and trembled under the intensity of her feeling. She kept rolling his name in her head. Habib, Habib. When she opened her eyes,

Fatima sat beside her, watching her with anxious eyes. Fatima handed Maggie a little jewelry case. "Hayes Jewelers, New York," it advertised on top. Inside was a small, beautiful diamond and sapphire ring. Fatima reached over Maggie's shoulder, plucking the ring out of its case and held the inside up for Maggie to see. There was an inscription: "For Miriam. A token. Habib."

"Miriam Khan gave this to my husband to present to Sheila someday. We were tempted to sell it, but Anwar said we should keep it for the day when Dhil arrived."

Maggie closed the case, then put her arm around Fatima's shoulders. "Come. Let's tell Sheila that you are both going to America with me."

Maggie cranked down the window and let the hot wind blow over her face as the rental car sped toward Islamabad. It hadn't been quite as easy as she had hoped, and she despised the consul for his hard-nosed opposition to Fatima and Sheila traveling to the United States. Without Charles's personal in-tervention, it would have been impossible to get temporary travel documents for them. Charles had left no stone unturned until he secured the permission for the two to enter the U.S. Although Maggie hadn't asked him to join her in guarantying the two women's living expenses until they could obtain legal status, Charles had insisted on becoming co-guarantor. This unanticipated gesture of Charles's went far beyond anything she had expected.

She looked out the car window, watching Punjab's fertile countryside slide by. Charles had always been a gentle man, she thought. He probably knew all along about Habib, but he had never complained or even commented on it. She hoped Clare was a better wife than she had been.

She turned and observed the two women in the back of the car. Both looked out the window. As if realizing that she was being examined, Sheila turned toward Maggie. For the first time, Maggie saw a beam lighten up Sheila's young face. Her shy smile took Maggie back to Habib and his peculiarly reticent expression when he felt happy and wanted to show it.

It had been their first intimate encounter. Habib had looked at Maggie in that same steady way he had when he wanted to say something but, for a reason she had never understood, elected to remain silent. And then he had smiled—that tender smile she came to realize was his way of showing love.

This trip would be her last, she knew. What more could she do? She hoped that Habib was alive and happy—well, if not happy, at least not in pain.

Glancing into Sheila's large, brown eyes, Maggie knew Sheila was Habib's message for her. It had been a long time in coming, but had at last arrived. She would take care of both mother and daughter until they stood on their own feet. And she would make sure Sheila went to college. One day soon, she would blossom into a lovely and brilliant woman.